"Thoroughly riveting as Backman weaves his story via multi-dimensional characters who are not just Chief Scientists but Stewards of ensuring Humanity's fragile continuance. ... Backman narrates this riveting drama using language of vivid sensory details as if one is watching a 3D movie."
— *Aasem @ Amazon*

"Excellent sequel to David's first book! So interesting to see how David weaved the lives of Kopono and family through the effects of his time travel and how decisions can affect so many aspects of people's lives. David's storyline makes you keep asking for more, but so interesting to get a personal side to his characters as decisions are made both in the past and future. David's writing style makes it easy to read and I look forward to more from this up and coming author."
— *Chuck @ Amazon*

"Backman's writing is so absorbing, and science is so reasonable, that the reader accepts the futuristic developments without pause. ... The author creates an evocative narrative of his exploration of love and loss, and of finding peace in decisions that have painful consequences. He has created characters who are intelligent, emotional, rational, and passionate. They range from lovable to truly unlikable, and he writes them with understanding, letting them speak like the rest of us and behave according to their nature. And somehow, the rich detail that makes them real is never burdensome to read. Reading this book was like exploring the detail of a Hubble image—rich, deeply moving, and poignantly beautiful."
— *rlfowler @ LibraryThing*

The Loss of What Is Past

DAVID BACKMAN

db

THE LOSS OF WHAT IS PAST

Editor: Barbara Kohl
Cover Design and Creation: David Backman

Library of Congress Control Number: 2025904967
Print ISBN: 979-8-9911897-4-3
E-book ISBN: 979-8-9911897-5-0

Fourth Printing, 2026
Apple Valley, Minnesota USA

THE LOSS OF WHAT IS PAST

Come, go with us; speak fair. You may salve so,
Not what is dangerous present, but the loss
Of what is past.

William Shakespeare, *Coriolanus,*
Act 3, Scene 2

Preface

This novel is the sequel to *The Lightning in the Collied Night* and *The Lightning in the Collied Night, 2ⁿᵈ Edition*. There are many reminders in this book about the characters and plots of those books, but you may enjoy this book more if you read *Lightning* first. And if it's been some time since you read *Lightning*, you may want to keep it handy while you're reading this book to refer to text from certain chapters.

Because there is no Table of Contents in the print edition of this book, here is an overview of the book's organization:

- **Prologue:** Two scenes that set up events for the rest of the story.
- **Chapters 1 through 46:** As in *Lightning*, each chapter has a date.
- **Epilogue:** Two scenes that look ahead, and also back, from the last chapter.
- **References:** Bibliography for sources used in writing the book, including *Opening the Great Depths: The Bathyscaph Trieste and Pioneers of Undersea Exploration* by Norman C. Polmar and Lee J. Mathers.
- **Timeline of Events:** A chronological listing of major events mentioned in or implied by this book. It's strongly recommended that readers wait until *after* reading the book to look at the timeline, as it contains spoilers.
- **Acknowledgments**
- **About the Author**

Prologue

January 23, 1960

Darkness is absolute and eternal in the Challenger Deep, the deepest point in Earth's oceans. It lies about seven miles below the surface of the western North Pacific Ocean, in the Marianas Trench. The pressure at that depth is almost incomprehensible—nearly 18,000 pounds per square inch. Nothing can survive except for microbes and small, soft-shelled organisms. For that reason, no human had ever explored the secrets of the Challenger Deep ... until this day.

* * *

Jacques Piccard checked the fathometer of the *Trieste*; it read just over 5,000 fathoms—30,000 feet. *About one mile to the bottom*, he thought. The Swiss engineer and oceanographer had designed the submersible, called a bathyscaphe, with his father Auguste. They'd designed the *Trieste* to withstand the crushing pressure of the Challenger Deep, and it had proven itself on a series of shallower dives into the Marianas Trench for the U.S. Navy's Project Nekton. This was to be the project's climatic dive—quite literally, a voyage to the bottom of the sea.

Piccard shivered in the dank, claustrophobic pressure sphere that protected him and his fellow hydronaut, U.S. Navy Lieutenant Don Walsh, from instant death. The shivering was due to enduring over three hours of damp cold—the cabin temperature was only 45 Fahrenheit—but also from the anticipation of achieving something no one had ever accomplished. The white pressure sphere had been meticulously crafted out of almost 16 tons of five-inch-thick steel. It hung down from the center of the white main hull, which resembled a giant bathtub. A round viewing port, fashioned from a block of tapered acrylic glass, made the sphere mimic a giant eyeball straining to see something in the black depths. But as of yet, there had been nothing for the two explorers to see.

"At our present pace, I think we have about one more hour to the bottom," Piccard told his companion. They'd stopped sending progress reports to their support tug, the U.S.S. *Wandank*, over two hours earlier, when their sonar/hydrophone voice communication system had inexplicably failed. They were on their own.

"Not quite long enough for a nap," the young lieutenant with close-cropped hair quipped. Walsh, a Naval Academy graduate and an experienced submarine officer and diver, was the officer-in-charge for the mission. He laid his notebook and pen on his lap, rubbed and blew on his frigid, stiff hands, and peered out the small porthole. "Not much on TV today," he joked to the scientist with black, damp, tousled hair.

Piccard chuckled, "No, I should say n—"

CRACKKK!

The entire vessel shook as they heard what sounded like a muffled rifle shot. *That felt almost like an earthquake!* Walsh thought as the pressure sphere rocked around them.

"What happened?" Piccard wondered aloud. He'd never heard nor felt anything like that in his many years of experience with bathyscaphes.

"Have we touched bottom?"

Piccard checked the fathometer. "I see no change in our rate of descent."

The two men waited anxiously for what might happen next ... but nothing happened. They turned off the instruments and the underwater telephone so they could hear better. Still nothing. They looked all around the tiny cabin. Condensation dripped from the sphere's walls and control panels, but they saw no leaks beyond the slow seepage that had started at about 18,000 feet.

Whatever that was, it doesn't seem to be life-threatening—at least, not immediately, Walsh thought.

The two explorers looked at each other, shrugged, and without further discussion continued their slow descent.

Piccard kept checking the fathometer; after about 30 minutes, it touched 6,000—36,000 feet. "Do you think we missed the floor?" he joked.

"Probably not," Walsh replied dryly.

I wonder if the fathometer is functioning properly, Piccard worried. He dumped some of the vessel's 20,000 pounds of iron shot ballast to slow their descent to one-half foot per second. They continued sinking into the black trench. They dropped past 37,000 feet, but the fathometer still gave no indication of the seafloor.

Finally, the instrument started indicating the ocean bottom at 37,500 feet. Walsh switched on the exterior arc lights. Piccard peered out the forward viewport while Walsh called out the distance to the bottom, in fathoms: "Thirty … 20 … 10 …." At eight fathoms, Piccard could finally see the seafloor. The vessel's guide rope lightly touched it at an indicated, and staggering, 37,799 feet—2,000 feet deeper than any recent survey.

As the *Trieste* hovered silently a few feet above the muddy bottom, neither man spoke; each kept his thoughts to himself at that historic moment. A dense white fog of diatomaceous ooze, loosened by the ballast they'd released impacting the ocean floor, billowed up around the pressure sphere.

Walsh picked up the underwater telephone. *It probably won't work, but there's nothing to see out there, yet*, he thought. "Pittsburgh, Pittsburgh, this is *Trieste*, we are on the bottom of the Challenger Deep at six-three hundred fathoms. Over." Pittsburgh was the *Wandank*'s radio call sign.

To their astonishment, a reply blasted from the phone's speaker 30 seconds later: "*Trieste, Trieste*, this is Pittsburgh. I hear you faint and clear. Will you repeat your present depth? Over," Lieutenant Larry Shumaker said, excitement evident in his voice.

Walsh answered, "Pittsburgh, Pittsburgh, this is *Trieste*, confirming depth at six-three hundred fathoms. Over." After a 15 second delay due to the seven miles of seawater above the *Trieste*, Shumaker acknowledged.

Walsh turned around to look out the aft hatch window. The white mud cloud had started to clear. As he looked up at the flooded steel and Plexiglas tube that connected the pressure sphere to the main hull, his heart skipped a beat.

"I know what happened—that noise, that jolt," he said quietly to Piccard. "It was the big viewing port of the entry tube that cracked."

"Oh!" Piccard exclaimed. Both men knew what that crack meant. If the entry tube's window failed and they were unable to blow the water out of the tube after surfacing, they would be trapped in the pressure sphere, 10 feet below the ocean's surface, for the four-day transit to Guam. Snorkels would provide fresh air, but all they had to eat were a few chocolate bars left over after their long descent. *And it won't be a very pleasant ride*, Walsh thought; he knew there were heavy seas with 25-foot swells on the surface.

"I think we should surface as soon as possible, so there's maximum daylight to check on the entry tube problem," Walsh recommended.

"Agreed," Piccard replied as he nodded once.

"But first ...." Walsh held out his right hand to Piccard, and they solemnly shook hands. Then they pulled two flags from a small watertight bag: a Swiss flag for Piccard, a United States flag for Walsh. While holding their respective flags, they took a selfie with a fixed camera supplied by *Life* magazine. Unfortunately, there were no exterior cameras to record for history what they were seeing at the furthermost depths of the ocean—a view never seen before by human eyes.

As Piccard turned to pull the ballast release lever, he glanced out the forward viewport. "What ... what is *that?*" he exclaimed in surprise.

Walsh peered out the porthole. *Yeah—what IS that?* He could barely make out a shape on the seabed. There, dimly illuminated by the vessel's spotlights, was a spherical shape that was half-buried in the diatomaceous mud covering the seafloor. He and Piccard had never seen anything like it. It didn't look like part of a ship, or anything else of earthly origin. It had a few projections on its surface and appeared to have suffered damage—*From pressure, or impacting the ocean floor, or both,* Walsh thought.

"We should take some photos," Piccard suggested. Walsh nodded, and Piccard detached the fixed camera from its mount, adjusted it for low-light exposure, pointed it out the porthole, and snapped several pictures. "I don't know how well these will turn out."

Walsh picked up the telephone. "Pittsburgh, Pittsburgh, this is *Trieste.* We're preparing to ascend now. The entry tube window is cracked, and we don't want to risk a longer stay. Also, we just saw what looks like a sphere of some kind half-buried in the muck on the bottom." *Whatever it is, it's been down here a long time,* Walsh thought. "We've never seen anything like it. We noted its location and took a few photos. Over." They waited for the response.

"*Trieste, Trieste,* this is Pittsburgh. Say again—you saw a *sphere?* Over."

Walsh replied, "Pittsburgh, Pittsburgh, this is *Trieste.* Affirmative. I estimate it's roughly the same size as our pressure sphere—about six or seven feet in diameter." A thought flashed through his mind: *Was someone else already down here—and they didn't make it back home?* "It has some projections on its surface. We can't see details, because it's covered with the same ooze that's on the seafloor. Over." There was an unusually long delay before Walsh and Piccard received a response from the *Wandank.*

"*Trieste, Trieste,* this is Pittsburgh. The captain says he'll report your discovery to USPACOM. Meanwhile, he requests you turn your camera over to him when you're back on board and not mention this to anyone else until he gets instructions from command. Please acknowledge. Over."

Walsh and Piccard looked at each other. The Swiss scientist was clearly surprised, and upset.

"But, this is an important discovery!" Piccard protested. "They cannot simply—"

"This is a U.S. Navy expedition, Jacques," Walsh interrupted with a hint of resignation. "They can do whatever they damn well please about what we found down here." He clicked the telephone back on. "Pittsburgh, Pittsburgh, this is *Trieste*. We acknowledge. We're heading for the surface. ETA …." He looked at Piccard.

"About three and a half hours."

Walsh checked his Navy watch; it read 13:29. "ETA is 1700 hours. If you could heat up the shower water, we'd greatly appreciate it. Over." Piccard grinned at Walsh.

After the usual delay, Shumaker's voice said, "*Trieste, Trieste*, this is Pittsburgh. Seventeen hundred hours and hot water, acknowledged. Congratulations to both of you for making history! We can't wait to hear all about it when you're back on the surface. Over and out."

"Hot showers, here we come," Walsh said as Piccard pulled a lever to release two tons of ballast. As they started to rise slowly toward the surface, the Navy officer took one last look at the mysterious object sunk into the ocean floor. *I'd give anything to know what the heck that is.*

2 October 2141

Kapono Ailana gazed out the window at the bright cerulean sky and the deep blue ocean seven miles below him as the electric Air New Zealand jetliner cruised above the Tasman Sea toward Australia's southeastern coast. Then he touched a button to darken the window, settled back in his seat, and closed his eyes.

What an eventful six days! the 36-year-old Hawaiian native thought wearily as he recalled everything he'd experienced since he traversed the Wagamese Wormhole and jumped 87 years into the future in his damaged spacecraft. First, there was his surprising rescue by Captain April in a sister ship that had somehow survived the world war of November 2057, followed by his meeting in Auckland with United Earth President Witi Ngata. Kapono smiled as he remembered finding out about his 86-year-old daughter, Yinuo Shen-Martin, and her son—his grandson—An. Then there was his joyful introduction to both of them, followed by a lengthy discussion about what happened to Earth, to Yinuo and An and their loved ones, and to Yinuo's mother, Lai Shen, over the past 87 years.

As Kapono thought about Lai, tears welled up under his eyelids and began to trickle down his left cheek. He recalled their last night together at the Prometheus Project base—*The best night of my life,* he thought—and their tearful farewell the next morning before he boarded his spaceship, *Chronos 3.* It was the first time he referred to Lai as *ku'uipo*—a Hawaiian term for the person for whom one's love is unbreakable and unlimited. And Lai in turn referred to him with the Chinese term *qīn'ài de,* which she told him means "my love." She used those same words in the video she recorded for him 30 years ago, two days before she died.

But, although his love for Lai was unbreakable, he realized with great sorrow that he would never see her again. United Earth had banned time travel due to the risk of tragic consequences from changing the past, and the Wagamese Wormhole had been destroyed by a thermonuclear warhead delivered by a probe launched from the ship that had rescued him.

"Kupunakāne?"

Kapono opened his eyes when he heard An say the Hawaiian term for *grandfather.*

"I must have dozed off. What is it, An?" He sat up in his seat and looked to his right at his grandson; Yinuo was napping in the aisle seat.

"Sorry to wake you, but we're coming up on Sydney," the 51-year-old man with graying black hair, Lai's green eyes, and a smile that reminded Kapono of his father said. "I thought you might want to see it from the air."

"I would. Mahalo, An," Kapono replied with a Hawaiian expression of gratitude.

Kapono had spent the past three days touring New Zealand's North Island and Auckland with An and Yinuo. Auckland was one of the few major cities unscathed by World War III. There had also been the inevitable introduction to the media of "the time traveller from the 21st century." Kapono was grateful to Witi Ngata for holding them off as long as he could. *The media folks seemed much "kinder and gentler" than I remember from the 2050s*, Kapono reflected. *Maybe that was because of the "love one another" aftereffect of World War III and the Love One Another movement that Lai started and Yinuo now leads.*

Kapono, An, and Yinuo were flying to Sydney, where An and Yinuo lived and where Lai, Yinuo, and many others had found refuge after the war. An told Kapono he was welcome to stay at his home as long as he wished. *And I may take him up on that*, Kapono thought, *while I get up to speed on my new job.* Yinuo had practically begged her father to take over for her as United Earth's chief physicist. She'd held that job for 35 years and was more than ready to retire.

Kapono un-darkened the window and peered out as the plane approached Australia's coastline, shielding his eyes from the bright sunlight. As Sydney came into view, his eyes opened wide and his mouth gaped at what he saw. "I had no idea!" he whispered to his grandson.

An leaned over slightly to better see out the window. "Sydney's central business district was devastated by the war, due to the importance of Sydney Harbour as a naval base." His voice became hushed. "Over two million people died. And so much of central Sydney was lost: the Opera House, Harbour Bridge, Bondi Beach, suburbs such as North Sydney and Newtown, the Royal Botanic Garden, the Rocks and Chinatown …." He trailed off. "All obliterated in an instant." He looked at his grandfather, his face a mask of sorrow. "I didn't know any of that, of course. But I've seen photos and holograms. It makes me sad that I and my generation never knew that Sydney."

An cleared his throat. "But the northern and southern suburbs fared much better. Mum and I live to the south, in Miranda. It's not far from Wedderburn Airport." The formerly small, private aerodrome had been expanded after the war to serve as Sydney's main airport due to the destruction of Sydney Airport and Western Sydney International.

Kapono had visited Sydney multiple times and had been to most of the sites An had mentioned. *I wish you could've seen that Sydney, too, An. There's so much of the world you'll never be able to see—including most of the Northern Hemisphere. Your world has virtually no crime—but at the cost of seven billion lives and global devastation. If only I could have returned to the past and warned them about World War III. If only ....*

* * *

An, Kapono, and Yinuo walked toward Yinuo's apartment on Pinnacle Street in Miranda; it was only a block from the light rail station. An wore a backpack, and Kapono pulled his daughter's roller bag behind him. Yinuo had asked to stop at her flat before they went to An's home to allow her to drop off her bag and change. As Kapono enjoyed the sunshine of the delightfully warm early spring day, he could see no signs of the nuclear holocaust that had ravaged the heart of Sydney.

"This is a lovely town," Kapono remarked to his grandson.

"Isn't it?" An replied. "Miranda and other shires south and north of Sydney were very fortunate. They were just beyond the edge of the firestorm. The wind on the day Sydney was bombed came from the southeast, so the mushroom cloud and radioactivity were pushed away from the city. When Mum and Nanna arrived here two years after the war, they settled in this area."

That's a story I'd like to hear more about, Kapono thought. Back in Auckland, Yinuo had summarized her and Lai's long post-war trek from northern Minnesota to Sydney, but she'd only hit the highlights. *And some of the lowlights,* Kapono thought as he recalled what Yinuo had told him about the harrowing journey.

"Here we are!" Yinuo said cheerfully. The short, gray-haired woman with her father's brown eyes and broad nose turned off the sidewalk toward the main entrance of a five-story white building with gray trim. Kapono and An followed her into the lobby and down the hallway to the door of her first-floor apartment. She stopped at the door and said softly, "Michelle Simmons 2018," and the door unlocked and opened. Yinuo turned toward Kapono. "Look it up," she said with a quick smile.

"I'll do that!" Kapono replied as he returned his daughter's smile. *But that name is familiar ... I think she was a noted Australian quantum physicist. And 2018 is the year I was born.*

They passed through the narrow foyer into the living area. "Power on, lights 50 percent," Yinuo said, and the entire ceiling illuminated with a soft glow. "It's not much, but it's all I need," she said unapologetically. "Make yourselves at home; I'll just need a few minutes." She pulled her bag into the bedroom and closed the door.

Kapono looked around the tiny flat. Although small, it did indeed seem to have everything one person might need: a study nook off the foyer, a compact bathroom with a walk-in shower, a storage closet, a strange-looking machine he guessed was some sort of washer and dryer combo, a large holographic TV on one wall of the combined living/dining/kitchen area, and a sliding glass door on the opposite wall, leading out to a small patio. He noticed the kitchen had an infrared cooktop, a refrigerator, and an odd, boxy appliance hanging under a cabinet.

"An, what's that?" he asked as he pointed to the white box.

"Food replicator," An replied. "Like a 3D printer, but it can make a variety of foods that taste *almost* like the real thing," he added with a sarcastic smile. "It's convenient, but I don't think Mum uses it much. She prefers to cook her own food when she's here—which isn't very often."

"Okay, thanks." Yinuo had told Kapono her job as chief physicist for United Earth required long hours and frequent trips to Auckland and Canberra. *I'm glad she asked me to take over for her—that's a tough job for an octogenarian.*

As Kapono looked around the small apartment, he suddenly had a thought. "An, I hope I'm not inconveniencing you and Linda by staying with you."

An shook his head, "No, not at all! We have a spare bedroom. And, as luck would have it, our long-term house guests—a mum and her two kids—just moved out. They lived with us for a couple of years while they were going through some tough times. But they're back on their feet now, and they found their own apartment."

Kapono remembered something Witi Ngata had told him in Auckland: *There's almost no homelessness and hunger now. If someone doesn't have a place to live or enough to eat, someone will take them in, or help them find shelter and food.* He looked at his grandson with an approving smile. "That was kind of you and Linda to help them out." *And I bet they didn't charge them a single dollar.*

"No worries. Besides, it was great having the two kids with us." His cheerful smile faded. "Linda and I couldn't have children of our own. We cared for many foster children when we were younger, but then Linda's work with the Peace Corps and my travels for construction projects made that impractical."

"I'm very sorry to hear that, An," Kapono said sadly. Although he'd known his grandson for only a few days, he thought he would have made an exceptional father.

"Thank you, *Kupunakāne.* Many couples were in the same boat after the war."

Kapono nodded, "I see." He remembered studying the long-term effects of radiation on fertility in one of his undergraduate classes at Cal Berkeley.

Then he noticed, out of the corner of his eye, something laying on the sideboard below the TV—and it was *very* familiar. "An, that pad," he said as he pointed to it, "looks like a holopad from my time."

"It is!" Yinuo said as she came out of the bedroom. "It was Mum's, from back in the 2050s. It's one of the few things of hers I have from that time." She picked up the pad with both hands and held it out to Kapono. "It had her calendar, her daily diary, some personal photos and videos, some e-books, and even a few movies." She added with a whimsical smile, "I think I memorized all the dialogue from *Interstellar,* I watched it so many times as a little girl."

Kapono carefully cradled the antique pad in his hands and lightly touched its screen. *I wish I could see Lai's calendar and diary—it would almost be like going back in time and being with her.* "Would you mind if I borrowed this for a while?"

"Not at all," Yinuo replied, then she frowned. "But, it's cactus." Seeing Kapono's puzzled expression, she translated for him. "Broken; it hasn't worked in decades. Its memory may still be intact, but finding someone who could extract it would be gnarly."

"I'm always up for a challenge," Kapono smiled enthusiastically at his daughter. "Did your mother leave any other calendars or diaries?"

Yinuo nodded, "Yes, on pads she bought over the years, after we arrived in Sydney. And, as you know, she was a stickler for details. I still have those files. Would you like to see them?"

"Very much. Mahalo."

"No worries, I'll grant you access and send you the links to them. And, that reminds me—we need to get you a pad from *this* century!" She'd already purchased a phone for her father in Auckland; unsurprisingly, his hPhone from the past wasn't compatible with 22nd century telecommunication networks.

"There's a shop a block from my house," An suggested. "Let's head over to my place, have tea—dinner, that is—and we can visit the shop tomorrow morning. Okay?"

"That's ripper!" Kapono replied with a sunny smile.

An laughed, "We'll make an Australian out of you yet, *Kupunakāne!*" He held out his hand. "May I carry that pad for you?" Kapono handed An the old device, and he carefully tucked it into his backpack. Then the three of them headed out the door toward the light rail station.

Kapono was overjoyed at the prospect of being able to see Lai's calendars and diaries. Then he had a thought that almost stopped him in his tracks: *If I could extract Lai's calendar and diary from her old pad, plus the newer files....* He shook his head in resignation. *Why even think about that? It doesn't matter—the Wagamese Wormhole is gone, and besides, time travel is banned. I need to live in, and focus on, the present.*

| 1 |

4 October 2141

Kapono walked with Yinuo out of the light rail station for the University of New South Wales Caringbah campus. She was taking him to meet the physicist he'd be working with on the antimatter research project she'd told him about a few days earlier in Auckland. As they approached the university's main buildings, he appreciated the symmetry and harmonious proportions of their New Classical architecture and the tranquility of the xeriscaped grounds with native trees and shrubs.

"This is a beautiful campus," he remarked to his daughter as they walked toward the physics building on the bright, mild spring morning.

"It is a beaut, isn't it? It's as old as I am, and I think it's held up quite well." She looked at her father. "It was very fortunate this satellite campus was completed right before the war. The main campus in Kensington was destroyed that day." As Kapono nodded solemnly, she added, "There was an international physics conference here then. Many leading scientists and scholars from all over the world were saved because of that conference."

"Fortunate, indeed," Kapono agreed as they entered the Michelle Yvonne Simmons Physics Building and climbed the main staircase to the third floor. Yinuo stopped at the door to a lab; a small sign on the door said *MYS310 - Antimatter Power Generation Research*. She placed her palm on the security scanner, and the door unlocked with a faint

1

click. Kapono opened the door for his daughter, then he stepped into the sunny, spacious, and tidy laboratory.

Yinuo led Kapono to a table where a black-haired woman in a terracotta lab coat was sitting, writing on a pad with a stylus. She looked up as Yinuo and Kapono approached.

"*Kia ora*, Aroha," Yinuo said cheerfully. "I'd like you to meet my father, Dr. Kapono Ailana. Dad, this is Dr. Aroha Whakatane."

"*Kia ora*, Yinuo," Aroha replied as she stood up and smiled brightly, then she reached out to shake hands with Kapono. "The famous time traveller from the 21st century! I'm so stoked to meet you, Dr. Ailana!"

"It's great to meet *you*, Dr. Whakatane. Yinuo has told me so much about you." He could tell from her name and facial features that she was Māori. He also noticed her deep brown eyes, which shone with wisdom and intense curiosity. "But please, call me Kapono—or just K, if you wish."

Aroha nodded, "And I'm Aroha, okay?"

"I know you have a lot to talk about," Yinuo said to Aroha and Kapono. "I have a meeting with Dean Sushkov." She looked at the digital clock on the wall. "It's almost lunchtime. How about you two have lunch, and I'll meet up with you afterwards. I should be finished by 1:30."

* * *

Aroha and Kapono found an open table in the university's bustling canteen and sat down with their trays of food. Aroha had suggested the barbecue snags with mashed potatoes to Kapono, and she'd chosen Chiko rolls.

"This reminds me of the cafeteria at Berkeley," Kapono said as he looked around the busy canteen while Aroha silently said a blessing over her food. "The food selections are a bit different, however," he added with a wink as he dug into his sausages.

"It's pretty decent fare for a university," Aroha opined as she took a bite of her Australian spring rolls. "Berkeley was in California, aye? Did you get your physics degree there?"

"My undergraduate degree, yes. I got my PhD at MIT." Then he realized both Cal Berkeley and MIT had been erased from the face of the Earth many years ago. "The Massachusetts Institute of Technology."

Aroha knew some details about Kapono's background due to the media coverage of his arrival in the future through the Wagamese Wormhole. But he knew very little about her, except what Yinuo had shared with him when she recruited him to work with Aroha on the antimatter project.

"How about you, Aroha? Where did you go to school?"

"I got my bachelor's in physics at the University of Auckland and my PhD at the Australian National University."

"What a coincidence—that's where Yinuo got her PhD."

"Aye, although there's very few graduate-level physics programs in Asia-Pacific."

"Oh … of course." He recalled what Yinuo had told him about the dearth of graduate degree programs in many disciplines since World War III. "Yinuo told me you were born in New Zealand."

Aroha nodded as she finished a Chiko roll. "Queenstown, on the South Island."

"I toured Auckland and the North Island with Yinuo and my grandson An before coming to Sydney. I've never been to the South Island."

"It's gorgeous," she said wistfully. "You really must see it someday. My mum still lives in Queenstown." She noticed the question that was in Kapono's eyes. "My dad was killed in the earthquake of 2120, when I was 14," she said as her wistful expression changed to one of sorrow.

"I'm so sorry," Kapono said sadly. "I know how hard it is to lose a parent when you're young. My mom died in a fire when I was four."

Aroha looked into Kapono's expressive brown eyes; their blend of intelligence and kindness captivated her. *His parents, his friends—everyone he's ever known—are gone,* she realized. Then she remembered what Yinuo had told her about her mother, and she smiled sympathetically.

"You know all too much about loss, don't you, Kapono? Yinuo told me about you and Lai," she said softly. Although Aroha had been just shy of six years old when Lai Shen died on Christmas Day in 2111, she vividly recalled that sad day. Her father, one of New Zealand's leading physicists, had worked with Lai and was grief-stricken about the loss of his colleague and friend.

Kapono nodded. "Yes …. I miss her very much." He smiled slightly, "But she had a long, full life, and she had such an impact on the world. I'm happy and grateful for that. And, I'm grateful to be with my daughter and grandson now. Lai left a video for me before she died. I have that, and I have my memories of her." *Plus her diaries that Yinuo shared with me ….*

Aroha smiled empathetically. "I have some choice memories of my dad. He … uhm … he saved my life," she added as her eyes began to glisten. "He pushed me out of the way of a falling beam in our house. My legs were crushed, but he took the full brunt of it."

Her legs were crushed? he thought with surprise. "Do you have bionic legs, Aroha?"

"Aye," she nodded. "You couldn't tell?"

"Not if you hadn't told me. Did you know bionic legs were invented at MIT over 100 years ago?"

"I did not know that."

"I imagine they've advanced a lot since the 2050s," Kapono said.

"Aye, they've been fairly commonplace since the turn of the century." She looked down at her prosthetic legs. "In some ways, they're better than the legs I was born with."

Kapono recalled what he'd read about the capabilities of bionic legs of his time. "Remind me to never challenge you to a race!" he kidded.

She chuckled softly. "Oh, don't worry about that. When I was younger, I had them adjusted so they'd mimic real legs in terms of performance. That allowed me to compete in netball and volleyball in school." Although she'd had her legs reset to their factory specs a few years ago, she never utilized their full capabilities in public as that would run counter to the core Māori value of *whakaiti*—humility.

"I've heard of netball. Isn't it sort of like basketball?"

Aroha laughed, "Well, it does involve throwing a ball through a ring on a tall post! But other than that, it's much different."

"Oh! I'll have to check it out."

"I'd be keen to take you to one of the Swifts' matches—they're the local pro team." Aroha had been recruited by the New South Wales Swifts during her 3rd year at the university, but she decided to focus on her Bachelor Honours year there, then her PhD.

"Thanks, I'd like that. I need to get acclimated to my adopted country," Kapono said with a smile. "And, I need to get up to speed on the antimatter project. Yinuo gave me some background on it, but I was hoping you could fill me in on the details."

"Gladly," she replied as she checked her watch. "We have some time before Yinuo returns."

Over the next half-hour, Aroha told Kapono about the work she and Yinuo had done to date on the matter/antimatter reactor design. She explained how they'd arranged for an ultra-high-voltage circuit into the lab and had acquired a minuscule, but extremely expensive, quantity of antimatter through the generosity of Australia's wealthiest billionaire.

"Due to recent advancements in superconducting magnets, Yinuo and I think the reactor can be quite small," Aroha explained. "Perhaps no larger than a soccer ball."

Kapono's eyes opened wide. "Really? That's amazing!" He remembered the large buildings required to house the fusion tokamaks and reactors of the 2050s. "And maybe," he added with his tongue firmly in his cheek, "we could use dilithium crystals to contain the reaction instead of magnets."

Aroha looked at him with a blank stare. "What in bloody hell are dilithium crystals?"

Kapono chuckled. "I'm sorry. Please forgive my weird, 21st-century sense of humor."

Aroha smiled graciously, "No worries, K." *I like a man with a sense of humour—even a weird one.*

* * *

"So, what do you think about the project?" Yinuo asked Kapono as they left the physics building and headed for the light rail station.

"It's really exciting! Fusion reactors were close to being commercially viable in my time. As you know, your mother worked on them before joining me on the Prometheus Project. But the potential for power generation from matter/antimatter reactions is much greater."

Yinuo smiled, "That's why we're spending a very large chunk of the university's physics budget on this project. And, what do you think of Aroha?"

"She's great. You made an excellent decision choosing her for the project. I'm really going to enjoy working with her, and learning from her."

"I'm glad you like her. Hiring her was the best decision I've ever made as United Earth's chief physicist—also the easiest decision. She's a brilliant physicist, and an exceptional person." She stopped walking and looked at her father. "In fact, I was thinking about asking her to take over for me as chief physicist—until you arrived, that is. I'd prefer to have a theoretical physicist in that role. I think it's a better fit for the job, plus there's a tradition of theoretical quantum physicists in that role, going back to the first chief physicist, my mum. What do you think? Will you take over for me?"

Kapono had told Yinuo back in Auckland that he'd consider assuming her chief physicist role, but that was before he knew Aroha was a candidate. "I, uh, I don't know. As you said, Aroha is an exceptional physicist, and I wouldn't want to stand in her way if you believe she's qualified to be chief physicist." He looked into his daughter's eyes. "Do you what you think is best. I'll accept whatever you decide."

She smiled knowingly. "I figured you'd say that. I want to give you some time to get started on the antimatter project. Let's talk about this again in a couple of weeks, all right, Dr. Ailana?" she said with a twinkle in her eyes.

"If that's what you'd like, Dr. Shen-Martin," Kapono assented with a smile.

They started walking toward the light rail station again. "You know, Aroha is single," Yinuo said offhandedly. "And I don't think she's dating anyone right now."

Kapono looked at his daughter and grinned. "Are you doing double duty as chief physicist and matchmaker now, sweetie?"

"I was just making conversation," she replied innocently.

They reached the station and boarded the next train to Miranda.

| 2 |

2 May 2144

Aroha sat slumped at her desk in the Antimatter Power Genera-tion Research lab. Widely considered the most talented experi-mental physicist in Australia and perhaps all of United Earth, she wasn't used to achieving anything less than exceptional results. *That's not going to happen this time,* she thought dejectedly as she tapped the stylus of her pad on the desktop and rested her tattooed chin on her left fist.

But there is ONE result from this project, she realized. *I think we've pretty much proven that generating usable energy from antimatter is impossible with current science.* Over the past two and a half years, Aroha had worked with United Earth Chief Physicist Kapono Ailana to design, build, and test a reactor that released energy from the annihilation of matter and antimatter. While they were able to sustain reactions for a few milliseconds, itself a tremendous achievement, the results were far short of what was necessary for practical power generation. And, those tests had nearly used up their precious, costly supply of antimat-ter.

But Aroha wasn't a quitter. She sat up and tapped rapidly on her pad with the stylus. She calculated she *might* have enough antimat-ter for a few more tests if she greatly reduced the amount used per test. She started to get out of her chair to prepare the reactor for a test using the smaller payload when she heard a *bleep* from the particle detector on the table behind her. The device detected and recorded subatomic particles emitted from the matter/antimatter reactions.

That was too, too weird, she thought as she looked at the detector's display panel. It showed that one type of particle had apparently just been created by the quiet reactor. Aroha raised her thick eyebrows when she read the details off the screen:

Type: UNKNOWN
Quantity: 1.0583422e10

Eeeeeh? Over 10 billion particles—but of WHAT? She realized the detector shouldn't have reported *any* particles, with no activity in the reactor.

She prepared the test and ran it. Immediately the particle detector bleeped again, and she stared at its display:

Type: Neutrino
Quantity: 2.883420190e12

That's more like it, she thought as she exhaled with relief. Neutrinos were a typical by-product of matter/antimatter reactions. *But ... what were those impossible other particles?*

Before she could investigate that question, Kapono walked into the lab. "Aloha! How are the tests going?"

Aroha smiled uneasily as she looked at the man who was one of the world's foremost theoretical physicists. He was wearing his customary Hawaiian shirt, khaki shorts, and flip-flops. Undeterred by the lack of Hawaiian shirts in post-war Australia, Kapono had found a tailor in Miranda who'd supplied him with a dozen shirts in a variety of traditional Hawaiian motifs.

"*Kia ora*, Kapono. They are ... *very* interesting."

The unusual uncertainty in Aroha's voice surprised Kapono. "How do you mean?"

"Just now I ran a test with an antimatter payload that was only one percent of what we've used for previous tests. I was trying to make the remaining antimatter last as long as possible. But," she continued as she turned toward the particle detector and pointed at its display, "*before* I ran the test, the detector reported over 10 billion 'unknown' particles."

Kapono raised his eyebrows. "*Unknown?* That *is* interesting! And also, quite impossible. Unless ...." His face assumed the far-away look it did when he was deep in thought. "What were the results of the test?"

"The results were similar to earlier tests," Aroha replied as she scrolled the detector's display with her finger. "Heaps of neutrinos."

"Hmm ... how about we—" Suddenly the particle detector bleeped again.

"That's what it did the last time!" Aroha exclaimed. She studied the detector display. "Take a look—again, over 10 billion of those unknown particles were emitted by the reactor ... somehow."

"Very strange," Kapono agreed as he looked at the detector's display screen.

Aroha ran a second test with the smaller payload, and the detector reported the expected number of neutrinos.

"Any ideas, K? I'm proper stuck on it. Anyway, *you're* the theorist," she teased.

"Was there any difference from earlier tests besides the much smaller payloads?"

Aroha shook her head, "No. Everything else was the same."

Kapono settled slowly into a swivel chair, and Aroha sat down beside him. "I can think of only one explanation. But ... it's going to blow your mind."

Aroha smiled enthusiastically, "Go ahead, blow away!"

Kapono looked into her eyes and said matter-of-factly, as if he were discussing the weather, "Tachyons. It has to be."

Aroha's deep brown eyes opened wide in astonishment and disbelief. "But tachyons are only *theoretical*—no one's ever observed them!"

"Until now?" Kapono smiled, tongue in cheek. "I can help you investigate this further, but I can't think of any other answer that fits the results." He licked his lips, clearly excited by what would be one of the most astounding scientific discoveries in history. "Think about it, Aroha ... tachyons can only travel *faster* than the speed of light, never slower. That explains how they showed up on the particle detector *before* you ran the tests. Also," he continued, "the less energy that's applied to creating tachyons, the faster they go. By greatly reducing the antimatter payload, it appears you provided just the right conditions to create tachyons—a *lot* of them."

Aroha sat back in her chair, somewhat overwhelmed by her apparent discovery after many months of dry holes. "It's incredibly exciting from a theoretical physics standpoint, but what would be the *practical* use for tachyons?"

Kapono pondered her question for several seconds. "Well, *theoretically*, they could be used to send messages of some sort to the past." Then his mind drifted into the realm where dreams became hopes, and from there, perhaps more. *Messages ... and what else?* "But there's many challenges in doing that. Huge scientific and engineering challenges, of course, but also the fact that using tachyons to send messages back through time could create some rather nasty paradoxes." He thought about the classic tachyon paradox of a spaceship sending a message to itself in the past, and when the message was received, the spaceship was to destroy itself. There would thus be no spaceship to send the tachyon message.

Aroha nodded. "A wee bit of a conundrum, ay?"

"Indeed," Kapono smiled vacantly. But his mind was still firmly planted in the realm of hope rather than the restrictions of physics. *What if it COULD be possible ...?*

| 3 |

16 March 2145

*T*his delay is bordering on yonks, Aroha thought with mild irritation as she sat in the APGR lab. She'd been waiting for over 30 minutes for Kapono to arrive, and she was starting to worry. *It's not like him. He's always so considerate and kind. Plus, those brown eyes of his....* She forced herself to derail that train of thought and returned her attention to the latest *Australian Journal of Scientific Research* on her pad.

Aroha didn't know why Kapono had asked her to meet him in the lab that morning. He'd said only that it was important, and he'd explain when he saw her. That was good enough for her. In the three and a half years she'd worked with him, she'd come to trust him completely.

She felt she had more than a workplace relationship with Kapono. *We're mates, really,* she thought. *Mates ... and maybe someday ....* She knew he'd left someone very close to him 90 years in the past. But she was with him nearly every day, in the present. She was patient. And, time was on her side.

She scratched what felt like an itch on her right thigh. After many years, it still surprised her whenever she thought she felt sensations in her bionic legs. She looked down at the caramel-colored synthetic skin covering her titanium alloy limbs. *ALMOST like the real thing,* she thought—and as she'd been reminded by some of the men she'd considered dating. She couldn't understand why her prosthetics should make any difference to them, or anyone else. She recalled Kapono's reaction when he'd first learned about her artificial legs. The fact her legs weren't "real" didn't matter to him. She smiled softly as she remembered his light-hearted remark: *Remind me to never challenge you to a race!* Her smile disappeared as she turned her thoughts back to the mystery in the lab.

Since her discovery of tachyons the previous May, she'd performed many additional tests with varying antimatter payloads. She confirmed that the less energy applied to generate the tachyons, the greater the number of tachyons and the faster—and farther back in time—they traveled. Happily, that behavior allowed her to stretch their limited supply of antimatter even further.

She'd hoped to write up her findings for the *Australian Journal of Scientific Research* and present them at the next meeting of United Earth's science committee, but Kapono had convinced her to hold off until they'd done more research. She knew he was busy working on theoretical research into potential applications of tachyons, but he kept saying he wasn't quite ready to share his research with her. *Any day now*, he'd told her—again—a few days ago.

Her thoughts were interrupted by a *bleep* from the particle detector—and, something else: she *thought* she saw a blue aura envelop the spherical matter/antimatter reactor, which was a bit larger than a soccer ball. It lasted for only a second. *Or, did I imagine that?* she wondered as she questioned her eyesight. She checked the detector's display screen; it showed over 600 billion tachyons had just been created in the quiet reactor—more than she'd seen from any of her tests over the past 10 months. *Plus, there was that aura ....*

She peered through the reactor's small, leaded glass viewport and was startled as she realized, *There's something in there!* She checked the radiation levels within the reactor to ensure they were safe, then unlatched the hinged reaction chamber door, opened it, and looked inside. There was a small metal cube, about three centimeters square, inside the chamber.

She carefully removed the tiny box from the reactor with tongs and set it on her desk. She studied the cube and noticed it had a lid.

She picked it up, opened the lid, and found a tightly folded wad of white paper inside.

This is bizarre, she thought as she unfolded the paper. On the paper was a hand-written message in black ink. She recognized the cursive writing—it was Kapono's.

> *17 March 2145, 10:40 a.m.*
> *Bring this note to me in the APGR lab at exactly 10:45 a.m. on 17 March. Tell NO ONE, not even me, about it before then.*
> *K*

"Bloody hell!" she whispered, then she thought, *Not just bizarre—definitely a bit gone!*

| **4** |

17 March 2145

Kapono sat at his desk in the APGR lab and finished writing on the piece of paper in front of him. Then he carefully folded the paper into a wad small enough to fit into a tiny metal box. He stuffed the wad into the box, closed its lid, and set the box on the desktop.

He leaned back in his swivel chair and looked at the dozens of quantum mechanics equations that covered the writing wall in front of him. *Time to put theory to the test*, he thought. *I wish I had Aileen's four-leaf clover now—and how fitting that would be.* It was St. Patrick's Day.

He smiled as he remembered the AI spacecraft pilot application he and a teammate had created for the Prometheus Project in the 2050s. They'd programmed Aileen with an Irish brogue and Irish slang, and an upbeat personality. Kapono had even taught the AI to sing, in a voice that resembled Sinéad O'Connor's. *Like interacting with a person*, Kapono recalled. *And, she was a damn good pilot, too.* Against impossible odds, Aileen had somehow guided Lai's crippled *Chronos 2* spacecraft a billion miles back to Earth and managed to crash-land it close to the Prometheus base. Lai had been critically injured, but she'd survived—and was instrumental in Earth's recovery after World War III. *If it hadn't been for Aileen ....*

Kapono picked up the metal cube and rolled his chair over to the matter/antimatter reactor. He opened the door to the reaction chamber, placed the small box inside, closed the door, and checked his watch: *10:41 a.m.* He confirmed the reactor's settings, then pushed the green button labeled *Engage* and rolled his chair away from the reactor, as if the additional distance would help him if the reactor were to go supercritical. There was a soft hum as its powerful electromagnetic field controlled the interaction of microscopic quantities of matter and antimatter. Then a blue aura enveloped the reactor for a fraction of a second. After the aura disappeared, the reactor shut down.

Kapono rolled back over to the reactor control panel, confirmed radiation was at a safe level, and opened the reaction chamber door. The small box was gone.

Now we'll see, Kapono thought as he looked again at his watch.

As he waited, his thoughts returned to Aileen, and AI in general. He'd noticed when he arrived in the future that the use of and attitudes toward AI were much different than in the 2050s. In the mid-21st century, AI had been entrusted with many different roles, from executive assistant to piloting spacecraft to managing missile defense systems. And AIs had been personified to the point where, as in Aileen's case, the line between AIs and humans had become blurred. But in the 2140s, executive assistants were *people*, and spaceship captains preferred to fly their own ships except for the most routine of tasks. Witi Ngata had told him AI hadn't been blamed for World War III. *That may be true*, Kapono thought, *but there's definitely less dependence on and trust in AI now than there was before the war.*

Kapono's thoughts were interrupted by Aroha entering the lab. He checked his watch and smiled appreciatively: *10:45 a.m.* "Aloha!" he greeted her as he stood up.

Aroha's expression was a mix of bewilderment and intense curiosity. "*Kia ora*, Kapono," she replied as she walked up to him and stretched out her right arm. "Do you know what this is?" She opened her palm—it held the small metal box. "It appeared in the reactor yesterday; the note inside it said to bring it to you now. That note is in your handwriting."

"Yes, I do." He motioned to the two closest chairs and smiled soberly. "Better sit down. This might take a while."

Over the next 40 minutes, Kapono summarized his research of the past few weeks into using tachyons to create a localized bend in spacetime. He explained he'd figured out how to control the tachyons generated by the matter/antimatter reactor to form a tachyon *bubble*. Theoretically, anything enclosed within the bubble would travel with the tachyons back through time. By adjusting the tachyon bubble's strength and direction, he could—again, theoretically—determine how far back in time, and *where* in the past the tachyons, and whatever was enveloped by them, would re-materialize.

Aroha listened in rapt attention. She understood most of it, but she realized, *I'm an experimental physicist, not a theorist. Besides, I haven't studied tachyons since grad school.* Thus she found what Kapono had explained to be a bit puzzling, but also incredibly exciting—and not a little scary.

"So, let me get this straight: you've devised a way to send matter to any point in the past, and to any place you choose?"

Kapono nodded. "Yes, that's basically it."

Aroha tried to comprehend the ramifications of Kapono's discovery. But all she said was, "Whoa, crazy …."

"Of course, it's mostly theoretical at this point. Except," he smiled triumphantly as he looked at the small metal box, "my little test worked. But there was no directionality there. It's a big leap to go from that test to sending anything to any time, anywhere on Earth."

"Why did you say, 'on Earth'?"

"Well, in order to focus the tachyon bubble for a specific destination, we need precise coordinates. Those are available for terrestrial locations, but not so much in outer space—not yet, anyway."

"Ah, I see." Her eyes swept over the myriad of complex equations on the writing wall; she looked at Kapono and smiled playfully. "You've been a busy beaver, haven't you?"

He chuckled at her reference to the famously unsolvable problem about the behavior of Turing machines. "I guess I have been! So, what do you think?"

"It's, uh, incredible. Really. I never dreamed our antimatter research project would lead to something out of an H. G. Wells novella," Aroha said, thinking of *The Time Machine*. "Except, his time machine could send *people* back through time, also." She noticed Kapono's expression changing to its familiar far-off gaze. "What?"

"Theoretically," he began in a hushed tone, "there's no reason the reactor *couldn't* send someone back through time."

"Bugger!" Aroha exclaimed.

| 5 |

10 January 2146

"Are you ready to make history, George?" Aroha asked the white lab rat she cradled in her hands. "Not that you have a choice, luv." She gently placed the rat into a small metal box provisioned with a thick layer of wood chips, a water bottle, and bits of kale, then closed and latched the perforated lid. She turned toward her phone sitting on the tabletop. "George and I are ready when you are, K."

"I'm good to go here, Aroha." Kapono's voice said from the phone. He was at An's townhome in Miranda. An was about two miles away, on-site at his latest civil engineering project: the infrastructure for the new Sydney Opera House being built at Taren Point. He was thrilled to be working with architect Eline Utzon, a descendent of the architect of the original opera house. An had mentioned to Kapono that he'd be away from home all that day when he called his grandfather to let him know Yinuo wasn't feeling well. Kapono promised to stop by her apartment that afternoon.

A perfect opportunity, Kapono had thought when his grandson told him about being out of the house all day. He and Aroha had been searching for the ideal place for their next tachyon spacetime-bending experiment. After several unsuccessful attempts over the past 10 months to direct the tachyon bubble to a specific location, their previous two tests had successfully sent a small metal box containing a variety of organic matter back in time one hour to the university's rugby field. They'd performed those tests in the middle of the night to avoid being seen. Confident of their ability to direct the tachyon bubble to a precise location, they were ready for the next step: sending a living creature back in time.

"Choice," Aroha replied. "Hang on a minute." She placed the box containing George into a recently-added shielded compartment within the spherical reactor, closed and latched the door, and checked the reactor's settings. "I've double-checked the antimatter payload, temporal variance, and coordinates. Ready when you give the word."

In the living area of the townhome, Kapono held his breath, then said into his phone, "Engage."

He stepped over to the sliding glass door overlooking the private patio and small back yard and saw something that hadn't been there the last time he'd looked, over one hour ago: a small metal box with a perforated lid. Grinning, he dashed outside, picked up the box, and opened the lid. The white rat was busy munching on a kale leaf.

"George, do you know you're the first living creature to travel backward in time?" George didn't seem impressed by his historic achievement. Kapono carried the box back into the house, set it on the dining room table, and picked up his phone. "Aroha, it worked!" he said excitedly. "George is here and appears to be okay. I'm going to check the video record now."

An had installed video cameras inside his townhome and overlooking the front and back yards so the mother of the family who'd stayed with them for two years could check on her children while she was away. Kapono opened the video monitoring app on his phone, selected the back yard view, and rewound the video playback by 70 minutes. Then he fast-forwarded through the recording until he saw a blue flash. He stopped the playback, rewound by a few seconds, and moved forward at normal speed until he again saw the burst of blue light, accompanied by the small metal box appearing in the yard. He checked the video's timestamp: exactly one hour before Aroha activated the reactor.

"Aroha, it worked *perfectly!*" he said jubilantly into his phone. "Both the time and location were spot-on!"

"Sweet as!" Aroha said happily. "Don't you think it's high time we let the world know about our discovery of tachyons, and your little time machine? There isn't a whole lot more we can do with the reactor, as small as it is. And, we're almost out of antimatter."

Kapono thought for a few seconds. "Well, maybe. I was thinking ... if we could build a bigger reactor chamber, one large enough for—"

"Yeah, nah! Get that thought out of your head, K!" Aroha knew Kapono very well from working closely with him for over four years. Thus she knew whom he'd left behind in 2054, and how much he longed to return to her. "First, it's a long way from sending a rat to the past, to sending a *person*. Second, you know the Council has forbidden anyone from travelling through time. And you know *why* they did that." United Earth's president and Council, advised by Yinuo, had decided years ago that the risk of a change to the past causing tragic consequences in the future was too great. Consequently, they ordered the destruction of the Wagamese Wormhole and outlawed time travel in any form.

Aroha's voice softened. "I know how much you love Lai. But you need to let go of the past, Kapono, and focus on your life, and your family and mates, in the here and now. From what you've told me, Lai would've wanted you to do that, don't you think?"

Kapono closed his eyes and nodded. "Yes—you're right. I do need to live in the present." *But I'm not so sure about what Lai would've wanted.* He remembered some of her last words to him, from the video she made right before she died: *More than anything, I'd like to see you again, my love.* He wiped his eyes with his left hand. "Mahalo for being a good friend, Aroha."

Back at the lab, Aroha replied into her phone, "No worries, Kapono." *It'd be choice if what I just told him was motivated only out of friendship and concern for his wellbeing.* But she knew those weren't her only motivations.

| 6 |

15 March 2146

Kapono opened the front door to An's townhome; his grandson had told him to walk in when he arrived. "Hello?" he said as he stepped into the sunny living area. He heard a door closing in the hallway, and then An entered the living area from the hallway.

"Thank you for coming, *Kupunakāne*," he said quietly as he approached Kapono and they hugged.

"How are you doing, An?" Kapono said as they stepped back from the embrace. He noticed his grandson looked tired and dispirited, and he had deep shadows under his eyes.

"I'm, uh, I'm okay," An replied with a faint, unconvincing smile.

"And how is Linda?" An's wife of 33 years was still on her long-term assignment in Northern California with the Peace Corps.

"She's well—she sends her love. She's trying to get a flight home as soon as it can be arranged. But, as you know, those are few and far between." The urgency in An's voice unsettled Kapono.

"How is your mother?" Yinuo's long-term exposure to radiation, especially as a toddler, from the nuclear holocaust of World War III had finally caught up with her; she'd contracted acute myeloid leukemia. Her hematologist-oncologist had told her and An the previous day that she likely had only a month to live, at best. An was caring for her at his home, just as she had cared for her mother near the end of her battle with pancreatic cancer.

"She has her good days and bad days." His faint smile returned. "Today has been a pretty good day. She's a battler. She's been looking forward to seeing you. Before we do that, would you like anything?"

"I'm good—thanks, anyway."

An led Kapono down the hallway to the main bedroom. An and Linda were using the spare bedroom upstairs, where Kapono had stayed for several months after he'd arrived in Sydney. As An opened the door for Kapono and he stepped into the sunny room, he had a feeling of *déjà vu*. The room's soft blue walls, large window with bright-colored shades, and oxygen container and medical monitor in one corner reminded Kapono of the room Lai had been in when she'd made the video for him just before she died.

Yinuo was reclined in a hospital-style bed; she opened her eyes and smiled welcomingly, but weakly, when she heard the door open. "*Makuakāne*," she said in a clear but strained voice, using the Hawaiian word for *father*. She tilted her head toward a chair at the right side of her bed. "Come and sit with me."

Kapono leaned over and lightly held her shoulders as he kissed her on her forehead, then he sat down in the chair. "Aloha, sweetie. How are you feeling?"

"Not too bad. Not up to playing any cricket, though." Kapono was glad to see the twinkle in Yinuo's brown eyes.

"Cricket season's over, anyway, Mum," An rejoined with a gentle smile.

Yinuo turned her head toward her father. "Tell me, how is the antimatter project coming along? I haven't heard much about it lately."

"We're making progress. Generating power from antimatter doesn't appear to be practical. But we're researching other ... opportunities."

Yinuo's eyebrows raised. "Oh? Like what?"

I guess now is as good a time as any, Kapono thought. He turned toward An. "There's something I need to discuss privately with your mother. Do you mind?"

"No worries. I need to get started on tea, anyway. I'll be in the kitchen," An replied, then he turned to the bedroom door.

"None of that replicator rubbish," Yinuo called out after him.

"I know, Mum. I'll make it myself." He looked at Kapono, "Are you staying for tea, *Kupunakāne?*"

"I'd like that. Mahalo, An."

As An closed the door behind him, Yinuo asked, "So, what's so secret that it's for my ears only?"

Kapono took a deep breath before revealing, "Aroha used the matter/antimatter reactor to generate tachyons."

Yinuo's mouth gaped open and she said nothing for a few seconds. "Holy dooley! That's … incredible!"

"Yes," Kapono nodded. "But we've discovered something else—something even bigger than tachyons." Yinuo asked *What?* with her eyes. *Might as well come right out with it*, Kapono thought. "We've been able to use the tachyons to bend spacetime, to … travel back in time."

Yinuo stared at Kapono while she processed what he'd just told her. Finally she said, "You're not joking."

"No, I'm not. We figured out how to send matter, even living beings, back through time to virtually any date and location we choose. We've tested it successfully with inanimate matter and with a lab rat." He paused. "I think it could be used to send a person back in time."

Yinuo's expression changed from surprise to shock as she realized where Kapono was going; she shook her head slowly. "Don't tell me you're thinking about …."

Kapono gently grasped Yinuo's right hand. "I know why you and your mother were against my returning to the past," he said softly. "You were afraid a significant change to events in the past, such as avoiding World War III in 2057, could have terrible consequences for the future. And, I understand what's behind your concerns." Kapono's discussion with Yinuo and Witi four and a half years ago about the perils of altering the past flashed through his mind. He'd reluctantly admitted to them that he couldn't be absolutely certain that the butterfly effect—a rippling of unintended changes through time—would not apply should he cause a change to history. "But I know how to avoid that problem."

Yinuo's expression changed to one of intense curiosity, tempered with apprehension. "How could you possibly do that? You're a fine physicist, *Makuakāne*, but you can't change the laws of physics."

He smiled in agreement. "No, I can't. But I can avoid impacting the past."

Kapono explained his plan to return to the past a few days after he'd traversed the Wagamese Wormhole and use Lai's detailed diaries and calendars, and other historical records, to ensure that she and Yinuo followed their destinies. He would stick close to them and remain in the background to avoid tampering with other events in the past.

Yinuo shook her head again. "Even if you're able to return to the past and avoid changing it, the Council has forbidden all time travel. You'd be a criminal!"

"If this works … who would arrest me?" Kapono replied with a wry smile.

Yinuo thought for a few seconds. "You have a point." She closed her eyes; when she reopened them, they were glistening. "I know how much Mum longed to see you again. It was very difficult for her right after the war, even after we reached Sydney. She never admitted it to me, but I know she was lonely. And," she looked into Kapono's eyes, "it would've been ripper to have known you when I was only an ankle biter, and for a long time after that—not just for the past few years."

"I would love to have known you all those years," Kapono said as he squeezed his daughter's hand.

"But even though you have all the details of our lives and other records, do you realise how difficult it will be to avoid changing history? There's a Chinese proverb: 'The flapping of a butterfly's wings can be felt on the other side of the world.'"

Kapono nodded as he recalled the scientific origin of the term *butterfly effect*: the world is so intricately connected, even one small change can have a much larger impact—for example, the flapping of a butterfly's wings ultimately causing a typhoon.

"I know it will be difficult," he admitted. "But, there's a good chance that any impact from the butterfly effect will be canceled by the Novikov self-consistency principle." Russian physicist Igor Novikov had postulated over 150 years earlier that the laws of physics will ensure that history remains consistent if a time traveler tries to change the past.

"With all respect to Dr. Novikov, Mum was never completely convinced his principle would hold up." She closed her eyes again as Kapono thought, *She seems to be getting tired.* After several seconds, she opened her eyes; her expression blended empathy and sadness. "Despite how difficult it will be to ensure history unfolds as it should, it'll be much harder for you to *allow* history to follow its course. Do you understand what I'm saying, *Makuakāne?*"

Kapono nodded solemnly. "I do. I know there were tragic events in your mother's life, and in yours, and in the lives of people close to you." *World War III was the biggest tragedy, but there were others,* Kapono thought sorrowfully as he remembered what he'd read in Lai's diaries. "I know I must let them happen. But at least I'll be there to support you and your mother, and help you get through those difficult times." *Well, support at least; there's only so much help I can give them without affecting future events.*

"I … I think I need to rest, now," Yinuo said wearily, then her lips formed a feeble smile. "Even though I'm more than twice your age, I can't tell you what to do. You must make that decision. I hope it's the correct one."

"I do, too. I hope you can forgive me for my selfishness."

Yinuo again looked directly into his eyes. "There is nothing to forgive, *Makuakāne.* You're the least selfish person I've ever known … other than my mum." She closed her eyes again.

I'm not so sure about that, he thought. Then he stood up and bent over his daughter. "Mahalo. I love you, honey," he whispered. He kissed her on her forehead, pulled her blanket up to cover her arms, stepped out of the bedroom, and quietly closed the door.

| 7 |

16 April 2146

Following the celebration of Yinuo's life at Elouera Beach, her friends and family gathered at An and Linda's home. Linda Shen-Martin had returned from Northern California five days earlier and thus was able to join An and Kapono at Yinuo's bedside when she passed away peacefully on the 13th of April. Linda would bring Yinuo's ashes with her when she returned to Northern California, to honor her request to scatter them in San Francisco Bay; Yinuo was born in San Francisco's Mission Bay neighborhood.

After several hours reminiscing about Yinuo's extraordinary life and sharing stories about her, the mourners began saying good night and returning to their homes. Aroha stayed to help An, Linda, and Kapono clean up. When the last remains from the reception had been deposited into the recycler and all the glassware had been sonic-washed and put away, Aroha hugged Linda and An and went up to Kapono in the living area. He was looking at something on a pad and lifted his head as Aroha approached.

"Yinuo's PhD thesis," he told her. "Did you know it was on tachyon theory?"

"I did not know that. Ironic, isn't it?

"Yes … it is," Kapono said softly.

"How are you doing, K?" Aroha asked gently.

He set the pad down on the coffee table. "I'm—what is it Australians and Kiwis say? 'She'll be right, mate'?"

Aroha smiled compassionately. "Legit."

"I'll be okay. Yinuo had a long, full life. But, I feel I hardly got to know her." Kapono had read in Lai's diaries about Yinuo's birth, her childhood, her graduations from secondary school and the University of New South Wales, earning her PhD in quantum physics at the Australian National University, her marriage to Liam Martin and raising their son An, and her career as a leading scientist for United Earth. *I would love to have been a part of her life all that time.*

"I don't know about that, K. From what you said about her at the service, I think you knew her pretty well." At Yinuo's memorial service, Kapono had spoken about how his daughter exemplified Hawaiian core values: *aloha* (an attitude of joy, love, and respect); *malama* (caring for, protecting, and nurturing); *lokahi* (harmony); *akahai* (kindness); *ahonui* (patience and perseverance), and *ike loa* (seeking knowledge and wisdom). "I think she would've really liked what you said about her."

"Mahalo. And, thank you for your help with the service and reception."

"No worries. I was happy to do it. Yinuo showed faith in me when she hired me to start up the antimatter project. She was always supportive and helpful—like a mentor, really."

Kapono smiled gently. "She told me that hiring you for that project was the best decision she ever made as chief physicist—also the easiest decision."

"Flatterer. I appreciate your saying that." She glanced at her watch. "Well, I'd best get along home." She put her hands lightly on Kapono's upper arms. "See you on Monday at the lab?"

"I'll be there. Good night, Aroha."

"*Pō mārie*—good night, Kapono." She retrieved her purse off the dining room table, said goodbye to An, and went out the front door. Kapono went over to An, who was still in the kitchen.

"Where's Linda?"

"She went off to bed. I don't think she's fully adjusted yet from the time change, plus the last few days have been hard on her. You know how much she loved her mum-in-law."

"I do. How are you holding up, An?"

"She'll be right," An replied, but his face contradicted his words. "I'm glad Linda won't have to return to California for a couple of weeks. Between her work with the Peace Corps and my construction projects, we don't get to see each other nearly enough."

"I'm glad you'll have some time together." He paused. *Should I ask him now? I guess there is no ideal time.* "An, there's something I'd like to talk with you about. It can wait, if you're tired."

"Now is fine. Should we sit outside?" Kapono nodded, and An opened the sliding glass patio door.

It was a mild mid-autumn evening; the clear sky offered an unusually good view of the constellations Centaurus and Triangulum Australe, and the Milky Way. The two men sat down in patio chairs and gazed up at the star-filled sky.

"Triangulum Australe is where the Wagamese Wormhole was, right, *Kupunakāne?*"

"Yes, that's right." He pointed at Centaurus. "And in the past, it was in Centaurus, in close conjunction with Proxima Centauri."

An turned to look at his grandfather. "Do you ever think about my nanna?"

"Yes, I do." *All the time.* "In fact, that's what I wanted to talk with you about."

"Oh? How so?"

Kapono explained in layperson's terms Aroha's discovery of tachyons and their follow-on work that proved they could be used to send matter, even a living creature, back to any point in time, anywhere on Earth. An's expression morphed from mild curiosity to astonishment as he realized where Kapono was headed.

"*Kupunakāne,* you're not considering using the reactor to send *yourself* back to the 2050s … are you?"

"I am." An started to protest, but Kapono interrupted him. "I know about the risks of changing the past. I've figured out how to mitigate that risk." He explained how he'd use Lai's diaries and calendars, and other details about events during the past 90 years, to avoid changing history, and how he planned to stay out of history's way as much as possible.

"I understand why you want to return to the past, to Nanna and Mum there. But, in addition to the risk to yourself from using the reactor for time travel, you'd be a criminal."

Kapono smiled slyly. "I'll be long dead before I could be charged with a crime."

An nodded. "But, what about the risk to yourself?"

"Aroha and I tested it on a mouse, and it worked perfectly." Kapono smiled to himself as he looked at the spot in the back yard where George had materialized after his short journey to the past. "There's no reason it shouldn't work with a human."

"Well ... if you feel you have to do it, I support your decision. But I'll miss you, *Kupunakāne*."

"And I'll miss you and Linda." *Until we meet again in the past.* "And I'm really glad you support my decision, because ... I need your help."

"How so? I'm no physicist, you know."

"I need an engineer to help me design and build a bigger version of the time machine. Would you do that?"

"I'm willing to help you, but I'm a *civil* engineer. I think you'll want help from a mechanical engineer, possibly also an electrical engineer."

"I realize that. But I don't know any mechanical or electrical engineers—none I'd trust with this little project, anyway. Besides, didn't you study those disciplines in college?"

"Sure, but that was a very long time ago." An looked away from his grandfather, into the dark night. *I'd be an accessory to a felony ....* After several seconds, he turned back to Kapono.

"I'll help you. I'll need to bone up on mechanical and electrical engineering, though."

"Mahalo, An. I'm very grateful. And, I'll ensure there's no way you can be associated with this."

An's eyebrows shot up, "How will you do that, *Kupunakāne?*"

"I have some ideas," Kapono said with a enigmatic smile. *But, for this whole thing to work, I'll need help from one more person....*

| 8 |

18 April 2146

"You're a bit gone, aren't you," Aroha declared matter-of-factly, her fists dug into her hips. She was exasperated by Kapono's revelation that he intended to travel back in time. *Someone's got to smack some sense into him,* she thought. "You're really acting the goat, Kapono."

He smiled ruefully and nodded. "Maybe I *am* foolish—crazy, even. But, you understand *why* I believe I have to do it, don't you?"

Aroha's expression changed from exasperation to empathy; she unclenched her fists and took them off her hips. "I do. It isn't called 'crazy love' for nothing." She stepped close to him and looked directly into his eyes. "But think *very hard* about what you'd be doing. Forget for a minute about becoming a wanted man and endangering your own life. You'd be risking all of history, K! Sure, you have all the details of Lai and Yinuo's lives. But one slip-up, one flap of a butterfly's wings, could mean the whole planet would be up the boohai!"

"'Up the boohai'?"

"A very bad day. *Many* very bad days, perhaps." *Unless Novikov was right ... but even Yinuo and Lai Shen didn't think so.* "You're the kindest, most considerate person I know. But taking this risk for the whole world because you *think* you've figured out how to avoid changing history is ...." Her expression was a mix of exasperation and incredulity. "Well, it's *arrogance.* I never thought I'd see that from you, of all people."

Arrogant? Aroha's accusation stunned Kapono. *I know my love for Lai is driving me to do this, but I've done everything possible to minimize the risks. Am I really being arrogant?*

Before he could reply, Aroha continued, "But we've had this discussion before. I think, in this matter, your ears are painted on."

"If by that you mean I'm not listening to you and don't respect what you're saying, that's not true. I hope you know I respect you more than anyone."

Respect—well, that's something. "And I hope you know how I feel about you." *But I doubt it ... love isn't just crazy—it's blind, too. I guess wishing for more than respect is acting the goat myself.* "That's why, despite my better judgement ... I'll help you." Kapono had told her he needed her help to not only operate the time machine, but also to ensure all evidence of that illegal act would be erased.

"Mahalo, Aroha!" Kapono exclaimed with joy and relief as he gave her a quick embrace.

"You're welcome. But," she continued with a puzzled frown, "exactly *how* are we going to pull off this disappearing act?"

"Besides purging the project files, including the backups, I think I know how to make the time machine disappear also," he explained as he turned his head to look at the soccer-ball-sized sphere sitting on a lab bench.

"But you'll need a much bigger machine for your trip back in time. Just how will I dispose of *that?*"

Kapono's grin reminded Aroha of the fabled Cheshire cat. "I've found a way to adjust the tachyon bubble so it envelops the entire sphere."

A smile spread slowly across Aroha's face as she understood what Kapono had just said. "Ah! Very clever, Dr. Ailana."

"Why, mahalo, Dr. Whakatane."

| 9 |

10 May 2146

An pushed on both sides of his forehead with his fingertips. He did that when deep in thought, especially when thinking about how to solve a big problem—which is exactly what he and Kapono needed to do. They were sitting at the dining room table in An and Linda's townhome, reviewing An's draft design for the larger time machine that would, hopefully, send Kapono back to the 2050s.

"*Kupunakāne*, do you realise how much titanium a sphere of this size will require? And how much it will *cost?*" The current matter/antimatter reactor was less than nine inches in diameter, not including the passenger compartment extension Aroha and Kapono had added for George. But the reactor designed by An, based on Kapono's specifications, would be nearly two meters—about six feet—in diameter. It had to be large enough to contain the matter/antimatter reaction and house Kapono in a shielded compartment.

"I imagine it'll cost quite a bit—more than I can afford, anyway," Kapono replied gloomily. *Even with Yinuo's generosity.* Kapono and An had been surprised to learn Yinuo bequeathed each of them over two million dollars. She'd led a simple, uncomplicated life and had spent very little of her earnings from her 35 years as United Earth's chief physicist on herself. She'd donated the remainder of her estate to the Peace Corps and the University of New South Wales physics department. Kapono was using his inheritance to fund the new, larger time machine. But titanium was hard to come by in the post-war world and very expensive when it could be found.

An removed his fingers from his forehead. "Maybe …." He looked at Kapono. "What did you say the passenger compartment of the current reactor is made of?"

"The shielding is titanium," Kapono realized with a start where An was going, "but the rest of the compartment is just steel!"

"And didn't you say that the more tachyons you need to generate and the faster they need to go—that is, the further back in time—the *less* antimatter you need?"

"That's right. Are you thinking what I'm thinking?" Kapono asked as his face broke into a wide smile.

"I believe so. What I'm thinking is, we don't need a bigger reactor. We can use the existing one. What we need is a bigger *passenger compartment*. And that can be fabricated with a 3D printer. We only need enough titanium for the shielding of the new passenger compartment." An looked at Kapono for confirmation.

"Yes! And that will make construction of the larger sphere fairly simple—and cheap! We can fabricate the components off-site and assemble them quickly in the lab."

"It wouldn't even need to be spherical, would it? It's easier and less expensive to print flat panels."

Kapono thought for a moment. "Actually, it does need to be spherical. The tachyon bubble has that shape."

"Ah, I see," An nodded. "A sphere it shall be, then. I need to run the numbers, but I think we can fit your budget, using printed metal for the new sphere and allowing for the titanium shielding."

"That's bloody fantastic!" Kapono replied, making An smile with amusement at how his Hawaiian grandfather was picking up the lingo.

This is moving along better than I'd hoped, Kapono thought happily. *But I'd better start working on other preparations*….

| 10 |

12 May 2146

I *hope third time's the charm,* Kapono thought as he opened the door to the modest storefront for Nguyen Vinh Antiquities and was welcomed by the tinkling of a bell hanging over the door. It was the third, and last, of the antique shops he'd visited in and around Miranda. *If they don't have what I'm looking for, I may need to look outside of Sydney.*

An elderly man with a deeply lined face and thin white hair fringing a bald pate looked up from behind a counter. "G'day, young man. How may I help you?"

He's probably never heard aloha, Kapono realized as he stepped up to the counter. "Good day, sir. Do you carry old foreign currency? Specifically, United States currency from around 100 years ago?"

The old man rubbed his chin. "Yes, I do have some of that. There's not much demand for it. But I picked some up at an estate sale a while back—a bloke from America who apparently didn't believe in banks. You realise, it's been worthless as currency since the war?"

"I know. My ancestors were from Hawai'i. I thought it would be nice to have as a … remembrance."

"I see. How much do you want?"

"How much do you have?"

"Let me check." Vinh opened an ancient olive-green filing cabinet standing behind him and removed a thick manila envelope. "It'll take a while to count it."

"No worries—I'll just look around."

As the shop owner counted the old bills, Kapono browsed through the dusty, crowded shelves and noticed the musty smell typical of antique shops. He spied a familiar stainless-steel box and smiled as he picked it up. *An hPhone! Well, I already have one of those, and I know mine works—just not in this time.*

He replaced the phone on the shelf and continued looking around at the treasures and near-treasures in the store, until he saw something perched on a shelf that made him stop and grin. It was a scale model of the original Starship *Enterprise* from *Star Trek*. Its registry letters and numbers, *NCC-1701*, were faded and barely legible. *It might be over 150 years old!* He checked for a price tag, but found none. He returned to the man at the counter. "How much is the model of the *Enterprise?*"

Vinh looked up from the neat piles of sorted bills in front of him. "That? Oh, it's priceless. It's likely the only one in Australia—maybe the entire world. But," he winked, "I could part with it for A$3,000."

"That's a little rich for me," Kapono admitted sadly. *Besides, I couldn't take it with me, where I'm going ... when I'm going.* "I think I'll pass. Thanks, anyway."

"No dramas." He finished counting the last few bills. "I have $22,540 in United States of America currency."

"That's great! Did you happen to notice the dates?"

"It's all pre-war, of course. Looks like they're all from between 2026 and 2053. Is that okay?"

"That's perfect. How much for all of it?"

Vinh rubbed his chin as he thought. "A$500. Or," he smiled dryly, "the currency *and* the spaceship for only A$3,200."

"That seems like a good deal. But I really only need the currency."

"All right," Vinh said with a hint of disappointment. He wrapped the bills carefully in brown paper, and Kapono paid him.

"Thank you. I'm glad I stopped in."

"Too right."

Kapono took one more glance at the dusty starship model on the shelf, then started toward the door. "Cheers!"

"Aloha, mate," the old man replied with a wave.

Kapono stopped, grinned, and turned back to the man behind the counter. "Mahalo, and aloha."

* * *

Kapono looked up from the e-book on his phone when the door of the doctor's examination room opened. A 30-something man with wavy brown hair, wearing a short white coat and carrying a pad, stepped into the room and extended his hand.

"Morning, I'm Dr. Smith," the urologist said with a welcoming smile.

Kapono stood up and shook hands. "Good morning, Doctor. Kapono Ailana."

"Please have a seat, Mr. Ailana," Smith said as he sat down in the swivel chair at the small desk next to Kapono, who sat back down as the doctor looked at his pad. "Someone made a blue on your medical record; it says your birthdate is 25 August 2018." He looked up at Kapono. "What's your actual date of birth?"

"That's not a mistake."

Smith's expression was a mix of bewilderment and irritation; then he remembered something from a few years ago. "Oh! You're the bloke who came here from the past, aren't you?"

"That's me," Kapono confirmed.

"Crikey! That makes you, what, 128 years old? You don't look a day over 40," the doctor joked.

"Vitamins," Kapono replied with a mischievous smile.

Smith chuckled, "Good on ya." He finished reviewing the medical record, then set the pad on the desk and looked at Kapono. "What can I do for you today, Mr. Ailana?"

"I want to get a vasectomy."

The doctor's eyebrows raised slightly. "I don't do those much anymore. Most people are trying to have *more* children these days. I don't know if you're aware of this, but many couples have trouble conceiving—it's an aftereffect of the war."

"I've heard about that," Kapono replied, thinking of what An had told him about his and Linda's struggles to have children.

"Right." Smith leaned back in his chair. "I can certainly do the vasectomy. But there's also male birth control—it's over-the-counter, you know. Very easy—and painless."

"But is it as effective?"

Smith shook his head. "Well, no—not nearly as effective as a vasectomy. I perform the minimally invasive type—it has the lowest risk of complications and lowest failure rate. And, just so you know, it's reversible. I have a 97 percent success rate with that. I've been doing a lot more of those than vasectomies, lately."

"That's good to know, but I don't need to worry about reversing it."

"Right. A vasectomy it is, then."

"How long does it take for the vasectomy to be effective, Doctor?"

"About 30 days. There used to be a longer waiting period, but the latest procedure has reduced that considerably."

"When could you do it?"

The doctor picked up the pad and tapped his fingers on its screen. "Let's see … if you could wait a bit, I have an opening after my next patient. It takes only about 30 minutes."

"That'll be fine. I can wait."

"Ripper." The doctor stood up, and Kapono did likewise. "Why don't you head back to the reception area, and my nurse will come get you when I'm ready."

"Great. Thanks, Doctor."

"See you in a little while, Mr. Ailana. Cheers."

Kapono found an empty chair in the clinic's waiting area, sat down, and started thinking about other preparations he'd need to make before his return to the past.

I'm going to need a government ID—a passport would probably be best, he mused. *I doubt anyone in Sydney can forge a United States passport from 2054. I'll just have to take care of that when I get there,* he decided.

| 11 |

26 June 2146

"I'll miss you, Pop," Linda Shen-Martin's voice said over Kapono's phone speaker. She was saying goodbye to her grandfather-in-law from Northern California's Sacramento Valley, where she was working with a Peace Corps team to rebuild communities. "I wish I'd had more time to get to know you better."

"I wish I'd had more time with you, also," Kapono said, his voice tinged with sadness and regret. "But the work you're doing with the Peace Corps is so important, and I'm very proud of you. I know Yinuo was, too."

"Thanks. I really miss her. I know this is important, but I've missed so much with my family." Linda's grandparents and father had passed away many years ago, and her mother died in 2139. *At least I was there for her near the end*, she thought sorrowfully. "I never thought, when Myrt Reinhart and I found *Chronos 4* in West Texas nine years ago, it would bring you here from the past. And then, a few years later, you'd find a way to return there. I thought—I hoped—we'd have more time."

Kapono remembered some of Lai's last words to him, from the video she'd left for him: *Life is short ... and you never know what's going to happen.* "I feel the same way. I hope you understand why I have to do this, and do it *now*." Not only was the supply of antimatter almost gone, but he was concerned someone would find out about his illegal time travel experiments and implicate An and Aroha.

"Yes, An explained it to me, but I don't know any details. He said I really don't want to know the details."

"He's right, Linda—you don't." *I don't want to implicate her in my scheme, too.*

"Pop, I'd like to talk longer, but I need to get back to the team. We're finalizing plans for new habitats for over 30 families. They've been living in tents and shacks for years. It's pretty exciting."

"That is exciting! But, before you go, I want to thank you for your love and support, not just for me, but for your mother-in-law, and for Lai." He recalled what Lai had said about Linda in the video she'd left for him. "You know, she thought you hung the Moon."

There was a pause before Linda replied, "Thanks for saying that. Lai was such an amazing person, and so kind to me. I miss her, too. I'm glad you'll be together with her again. I know how much she missed you." It sounded like she cleared her throat. "I need to go now. I love you, Pop."

"I love you, too, sweetie. Aloha, *a hui hou.*" The call ended. *The great thing is, I will see her again someday, if this works. And An, too.* He turned toward his grandson, who was sitting with him in the living room of An and Linda's townhome. "It's time," he said quietly as he stood up. An stood also and hugged his grandfather.

"Be careful, *Kupunakāne,*" An said in a strained voice. He broke the embrace. "I don't suppose you can give Nanna my love?"

"I'm sorry—that won't be possible," Kapono said sadly. *But I need to make sure he'll be able to do that himself, someday, in my life-to-be.* "Thank you again for all of your help. I never could have done this without you."

"You're welcome. I hope I won't regret it later. But," he realized as he smiled reluctantly, "I guess I won't know if anything changes—will I?"

"No," Kapono acknowledged. "But I'm going to do everything I can to make sure there's no changes for you not to notice."

"Fair dinkum. And Aroha will take care of, uh, tidying things up at the lab?"

"Absolutely. You won't get any unexpected knocks on your door." Kapono had done everything he could to minimize the exposure for An and Aroha. Only Kapono, Aroha, and Dean of Physics Lev Sushkov had access to the lab, and Sushkov hadn't come to the lab for many weeks. An and Kapono fabricated the larger components for the time machine at a commercial 3D printing facility, then assembled them in the lab in just the past few days.

"That's good. I wouldn't want Linda to have to visit me in prison when she returns home," An said with an apprehensive smile.

"Neither would I!" *I'd never forgive myself if An or Aroha get into trouble because of this.* "I should go." He started heading for the front door, and An followed him. Kapono hugged him one last time. "Aloha, *a hui hou.*"

"You said that to Linda, too. What does that mean?"

"Until we meet again."

∗ ∗ ∗

Aroha paced nervously back and forth in front of the large metal sphere—the time machine Kapono and An had built—at the Antimatter Power Generation Research lab. She started thinking, *What can I say to make him—* when the door opened and Kapono stepped into the lab.

"Aloha, Aroha. Is everything ready?"

She hesitated, and looked at Kapono with uncertain eyes. "Aye, but …."

"What's wrong?"

She walked up to him and grabbed his upper arms. "*This* is wrong! I don't know what I can say to you to make you see that!"

"Probably nothing," he admitted with a small smile. "You've explained why this is, logically, a terrible idea. But not every decision is logical. There's that 'crazy love' we've talked about."

"Aye, there's that," Aroha said softly. "And, about that … there's another reason I don't want you to do this."

"What's that?"

She looked into his eyes. "I love you, Kapono."

"I love you, too, Aroha. You're my closest friend." Then the full meaning of what she'd just said hit him, as if someone had shaken him awake. "But, that's not what you mean—is it?"

"No. I'm *in love* with you. Love really *is* blind, isn't it?"

Kapono chuckled softly. "In my case, I guess so!" He took Aroha's hands in his. "I hope you know, I think the world of you. And I *do* love you—just not in the same way you love me. I already have my *ku'uipo*—the one person for whom my love is unbreakable and un-limited. And, that's why I *must* do this—logic, even common sense, notwithstanding. I hope you can understand."

She wiped her nose with her sleeve and nodded. "Aye ... I under-stand what love can drive people to do." She closed her eyes as she remembered the day three weeks earlier when she'd considered using up the project's remaining antimatter to prevent Kapono's return to the past. *I have to let him go,* she decided, and she opened her eyes. "All right—let's do this."

Kapono hugged her tightly. "Mahalo." They broke the embrace, and he turned toward the large sphere. "Coordinates and temporal variance all set?"

"Aye. And there'll be just enough antimatter left for the Great Dis-appearing Act."

"How far back do you think that will be?"

"I estimate about 1,600 years."

Kapono smiled approvingly, "That's perfect."

Aroha powered up the matter/antimatter reactor. "The boarding door is about to close," she said with a reluctant smile.

Kapono checked his jacket pockets one more time to ensure he hadn't forgotten anything, then he picked up the small bag that held the all-important pad with Lai's diaries and calendars. "All set," he replied. He kissed Aroha lightly on her forehead. "Aloha. I'll never for-get this—and you."

"I know I won't be forgetting you anytime soon. Be careful, K."

She held the small door of the sphere's shielded passenger compartment for Kapono as he climbed into it; it was barely large enough for him to sit in a fetal position. He gave her a thumbs-up sign, and she closed and latched the door. Then she once again checked the coordinates and time displacement, confirmed the magnetic field in the reactor was at full power, hesitated for a second, and pushed the *Engage* button.

There was a faint hum, then a burst of blue light. The reactor shut down. Aroha peered into the sphere's passenger compartment through its small viewport and saw it was empty. She stood motionless by the sphere for several seconds, then wiped her eyes and loaded the last of the antimatter and an equal amount of matter into the reactor.

She adjusted the size of the tachyon bubble such that it would envelop the entire sphere, then she reset the coordinates for the surface of the Pacific Ocean above its deepest point—the portion of the Marianas Trench known as the Challenger Deep. She checked the target date—it read *12 March 547*. Based on what she knew about the history of exploration of the Challenger Deep, she realized she would be the last person to see the sphere until the middle of the 20th century.

She picked up a hammer from the lab table and smashed the glass viewport of the sphere's passenger compartment to ensure the sphere would fill with seawater and eventually sink to the bottom. Then she pressed *Engage* and quickly stepped back from the sphere, to the opposite side of the lab. Again there was a faint hum, but this time the blue glow enveloped the entire sphere. Then, it vanished.

After she confirmed the hyper-power circuit had shut down automatically, she thought, *I should double-check Kapono's clean-up work.* It wasn't that she didn't trust him; he'd recommended she confirm his part of the Great Disappearing Act. She logged into the project's archive, confirmed that all files and data regarding her discovery of tachyons and Kapono's time travel research were gone, then she logged into the university's archive to ensure all backups had been deleted. *Spick-and-span*, she thought as she exhaled with relief. She logged off from her workstation, glanced at the blank writing wall, and headed for the door.

Just as she was about to grasp the lab's doorknob, Lev Sushkov, dean of the University of New South Wales physics department, opened the door and stopped short when he saw Aroha.

"Oh, *kia ora*, Dr. Whakatane!" Sushkov exclaimed with mild surprise.

"*Kia ora*, Dr. Sushkov," Aroha replied, trying to keep her voice steady while her stomach did flip-flops. *Why is he here NOW?* she worried. *Does he know something?* "May I help you?" The tall, gray-haired man stepped into the lab.

"I hope so. I was taking a Sunday stroll when I saw a blue flash coming from the windows of this lab. I thought perhaps my mind was playing tricks on me. But then, a few minutes later, I saw another blue flash, brighter than the first. I thought I'd check it out. Can you tell me what I saw?"

"Hmm ...." Aroha pretended to ponder the dean's question. "Sometimes, I've noticed the ultra-low-E glass in this building can cause reflections in various hues. Perhaps that's what you saw."

"Perhaps. I've never seen anything like that before, however." He seemed to set the mystery aside. "So, how is the antimatter project going? I haven't been keeping up with your progress as I should." His expression became somber. "Dr. Shen-Martin used to take care of that for me ... and many other things."

"We just wrapped it up. I regret to tell you that we learned it doesn't appear feasible to generate power from matter/antimatter reactions. The cost would be astronomical for the amount of energy released."

"That's unfortunate," Sushkov said sadly. "I know you and Dr. Ailana worked long and hard on it." He looked around the lab. "Where is Dr. Ailana? I haven't talked with him in quite a while."

"I'm not sure," Aroha replied. It was the truth, albeit not the complete truth. "Perhaps he's gone walkabout, out in Woop Woop." *I can't tell him Kapono did a runner—disappeared without a trace.*

Thinking Aroha was joking, Sushkov smiled with amusement. "I can catch up with him later." He looked around the lab again. "Where's the reactor you and Dr. Ailana built? I was hoping to see it."

"Oh, we disposed of that, since the project is done."

"I see. Someplace safe, I hope?"

"Aye—very safe."

Sushkov nodded, "Good. I look forward to reading your report, Dr. Whakatane."

"I'll have a draft for you by the end of the week, Dr. Sushkov."

"Excellent. Well, I need to head for home—my wife is probably wondering what's become of me." He opened the door, then turned to look at Aroha. "You should take off the rest of the day, Doctor—it's lovely weather for this time of year."

"I'll do that. Thank you for the suggestion."

"Cheers!" Sushkov said as he went out the door. Aroha sank back against a lab table and let out a long breath.

* * *

Dr. Kapono Ailana never returned from walkabout, and the motive for his deletion of all files and data from the antimatter project remained a mystery. There was an intensive nationwide search for United Earth's chief physicist, but it was called off after two months when there was no sign of him. For the second time in his life, he was officially declared missing and presumed dead on 25 August 2146—his 41st birthday. Or his 128th birthday, depending on how one chooses to mark the passage of time.

An led a moving memorial service for Kapono at Elouera Beach. He, Linda, and Aroha were convincingly sorrowful. But Aroha's sadness, and her tears, were no act. As she stood with other mourners on the sunny, windy beach listening to An's touching tribute to his *kupunakāne*, her thoughts were about what might have been, had the man she loved not vanished in a blue flash two months earlier.

Haere rā, luv. I hope you're safe… and happy.

| 12 |

November 12, 2054

The oft-patched brick surface of the narrow, dead-end alley in Boston's Charlestown neighborhood glistened from a recent rain shower. The alley was pitch dark, illuminated only by a waxing gibbous Moon and dim light from the adjoining street.

Suddenly, the darkness was interrupted by a brief, bright blue flash. The blaze of blue light disappeared into the night, revealing a man sitting in the middle of the alley, coiled in a fetal position.

Kapono was stunned and disoriented. He fell backward, catching himself with his hands. He sat in the damp alley for a minute while his head cleared, and he looked up and down the alley. *No one here. So far, so good.*

He slowly stood up, brushed off the seat of his black slacks, reached into a pocket of his black leather jacket for his hPhone, and turned it on. As he expected, there was no 8G service—his phone plan had been canceled after his disappearance on October 19, 2054. But he was able to connect to a public Wi-Fi network. A grin flashed across his face as he saw the date and time on his phone: *November 12, 2054, 10:32 p.m. Perfect!* he thought, appreciative of Aroha's precision. *I'm at the right time. But, am I in the right PLACE?*

He checked the maps app on his phone. *It looks like I'm in the right area,* he thought with relief. He walked to the alley's entrance and looked up and down the street. Mist rose from storm sewer grates, and cars splashed through puddles in the potholes of the worn pavement. He noticed with relief that nearly every car had Massachusetts license plates. Then he recognized the second building to his left: *Lai's apartment!* He'd found a photo on Lai's pad of Lai and a Secret Service agent named Hannah Ochrankyne standing in front of the building in running togs. He checked the map on his phone to ensure it was the right place—it was: Main Street.

He knew from Lai's diary that she was returning from her trip to Honolulu and Maui that night, and her flight from San Francisco was scheduled to land at Logan soon. He'd picked that day, time, and place to return to the past because he knew within a specific time window that Lai would be arriving alone at her apartment. He checked her flight status on his phone and saw her plane had just landed. *She should be getting home in about an hour*, he figured.

As he thought about how to kill that time, he spied a pizza place across and down the street. He smiled from a memory from nearly five years earlier of another pizza place, in eastern Kansas—although it was only a few weeks ago by the present calendar. He crossed the street and headed for the pizzeria.

* * *

An hour later, a driverless rideshare car pulled up at the curb just down the street from Lai's apartment building. The trunk popped open, and Lai climbed out of the back seat, grabbed her roller bag from the trunk, and closed the trunk lid.

As the car pulled away from the curb, she started walking toward the front entrance to her building and noticed the dark form of a man in black slacks and a black leather jacket standing about five meters from the apartment entrance. *Damn*, she thought nervously, *I hope I don't have to remember my Wing Chun lessons from 17 years ago!*

She avoided eye contact with the man in black and started to walk briskly past him when she heard him say quietly, in a voice that was eerily familiar, "Lai." She froze, then swung around and looked at the man's face, first in disbelief, then utter shock. The man smiled tenderly at her as he said, "Aloha, *ku'uipo.*"

"*Kapono!*" Lai cried out with joy. She released the handle of her bag and rushed to him, grabbed the sides of his head, stretched up on her toes and kissed him passionately. She broke off the kiss and released his head, holding his arms instead. "But, how could you *possibly* be here? The wormhole is gone!" Then she noticed he looked older than when she'd last seen him, less than one month ago from her perspective; his hair had a touch of gray.

"That's a long story. We should go inside." He looked at her bag standing behind her on the sidewalk. "Can I help you with your bag? You're probably tired after your long trip, huh?"

Lai realized Kapono had said almost exactly those same words to her when he'd welcomed her to the Prometheus base two years ago. And she also remembered how she'd rudely dismissed his offer of help. Grateful for the opportunity for a do-over, she replied, "Thank you, sir—I'd appreciate that." He grabbed the suitcase handle and a small bag he was carrying with his left hand and Lai's hand with his right, and they walked together toward the entrance of the old brick building.

Lai opened the door of her second-floor apartment and they stepped inside. Kapono looked around the small flat as Lai removed her coat and hung it on a peg by the door. "This is great!" he remarked as he appreciated the living room's fireplace, tall divided-light windows, built-in bookshelves, oak floors, and brick accent wall, and the tiny but quaint kitchen. "It has a lot of character."

"Thanks! I like it. I'm not here much, though." She'd rented the apartment in Charlestown to be close to Daniel Bennett's townhome. In the past two weeks she'd spent most of her time working with him on their fledgling Love One Another movement.

"If you want to hear that story now, you might want to make some coffee—it really is long."

She embraced him again. "I *do* want to hear your story, my love. But it's late, and I *am* pretty tired. So, how about we wait until morning for that story?"

"Sounds good." He took off his jacket and hung it beside Lai's coat. Lai started heading for the bedroom, and he wasn't quite sure what to do. He looked at the sofa. "I'll just, uh, crash here, okay?"

Lai turned around and stared at Kapono. The look on her face told him, *Are you out of your mind?* She walked back to him and grabbed the front of his shirt. "No sofa for you, mister. I'm not *that* tired." She started pulling him toward the bedroom door, then she stopped, released her grip on his shirt, and turned around with an apologetic expression. "Uhm … I didn't plan on any gentleman callers."

"Don't worry," he said with a smile, "I took care of that before I came back." *In more ways than one. Looks like she doesn't know, yet.*

Lai grinned, "Well, aren't you the thoughtful one!"

| 13 |

November 13, 2054

Kapono looked at Lai's face as she slept beside him. It was softly illuminated by rose-colored early morning sunlight filtering through the sheer curtains on the bedroom window. *She's so beautiful,* he thought as he lightly stroked her hair with his fingertips. She smiled sweetly and opened her eyes.

"Morning, love," she said sleepily, then she yawned. "What time is it?"

"About six-thirty." He leaned over and kissed her. "Sorry if I woke you up."

"You didn't." She wrapped her arms around him and returned his kiss. "I need to get up, anyway. I want to hear your story!" She groaned as she stretched both arms over her head. "I'll make us some coffee, if you want to hop in the shower."

"Or," he said with a mischievous smile, "we could jump in the shower together and save water. And, I'll wash your ... back."

Lai's eyes sparkled as her lips turned up in a playful smile. "I like how you think, Doctor."

* * *

"This coffee is wonderful!" Kapono exclaimed with delight after his first sip. Lai had brought some Kona coffee back with her from Hawai'i. He hadn't had any since he'd visited his father in Maui the previous November, by the current calendar—but nearly six years ago in absolute time for the Hawaiian physicist.

"Isn't it incredible? Governor Peleke introduced me to it when Daniel Bennett and I met with him in Honolulu about LOA—Love One Another." She and Kapono were sitting on the red overstuffed sofa in the small living room. "Did you find out anything about my work with Daniel on LOA when you were in the future?"

Kapono nodded, "I did." *Including some things I can't share with you,* he thought sadly.

"But now," she said as she set her mug on the coffee table, "I want to hear your story—every last detail. Starting with, how the heck did you make it through the wormhole and back to Earth in the future? We thought your ship had been hit by a micrometeorite, then the black hole blew up, and the wormhole with it."

Well, not EVERY detail, he thought. "I was very lucky. That micrometeorite barely missed me, but it punched a couple of holes in the cabin and took out the guidance computers and communications. But Aileen and I used Plan H. It worked!" Plan H was the scheme Lai and Kapono had devised to allow him to fly *Chronos 3* manually, with help from the Aileen AI pilot app on his hPhone, if the ship's guidance computers failed. "As for how I made it to Earth ... I'm sorry, but I'd better keep those details to myself."

"Oh, okay," Lai said with disappointment. "Can you tell me anything about how you got back here to the past?"

He took another sip of coffee as he decided how much he could share. "What do you know about tachyons?"

"I studied them in college and grad school. They're hypothetical subatomic particles that, theoretically, can only travel faster than the speed of light. And they may be able to travel backward in time. Why?"

Kapono set his cup on the table and looked directly into Lai's eyes. "What if I told you they're not hypothetical—they're *real*?"

Lai's eyes opened wide and her mouth gaped open in shock. "Holy shit! You discovered tachyons?!"

"Someone I worked with in the future did. And, what if I told you that what you said about tachyons being able to travel backward in time is true? And that they can be used to send matter, even people, back through time."

An amazed smile spread across Lai's face. "I'd say ... seeing is believing!"

Kapono chuckled, "Right!"

"You've got to tell me how you did that! The quantum mechanics must be incredibly complex."

"They were pretty hairy," Kapono agreed, thinking about the maze of equations that were on the writing wall of his lab in 2146. "But I think it would be best if I don't share those details with you. The less I divulge about the future to you and others, the better. There's too great a risk of endangering the future by accidentally changing the past."

"I don't understand," Lai said with a puzzled expression. "Current theory is that the butterfly effect won't apply for the quantum mechanics of time travel."

Kapono nodded. "Yes, but there was subsequent research by ..." he almost slipped and said *you and Yinuo*, "... top quantum physicists that cast uncertainty on whether or not the butterfly effect would apply. Thus, I devised a plan to ensure my presence in the past doesn't change history in any significant way."

He explained how he would use her diaries and calendars, plus other details about events after 2054, to avoid changing history—and specifically, Lai's path through history. "It's essential that people who know me don't learn I've returned to the past: Katherine and other Prometheus team members, for sure, and also José de la Cruz, Senator Wilkes, and the rest of the Prometheus Oversight Committee." Katherine Etter was the Prometheus project director and had hired Kapono and Lai for that project.

"How will you manage that? Are you going to hole up in my apartment all the time?"

"Well, no." *Maybe a lot of the time*, he realized. "I *am* going to keep a very low profile. I want to be with you as much as I can. But I won't be able to go everywhere with you." *It's just as well she does as much as possible on her own.*

"Okay," Lai agreed. "Just having you here *at all* is more than I ever dreamed of!"

Kapono looked at her with love. "Likewise for me. I couldn't bear to live with 'the loss of what is past.'"

"That's from *Coriolanus*!" she exclaimed in surprise. "Not one of the Bard's best-known plays. How the heck do you know that?"

"I had some time on my hands in the future," Kapono explained. "I decided to become a more well-rounded individual and got acquainted with some of the classics: Shakespeare, *The Great Gatsby*, *1984*, *Stranger in a Strange Land*, *Escape from Kharkiv*, *Wuthering Heights*, *Tiananmen Square*, *To Kill a Mockingbird*, and others."

"I'm impressed!" Lai said with admiration. "You know how much I love Shakespeare, but I haven't read most of those books—although *Tiananmen Square* was my favorite book when I was a teenager."

"Speaking of Shakespeare, and 'What's in a name?' … I'll need to use an alias."

Lai's eyebrows lifted. "Really? I guess that makes sense. So, what do I call you?"

"*You* can call me Kapono, when we're alone. Otherwise, allow me to introduce you to Kai Mililani."

"Pleased to meet you, *Kai*," Lai winked. "How did you come up with that name?"

"Kai means *ocean*. You know how much I love the sea."

Lai nodded. "Yes. It's perfect. And, I can still call you K," she said with a smile. "How about the last name?"

"Well, that means … *heaven's love*," he said sheepishly.

"That's perfect, too." She took another sip of coffee. "So … how will you get around *at all* as Kai Mililani? You didn't happen to bring a fake ID with you, did you?"

"No, I didn't. I'll need to get one—a passport, preferably. Just where, I don't know." He looked up at Lai. "I don't suppose you have any ideas?"

Lai was amused Kapono had asked her if she knew anyone who could forge a passport. "I hope you realize that I don't normally associate with those kinds of people." Then she started thinking seriously about his question and remembered something—some*one*—from fifteen years ago, and smiled tentatively. "But, I *might* know someone who could help you."

"Really?" Kapono said in surprise, and relief.

"Yeah." Lai paused. "Remember when I told you about my time in prison when I was 20?" Kapono nodded. "Well, I didn't tell you the whole story. Some of the other inmates, they, uh, made me their personal punching bag."

"Oh, Lai!" Kapono exclaimed as he reached out to hold her left hand.

"It got pretty rough. But then the most badass woman there—we all called her Queen—took me under her wing." *No need to go into details about that,* Lai thought. "I had one friend in there; her name was Min. After Queen started protecting me, Min became the next target. I begged Queen to protect Min, too. We … uhm … reached an accommodation about it." Lai paused and took another sip of coffee. "Min told me that if I ever needed a favor from her, to let her know."

"What was she in prison for?"

"Counterfeiting," Lai replied as she blinked.

"Ah! Do you know how to reach her?"

"I did—she sent me her phone number when she was released from prison. I'll try to track her down. If she's no longer in that business, maybe she knows someone who is."

"Mahalo. But, Lai, you realize aiding and abetting a felony is a felony, right?"

"Yeah—I know." She squeezed his hand. "The things we do for love, huh? Guess I'll need to make a trip to the bank and get some cash—probably a *lot* of cash."

"Don't worry about that. I brought some with me."

"Where the heck did you get 21st century U.S. currency?" Lai asked in amazement.

"An antique shop in … the future." *I've got to be careful—I almost slipped again.*

Lai laughed. "You've really thought of everything, haven't you?"

I sure hope so, Kapono thought uneasily.

"Oh, I forgot to mention—when I was in Maui, I met your father, and Akela!" Lai said happily. "But I guess you already knew that."

"Yes. I'm so glad you got to meet my dad."

Lai's eyes glistened. "He was hella kind to me, K. And, he really misses you." She paused and set her mug on the coffee table. "Assuming we can get you that ID, is there any way you could go see him?"

He looked at the morning sunlight streaming into the living room windows for a couple of seconds, then turned back to Lai. "I don't think that would be a good idea," he said softly.

She looked at him, her face a mix of sympathy and sorrow. "It must be so hard for you to know the future and not be able to tell me, or anyone else, about it."

"Just like Prometheus," Kapono said with a grim smile.

"Huh?" Lai looked quizzically at him.

"You know our project was called Prometheus because he could see the future." Lai nodded. "I found out that, although he could see the future, he couldn't share those details with anyone else." *So I can't tell you our daughter's son told me that 87 years from now.*

"Oh! How ironic."

"Yes." He reached out to hold Lai's hand again. "Lai, there's events that will happen that will be … difficult for you, and for people close to you. I wish more than anything I could help you, and them, avoid those events. But I can't. The risk of causing a more tragic future is too great. I hope you understand."

"I do," Lai said quietly as she nodded once.

"At least I'm here to give you my love and support through those tough times. That's why I returned to the past."

"And I'm so glad you did!" she replied as she blinked her moist eyes. "Having you here with me, when I thought I'd never see you again, means so much to me—more than you could ever know." She smiled reflectively. "Maybe *not* more than you could know. I keep forgetting about my diary. I'm pretty wordy, huh?"

Your diary—and a video you'll make for me. "And I'm really glad for your attention to detail," Kapono said with a smile. *I have to be sure she keeps making entries in her diary and doesn't mention me in them. Otherwise, there could be one heck of a temporal paradox!*

| 14 |

December 2, 2054

Kapono heard his phone buzz and saw *Lai* on caller ID. He set *The Complete Works of William Shakespeare* he'd been reading down on the sofa in Lai's living room and picked up the phone from the coffee table.

"Hi, honey! How did the presentation go?" Lai was at the University of Kansas with Daniel Bennett and his senior Secret Service agent Ben Abwao for the public debut of the Love One Another concept. Kapono hadn't accompanied her to Lawrence, nor on her trip to Honolulu several days earlier to meet with Hawai'i's leadership about LOA, due to his need to stay in the background. From reading Lai's diary, he knew all about her trip to Lawrence, but he suspected she'd enjoy telling him about it.

"Hi, love! I think it went really well. The hall was packed, and Daniel's presentation was great. There were lots of questions afterward. And," she continued excitedly, "guess who was here? Do you remember Klement, from the bowling alley?"

"I do," Kapono replied.

"Oh, of course you do—that damn diary. Anyway, he came up to me after the session and told me how sorry he was about what he said to me back in October. You were right about him—he *was* having a really tough time back then. His son was killed when the *Enterprise* was hit by that Chinese missile last year. We had a really nice chat."

"So, you forgave him?"

"Of course! And he forgave me. And, he asked about you."

"What did you tell him?" Kapono knew what Lai had written in her diary about her meeting with Klement Sedlák, but he asked the question to see what impact his return to the past might have on even small events.

"The truth. Well, as close to it as I could get. I told him you're in a better place now. And, you are!" Kapono could tell Lai was grinning, even though there were no holograms for the call.

"Yes, I am," Kapono agreed, smiling partly because what Lai had told Klement matched her diary's account exactly.

"Hey, I need to get back to Daniel and Ben pretty soon for the drive to the Kansas City airport. But before I do that," Lai said in a quieter voice, "is there anything you want to tell me?"

Kapono chuckled softly. "You know there's *many* things I want to tell you, but I can't. Are you thinking of something in particular?"

"After we got to the hotel last night, I went to the local pharmacy and bought a test," she continued in an even quieter voice. "I had this … feeling. I took it this morning." She paused. "The rabbit died. Please tell me you already know."

"I do. How do you feel about it, sweetie?"

"I'm probably the happiest person on Earth right now!" Lai's joyful voice said over the phone speaker. "And I'm so happy, and grateful, that you're here with me—and our child."

I wonder if Lai is thinking about her alternate future, in which she had to raise our child on her own. "I am, too." He couldn't tell her he'd met their daughter in the future, but not until she was 86 years old, and he'd only known her for a few years. *Now I'll be with Yinuo for many years. And I won't have to bear the pain of outliving my child … again.*

"I'm so excited, I already started thinking about names," Lai confided. "Too soon?"

"Nah," Kapono said as he thought, *THIS will be interesting!* "What did you come up with?"

"Well, if it's a boy, I was thinking … Keone." Kapono blinked; Lai hadn't put into her diary her thought about naming their child, if it were a boy, after his father.

He cleared his throat. "I'd like that. What if it's a girl?"

"If it's okay with you, I'd like to name her after my mother, Jun. Your returning to the past made me think about how much I miss her … and my father." Her parents had been suddenly and tragically killed just under 10 years ago.

Uh-oh, Kapono thought. *Her name might not make any difference to history—but I don't want to risk it.* "That would be great. But, I was wondering—were there any other names you were thinking of?"

"Why do you ask?" Lai said, puzzlement evident in her voice. "Unless … oh, shit. Do you think it will matter?"

"I don't know. It might."

"Okay." There was silence from the phone as Lai thought for a few seconds. "You might think this is weird, but after you spent the night in my quarters before you left on your mission, I started thinking, *what if?* It was the, uh, right time of the month for me to consider that possibility. And I started thinking about names even then."

"I don't think that's weird. Did you think of any girl's names?"

"One: Yinuo. It means *promise*. I thought it fit, given your promise that night to return to me and my promise to wait for you and finalize the quantum mechanics for your return trip."

"That's a beautiful name."

"So, it's a girl, right?"

"Well, you'll have to ask your doctor about that," Kapono said regretfully.

"You're terrible, you know that?" Lai said with mock annoyance. "I'll go see her when I get home. Oh—before I return to Boston, I'm going to make a side trip to the Bay Area, then I'm going with Daniel to Kaleo's inauguration on the seventh." Kaleo Peleke had been re-elected governor of Hawai'i the previous month. "Wait—you probably already know all that, huh?"

"Yes, but I love hearing it directly from you." Kapono knew Lai was going to visit the man who'd date-raped her in high school and the man responsible for her imprisonment when she was a sophomore at Stanford ... to forgive them. "And, I'm very proud of you."

"Thanks, but I haven't done anything yet. It's ... this is going to be really hard, K. I don't know if I'm up to it."

"I know you can do it," Kapono said confidently. "You need to trust in yourself more, Lai."

"Funny, that's what Daniel told me the other day. I wish you could meet him. He's a hella wise man, and kind. I really misjudged him."

"I *would* like to meet him. But I think the fewer people who know I'm here, the better."

"Yeah, you're right. Speaking of Daniel, he's waving at me now. Got to go. I'll call you when I land in San Francisco tonight. I love you."

"Aloha, sweetie. Have a good flight." Kapono set his phone back on the coffee table. *If only I could talk with Daniel ... the counsel of a former president, with all of his life experience and perspectives on the world and on history, would be invaluable.* After a minute deep in thought, he picked up the large leather-bound book he'd found on Lai's bookshelf and continued reading Act 1 of *A Midsummer Night's Dream*:

> *Or, if there were a sympathy in choice,*
> *War, death, or sickness, did lay siege to it,*
> *Making it momentary as a sound,*
> *Swift as a shadow, short as any dream;*
> *Brief as the lightning in the collied night*
> *That, in a spleen, unfolds both heaven and earth,*
> *And ere a man hath power to say, Behold!*
> *The jaws of darkness do devour it up:*
> *So quick bright things come to confusion.*

I sure hope all this doesn't come to confusion, Kapono thought apprehensively.

| 15 |

January 17, 2055

"Are you sure about this, Mr. B?" Ben Abwao asked Daniel. They were in the kitchen of Daniel's old townhouse in Boston's Charlestown neighborhood. Daniel was pouring himself a cup of coffee, and Ben had stepped away from his matrix of video monitors in the butler's pantry to join him. "We don't know much at all about this man."

Daniel looked up from his coffee cup and smiled affectionately at the tall, burly Secret Service agent who'd kept him safe for over 20 years. "Thank you for your concern, Benjamin. Although I sometimes complain about your being overly cautious, I *do* appreciate your diligence. But," he rationalized, "I think it's okay. You saw his message to me requesting this meeting. Only a *very* close friend of Lai's would know what he knows. And, I trust her implicitly."

Three days ago, Daniel Bennett had received a message on his phone from someone named Kai Mililani, asking to meet with him at 9:15 a.m. on January 17 regarding an urgent matter. Ben was able to find hardly any information about Mr. Mililani. But he claimed to be a friend of Lai's, and he gave details of Daniel's private conversations with her. For example, the message said that after their presentation at the University of Kansas in December, Daniel told Lai, "Love is patient" when she apologized for taking so long to forgive him for his signing the American Security Act into law in 2036—an action that ruined the lives of millions of Americans and indirectly led to the death of Lai's parents.

"All right, Mr. B," Ben acquiesced, then he checked his watch. "It's almost time." He headed back to his monitoring station to watch for the mysterious visitor.

"Thanks, Benjamin." Daniel walked back to the living room with his coffee and sat down on the off-white linen sofa. It was a clear, cool day in Boston; the early morning sunlight brightened the traditionally-furnished room. Then the front doorbell rang, and Daniel watched as Ben unlocked the hardened door with its built-in 3D scanner, greeted the visitor, and showed him into the living room. Daniel stood up and offered his right hand.

"Welcome to my home!" Daniel said graciously. "Please, have a seat." He motioned to the love seat opposite the sofa.

"May I take your jacket, Mr. Mililani?" Ben asked.

"Thank you," the visitor replied as he shook Daniel's hand, then removed his leather jacket and handed it to Ben.

"Would you like anything? Coffee, perhaps?" Daniel asked as Ben hung the jacket in the foyer, then returned to his station in the kitchen.

"No, thank you, sir," the visitor said as he sat down on the love seat. "Thank you for seeing me, Mr. President."

"Maybe Lai told you I'm not big on titles—especially really old titles like that one. Daniel is fine. May I call you Kai?"

Kapono smiled awkwardly. "Well, sir—Daniel—my name isn't actually Kai Mililani."

"Oh, really?" Daniel replied with raised eyebrows.

"No. My name is Kapono Ailana."

If Kapono had a feather, he could have knocked Daniel over with it. "You don't say? That's amazing—some wicked pissah!" Daniel exclaimed in his Boston accent. "Lai's told me a lot about you. But, I thought you were dead, or somewhere in the future." He grinned, "Obviously, neither is true. I wonder why Lai didn't tell me you're in town."

"Because," Kapono said quietly, "I asked her to not tell anyone about me."

"Why is that?"

"Because I *was* somewhere in the future. Two months ago, I returned to the past—that is, to the present, from your perspective."

"Now *that's* a wicked pissah if there ever was one!" Daniel exclaimed in total shock. "But, how is that possible? Lai told me the Wagamese Wormhole was destroyed."

"I discovered there are other ways to travel through time," Kapono said with a thin smile. "*One* other way, at least."

"Well, I'll be damned," Daniel whispered. "I'd love to know how you managed that—assuming you'd tell me, and I'd understand it. But then, I don't suppose you can tell me much of anything about the future, is that right?"

"Maybe not," Kapono said with an odd expression.

Daniel studied his face. "Does Lai know you came to see me?"

Kapono shook his head once. "No, sir. That's why I asked to see you today, at this time. I knew Lai wouldn't be here." Kapono knew from Lai's diary she was out jogging with her friend Hannah, the other Secret Service agent on Daniel's detail. He'd obtained Daniel's personal phone number from Lai's contacts list.

"I see," Daniel said. "I guess you know a lot about what's happened since you went through that wormhole." He sat back in the sofa. "How can I help you? What was the 'urgent matter' you needed to talk with me about?"

Kapono paused as he collected his thoughts and wondered if he should continue. Then he took a deep breath and plunged ahead. "You're correct that I know a lot about what's happened in the past few months, and what *will* happen in the years to come. Many wonderful things will happen," he said as he thought about Lai's pregnancy and the surging Love One Another movement. "But also, some horrifying things." He looked into Daniel's eyes with a somber expression. "I'm sorry to say, I need to talk with you about one of those terrible events." He looked toward the kitchen. "Can Mr. Abwao hear us?"

Daniel shook his head. "He's busy watching the security monitors."

In a subdued voice, Kapono told Daniel about what would happen on November 13, 2057. Daniel listened intently, first with curiosity, then with increasing shock that segued to horror as Kapono described World War III and its aftermath.

"Seven billion people!" Daniel repeated in an anguished whisper. "And most of the world turned into a wasteland. All because of a *mistake?*"

"Yes," Kapono said softly, "and miscalculations."

Daniel's face was a study in sorrow. "We, uh, we analyzed scenarios like that when I was in the White House," he recalled in a subdued voice. "We always feared a mistake could trigger a nuclear incident, perhaps a full-blown war. And, you know, something like that happened back in '27, and a few times before that." Kapono nodded. "On those occasions, some brave soul always managed to say, 'Stop! We must not do this!'" He looked up sadly at Kapono. "But, not this time. You said the speed of the AI defense systems will leave no time to correct the mistake, is that right?"

"Yes," Kapono confirmed.

"Why are you telling me this, Kapono? And, why *now?*"

Kapono studied his clenched hands for a few seconds, then looked up at Daniel. "Because I need your advice, Daniel. Lai told me you're the wisest person she knows. I'd greatly appreciate your opinion on this."

"On what, specifically?"

"About whether I should try to stop World War III."

Daniel looked at Kapono in utter amazement. "What do you mean, *if* you should stop World War III? How could you question for *one second* stopping the slaughter of seven billion people and the destruction of most of the world?!"

Kapono nodded slowly. "I know it must sound ridiculous. But ... it's not that simple, Daniel."

Kapono explained what happened to Earth after it pulled itself out of the devastation of the war, but he said nothing about Lai's crucial role in shaping the post-war world. He also explained the dangers of changing the past and the potential for a different, more tragic, future. Then he stopped, and Daniel sat silently for several seconds, deep in thought.

"Okay … I think I understand your dilemma, now." He leaned forward on the sofa. "Have you read the RAND Corporation's report, *The Future of Humanity*? I know Lai's seen it."

"I have—and the other reports." Three Top Secret studies published in 2049 predicted with near certainty the total devastation of the human race by war or ecological collapse, or both, within 60 years.

"From what you told me, the post-war future is considerably brighter than that, despite the terrible cost. Three billion people survive, and within 80 years they live in a world with almost no hunger and homelessness, and virtually no violent crime—a world where everyone loving each other isn't just a dream." He looked into Kapono's eyes. "Maybe that's a future worth keeping, despite the high cost. Perhaps the alternative would be much worse."

"Yes, perhaps … that's what Lai and Yinuo told me."

"Yinuo?"

Kapono started to berate himself for letting that detail slip out, but then he thought, *It doesn't matter.* "Lai is three months pregnant with our daughter." A grin started spreading across Daniel's face. "Lai can't know that you know," Kapono pleaded. "And you can't tell anyone else about it. Hannah knows already; Lai was planning to tell you after the rally in Honolulu."

Daniel made a zipping motion across his mouth. "My lips are sealed—about *everything* you've shared with me." He looked at Kapono with a puzzled expression. "Why did you tell me so much about the future? Aren't you worried I'll mess up and reveal it to others?" Kapono started to reply, but Daniel's mouth gaped open knowingly as he realized why Kapono had felt safe telling him so much about the world-to-be. "I'm not going to be around for any of that … am I?" he said very quietly.

"No. I'm sorry, Daniel," Kapono said softly, regretfully.

A reflective smile formed on Daniel's lips. "I'll be 86 in a few months. I've had a good run—'fought the good fight.' No regrets." He paused and reconsidered. "Well, just one. But Lai helped me make up somewhat for that mistake. She's really special. But I'm sure you know that. And she really missed you. I'm so glad you're here with her again."

"Me, too."

"We're leaving tonight for the big LOA rally in Honolulu on the 20th. You're from Maui, right? I don't suppose you could join us?"

Kapono shook his head regretfully. "I don't think that would be a good idea."

"No, I suppose not. We're stopping in Minneapolis en route, to speak about Love One Another tomorrow—MLK Day—at the University of Minnesota. As you probably know, that's Lai's alma mater." Kapono nodded. "Encouraging people to love one another on MLK Day—I think that's appropriate, don't you?"

Kapono smiled and nodded, "Yes, it certainly is." He thought for several seconds about his discussion with Daniel, then straightened up on the love seat. "I should be going—Lai and Hannah will be back soon." Both men stood up. "About World War III … I've decided what I'm going to do. Thank you, Daniel—or, as we say in Hawai'i—mahalo."

"You're welcome, Kapono. But I didn't do much."

"But you did. You listened. You helped me make the right choice. And you've been such a great help to Lai, as her mentor and her friend—and so much more. But I have to stop there. You understand, don't you?"

"Yes, I do. And I understand that you can't tell me how and when I'll die. But, could you tell me at least—is there any meaning to it?"

Kapono smiled compassionately at the bald, elderly man standing before him. "Oh, yes. And, more than that—it involves an act of great love."

Daniel's eyes filled with tears. "I like the sound of that."

| 16 |

January 20, 2055

Daniel sat on a folding chair in the *Keliiponi Hale*, or Coronation Pavilion, waiting for the Love One Another rally to begin outside the historic Iolani Palace in Honolulu. He was thinking about the LOA event he and Lai had led two days earlier at Northrup Auditorium on the University of Minnesota's main campus in Minneapolis. As usual, he'd delivered the main presentation, but Lai had answered most of the questions during the Q&A session that followed. He reflected on her poise, grace, and passion as she'd delighted the overflow audience with her insightful impromptu responses.

He looked over at her; she was talking with Ben about 15 feet away. Ben's six-nine frame, nearly two feet taller than Lai, towered over her. *She seems absolutely terrified about speaking to a crowd*, Daniel thought, *but when she talks extemporaneously, she's great.* Then he realized why: *She's speaking with her heart then. And that's what people need to hear.*

Governor Peleke walked over to Daniel; he stood up to greet his long-time friend and protégé. "Aloha, Kaleo!" Daniel said with a warm smile as the two men embraced. "Thank you for hosting us here today."

"Aloha, my friend. I'm so glad you and Lai could come. Is there anything you need?"

As Daniel and Kaleo reviewed the final preparations for the rally, Lai joined them. She waited for a break in their conversation, then she said cheerfully, "Good morning, Governor—sorry, Kaleo!"

"Aloha, Lai!" Kaleo replied. "It's a beautiful day to officially kick off the LOA movement in Hawai'i, isn't it?" And it was—bright sunshine with only a few clouds in the sky, about 70 Fahrenheit, and the large crowd seemed energized and in a good mood.

"Yes, it is!" Lai replied. "And thank you again for all your help and support, including for today's rally. We wouldn't be where we are today without you."

"You know I believe in what you and Daniel are doing. I'm glad to help in any way I can." Then Kaleo saw his press secretary motion to him. "I'm sorry, I need to attend to something. I'll be right back." He left Lai and Daniel and walked over to the staffer.

"Are you all set?" Lai asked Daniel.

It's time, he decided. He grimaced, as if he weren't feeling well.

"Is something wrong?" she asked, her voice tinged with concern.

"Uh, yeah. I ... my voice isn't doing so well," Daniel replied in a raspy-sounding voice, then he coughed once. "It must be from that cool, dry air in Minnesota."

"Oh, that's a shame!" she replied with a hint of skepticism. "Maybe you could keep it short—just hit your main points."

Daniel looked at her with an apologetic expression. *I don't like hitting her with this at the last minute, but I think it's better that way—she won't have time to agonize over it. I know she's ready.* "Lai, I don't think I can get up there and talk today. You'll need to speak for us."

"Daniel, you know I've never done *anything* like that before!" She glanced over her shoulder at the crowd, which was growing larger by the minute. "There's *thousands* of people out there! And, I don't have anything prepared! Maybe you could, uh, gargle some warm salt water, or something?"

Daniel put his hands lightly on her shoulders and looked into her eyes. "Lai ... you need to do it. You'll be fine. You don't need anything written down—just speak from your heart."

Kaleo's press secretary, Thomas, walked up to them. "Are you all ready? The governor's about to make his opening remarks."

Lai started to respond, but Daniel told Thomas, "Yes, we're ready." Noticing Lai's panicked expression, he held her shoulders more firmly and told her, "*You're ready.* I'll be right beside you."

After Kaleo introduced Daniel and Lai to polite applause, Lai looked apprehensively at Daniel. He smiled reassuringly at her and said quietly, "You've got this."

She walked slowly up to the podium stand and pulled the microphone down to her face with shaking hands; Daniel took a couple of steps to stand behind her. "Aloha! I'm … uh …." Realizing most people in the crowd could see only the top of her head poking up from behind the hulking Kevlar-lined podium enclosure, she pulled the wireless mic off its stand and side-stepped to her left. Daniel moved out from behind the podium enclosure to stand at her left side.

"There—that's better!" There was good-natured laughter from the crowd. "Let's try that again … aloha!" *ALOHA!* the crowd roared in reply.

As Lai began sharing with the crowd the details of her transformation from a bitter, angry, hateful person to one who had embraced love and forgiveness, Ben was desperately trying to signal Daniel to move back behind the armored podium stand. Finally, he caught on and shuffled behind Lai to stand behind the bulletproof enclosure, to her right. But Lai was still out in the open as the crowd listened attentively to her, mesmerized by her heartfelt story.

Daniel was beaming. *She's come such a long way. And now, standing up in front of this huge crowd, baring her soul—she's such a different person than when I met her just three months ago.*

Then Daniel noticed something—*someone*—moving in the crowd in front of them, about 10 rows back from the pavilion. They were coming toward the podium. Ben had noticed the movement, too. He stepped closer to Daniel and Lai and started to ask Hannah, who was stationed in the crowd, to check it out. But suddenly the person stopped, raised his right arm, and pointed a pistol directly at Lai. "*Death to Chinese devils!*" he yelled. Then he pulled the trigger.

As the man shouted and fired three shots—*POP! POP! POP!*—Daniel did the only thing he could think of: he bent his left leg at the knee and toppled over on top of Lai, knocking her hard to the concrete floor of the pavilion. As he fell, he felt a sharp burning sensation in his chest. *Is that what it's like to be shot?* he wondered. Then Kapono's words about an act of great love popped into his mind before darkness and silence enveloped it.

* * *

Daniel heard what sounded like Lai crying out, *"Oh my god!"* He opened his eyes and discovered he was lying face-up on the hard pavilion floor, with something soft propping up his head. He saw Ben and a woman he didn't recognize kneeling at his right side; they were doing something to his torso, which he noticed was covered with bright-red blood.

He looked into Ben's worried and distraught face. "Benjamin ...." he said weakly.

"Mr. B, you just lie still—EMS will be here soon," Ben replied in a calm voice that almost masked his concern about the man he'd protected for over two decades.

Daniel nodded once. "How's Lai?" She shifted to a kneeling position at his left side so he could see her.

"I'm fine, Daniel! Don't worry about me!" She started crying, "You shouldn't have done that! *Why the hell did you do that?*"

Daniel attempted a smile. "It ... it seemed like a good idea, at the time." He noticed a large, bloody bruise on Lai's forehead and worried, *I hope Yinuo's okay.* "That's a nasty bump on your head. Sorry about that ... I'm not as spry as I used to be." He heard the EMS siren in the distance, growing steadily louder, and looked again at Ben. "Benjamin ... listen to me."

Ben leaned down closer to Daniel's face. "Yes, Mr. B?"

Daniel coughed once. "This … this is on me," he gasped. "You and Hannah did everything right … everything you could, to protect Lai and me. Don't give … give it another thought."

Ben grasped Daniel's right hand. "We're going to get you fixed up, Mr. B. Then we'll have a talk about following Secret Service directions better, okay?"

Daniel smiled faintly. "Sounds like a plan." He looked at Lai. "I'm so proud of you. You … you were doing great up there. You're … a natural."

Lai held Daniel's other hand. "I don't know about that, Daniel. We need you—*I* need you! I can't do this without you!"

Daniel gripped her hand. "You *can* do it, Lai … I *know* you can. I believe in you. I heard you today. You're ready … everything you need, you have in there," he said softly as he lifted his hand and pointed toward her heart. "*Trust in yourself.*" Then his hand dropped. "Thank Kapono for me … okay?"

Lai's expression changed instantly from extreme sorrow to total shock. *And something else*, Daniel noticed—*anger?* "I, uh … I will, Daniel," she replied.

As Daniel looked into Lai's tearful eyes, the darkness and silence returned.

* * *

Lai and Hannah sat quietly next to each other in the emergency room waiting area at Queen's Medical Center in downtown Honolulu. Ben had insisted on staying close to Daniel and was keeping watch just outside the operating room. Lai's head was bandaged; she'd already been treated for the scrape on her forehead and a concussion. The two women waited anxiously for any word about Daniel.

Kaleo and Thomas walked into the lounge. "I'm so sorry for my delay getting here," Kaleo apologized as he approached Lai and Hannah. They stood up, and Kaleo embraced Lai first, then Hannah.

"No need to apologize, Kaleo," Lai replied. "I know how busy you are. I'm grateful you and Thomas are here." They exchanged greetings with Thomas, then he and Kaleo sat down across from Lai and Hannah.

"Is there any news?" Thomas asked.

"Not recently," Hannah replied. "President Bennett's been in surgery for over three hours. The hospital's senior cardiac surgeon, Dr. Imai, is leading the surgical team."

"She's the best," Kaleo affirmed with a nod.

"Do you need anything?" Thomas asked the others. "I can run down to Café Aloha—they have Starbucks and other beverages, and food."

I really could use some coffee! Lai thought. *But the ER nurse said no caffeine for at least 24 hours.* "Thank you, Thomas. Maybe some orange juice, if they have it." Thomas nodded and looked at Hannah.

"I'm good, thanks for asking," Hannah said.

Thomas walked down the hall toward the elevator. A couple of minutes later, Dr. Imai and Ben entered the lounge; the doctor recognized Kaleo.

"Governor! Thank you for being here." She looked at all four of Daniel's friends. "Let's go into the consultation room, all right?"

The doctor led them to a small room just down the hallway from the lounge, invited them to sit down at a round table, closed the door, and joined them at the table.

"As you know," Dr. Imai began in a quiet voice, "President Bennett suffered serious damage to his heart, and also some damage to his left lung. Unfortunately, the damage to his heart was beyond our ability to repair." Lai's, Hannah's, Ben's, and Kaleo's faces fell. "A heart transplant wasn't practical—no donor was immediately available. We hoped we could perform a heart *replacement*. The hospital has some of the latest artificial hearts in inventory."

Lai's phone buzzed. She quickly glanced down at it and was surprised to see a message from Kapono. But she was utterly shocked when she read it:

> *I'm here. Meet me in the chapel as soon as you can—Queen Emma building, Level 4. K.*

She slipped the phone into a pocket of the FBI jacket she was still wearing from after the shooting and returned her attention to Dr. Imai, whose expression had turned sorrowful.

"But," she continued, "his condition deteriorated rapidly. In the middle of the replacement operation, his heart and breathing stopped. We wanted to continue, but the president had a do-not-resuscitate directive. That prohibited us from performing cardiopulmonary resuscitation." She paused and looked sadly at each of them. "I'm very sorry. The president is gone."

"*No!*" Lai cried out in anguish. *It should have been me!* Hannah and Kaleo, sitting next to Lai, did their best to comfort her. Then she realized, *They're hurting, too. Kaleo and Ben knew him for over 20 years.* She began to console them, and Hannah.

"I'm sorry, but I have another patient awaiting surgery," Dr. Imai said. "I'm so sorry for your loss. We have a chaplain, if you'd like to talk with him. I can call him, if you'd like."

"Thank you, Doctor. Perhaps later," Ben replied quietly.

"Doctor, I'm the president's executor," Kaleo said in a strained voice. "I can take care of the short-term administrative details." He knew the White House would be involved in preparations for the state funeral.

"Thank you, Governor. I'll let our patient relations director know."

After the doctor left, Lai said, "I think I'd like to visit the chapel for a few minutes."

Ben and Hannah looked at each other in surprise; Lai had told them she was an atheist. "Would you like me to go with you, or get the chaplain for you?" Hannah asked.

"Uh, no, thanks. I'd just like to be alone for a little while. I hope that's okay."

"Of course," Ben replied gently. "Hannah and I can help Governor Peleke—if you need our assistance, Governor?"

"Mahalo, Benjamin. I'd appreciate that." He turned to Lai. "Take whatever time you need."

"Thank you, Kaleo … all of you."

After Lai left the consultation room and walked at a suitably somber pace to the elevator, she rushed to the hospital's Queen Emma building and the non-denominational chapel there. She pushed open the door to the chapel. As she stepped into the small, hushed room, she was overcome by feelings of peace and serenity, as if her entire body were wrapped in a warm embrace. The chapel was softly illuminated by candles and filtered sunlight from a skylight.

Then she saw a man with gray-tinged black hair, wearing a Hawaiian shirt, sitting in the front row of chairs with his head bowed. As she approached him and recognized him, she sighed in relief.

"Kapono!" she said as quietly as she could manage. He turned around and flashed a smile, then stood up.

"Hi, honey," he said in a hushed voice that blended sympathy and sadness. He hugged her tightly. "I'm so sorry." He saw the bandage on her forehead and noticed her eyes were red from crying. "How are you doing?" She pulled away from his embrace and glared at him.

"You would know, wouldn't you," she said sarcastically. And Kapono noticed something else in her voice—something he hadn't seen from her in a long time: anger. He started to respond, but she brusquely interrupted him. "Why are you here? Don't you think you're a little late?" she seethed.

"I knew you'd be upset, and I thought I could help," he said softly.

"'Upset' doesn't *begin* to describe how I'm feeling right now!" Lai shot back. She seemed to Kapono to be infuriated at him. "How could you let this happen?! And don't give me that 'I can't change the future' bullshit! He shouldn't have died! *It should've been me!*" Her eyes filled with tears again.

Kapono cradled her arms gently in his. "Lai, I know this doesn't make sense to you right now. Death by violence never makes any sense. But, please believe me—this had to happen. You *had* to live."

The anger on Lai's face subsided, supplanted by bewilderment. "*Why?* Why couldn't it have been me, instead of Daniel?"

"I wish I could tell you—but I can't. I know you don't understand that right now. But Daniel understood."

"How could you possibly know what Daniel understood?"

"Because … I met with him three days ago in Boston, while you were out jogging with Hannah."

Lai's mouth gaped open. "Why did you do that? I thought you had to keep a low profile!"

"From what you told me about Daniel, I thought he could help me make a big decision I'm facing. And, he did. He figured out the reason I revealed some of the future to him was because he wouldn't live to see that future. I shared with him that his death would be meaningful, and it would involve an act of great love. He seemed at peace about that."

As Lai wiped her eyes, the meaning of Daniel's request to her finally became clear. "He asked me to thank you for telling him that. What, uh, what was the decision he helped you make?"

Kapono smiled regretfully. "I can't tell you that. But remember, whatever happens, I'm here to help you get through it." He paused. "What I *can* tell you is, Daniel loved you very much. And he had immense faith in you."

"Yeah, I know. He told me, right before he died. I'm going to miss him so much, Kapono." She pressed herself against him, her head on his shoulder, and he held her tightly as she composed herself. Then she stepped back from the embrace. "How did you get here? That fake ID must've worked."

"It did!" It turned out Lai's friend from prison did know an expert in forging passports, and Kapono had used most of his cash to pay for it. Knowing Lai would be devastated by Daniel's death, Kapono had decided to risk a flight to Honolulu. He'd paid for the flight using an

American Express card Lai had given him. He'd arrived in Honolulu very early that morning to avoid being seen by anyone who might know him from his years living in Maui.

"Well, that's good to know. And," she said as she reached out to hold his hands, "I *do* appreciate your coming here. I'm really glad to see you, my love." She put her hands on the sides of his head and pulled it toward her face for a long, soft kiss. Then she released his head. "I probably need to get back with the others, now. I bet they're wondering where the heck I am."

"I understand. My flight back to the mainland leaves in a few hours, anyway. Send me your travel plans when you know them, okay?" Her diary didn't contain those details; he was unsure if she'd be returning to Boston or flying directly to Washington for the funeral of the former president.

"Will do." She hugged and kissed him one more time, then he bid her aloha and headed for the door.

Just outside the door, Hannah was peering through its small window to see if Lai was in the chapel. She saw her embracing and kissing Kapono. *I wonder who THAT is.* Then Kapono opened the door, nodded once at Hannah, and walked down the hall toward the elevators. Hannah stepped into the chapel and approached Lai.

"There you are! We were beginning to worry about you," Hannah said.

"Oh, hi, Hannah!" Lai replied in surprise, wondering how much her friend had seen. Then Hannah answered that question.

"Who was that good-looking guy? Looks like you know each other pretty well," she said with a wink.

"Oh, he's, uh, an old friend who happened to be visiting someone in the hospital," Lai said honestly, if not with complete honesty. "I told him what happened, and he was sorry to hear about it."

"I see," Hannah replied. *That was quite a kiss for an old friend.* She felt a hot tingling sensation in the back of her neck—a feeling she got whenever something about a situation didn't add up.

| 17 |

January 25, 2055

Lai walked up to the coffee service table in the East Room of the White House. Her head was pounding from the nearly constant headache she'd suffered since Daniel had saved her life by knocking her to the floor of the pavilion in Honolulu.

"Regular or decaf, Dr. Shen?" the elderly waiter asked with a friendly smile.

Lai was taken aback; she noticed the waiter's name badge. "You know me, Morgan? And, regular, absolutely—black, please." *And that'll do it for my caffeine ration for today.*

"Yes, ma'am. I watched you give the eulogy for President Bennett on TV this morning. I think he would have really liked it," he said as he poured coffee into an ornate bone china cup and handed the cup and saucer to her.

"Thank you for the kind words, and the coffee. How well did you know the president, Morgan?"

"I was on the White House staff back when Mr. B—that's what he asked us to call him—was president, and vice president before that. He was one in a million."

"Yes, he sure was," Lai agreed in a weary voice.

Morgan studied Lai's face. "Are you okay, Dr. Shen? Forgive me for saying it, but you don't look so good."

Lai managed a polite smile. "Thanks for asking. I'm, uh, doing okay … given the circumstances."

Morgan nodded empathetically. "I understand. I really wanted to attend the service this morning, but I had to help set up for the reception. I know a lot of the folks who were there, and who are here at the reception. You get to meet a lot of interesting people when you work in the White House for over 30 years."

Lai considered the gray-haired man in the black waiter's jacket. "Would you like a break, so you can say hello to the people you know here? I'm glad to fill in for you. I'm an expert coffee pourer," she said with a wink.

"Oh, ma'am, I don't …. Are you sure?"

"I insist. I really don't mind being this close to a big pot of coffee. Take your time. I'll be here for the duration."

His face lit up in a grateful smile. "Thank you, Dr. Shen! That's so kind of you. I'll just be a few minutes." He headed for a group of people who were conversing about 20 feet away.

Lai stationed herself alongside the coffee table and reached into a slit pocket in her dress for a pain pill, then remembered she'd taken the pill that morning. *Dammit.* She took a sip of hot coffee. *Thank you, Kaleo,* she thought as she savored the delicious coffee. Kaleo had arranged to have Kona coffee, Daniel's favorite, served at his funeral reception.

She looked down at her black, long-sleeved Ralph Lauren cashmere dress. It was only the second time she'd worn it. The first was 10 years ago, at her parents' funeral. *I won't be able to wear clothes like this much longer,* she realized. *Heck, I won't be able to see my feet before long!*

As she waited for customers, she surveyed the room. It was filled with Daniel's friends and people he'd served with in the White House and Senate. There were even a few of his Stanford classmates and football teammates. Lai had already offered her condolences to Daniel's long-time personal secretary, Masha Valentyna; his house manager, Anton Norgaard, and Anton's partner Michael; the late President Aida Pendamai's two children and their families; and many other mourners.

Sadly, Daniel had no living family. His fiancé Sahra had been tragically killed in 1993, and he'd never married. His sister Maria, a Catholic nun, had died six years ago. Thus, Kaleo and Lai had made his funeral arrangements, working with White House staff on the logistics for his lying in state at the Capitol, the funeral service at the National Cathedral earlier that day, the reception at the White House, and finally, the transport of Daniel's coffin on Air Force One to Boston, where he would be laid to rest with his parents and sister in his family's plot in Forest Hills Cemetery.

Lai looked for Kaleo but didn't see him. *I don't know what I would've done without him,* she reflected. He and his staff had taken care of returning Daniel's body to Washington and the myriad of other details leading up to the graveside service in Boston. He'd also been so helpful to Lai and Daniel in starting the Love One Another movement. *But, all that effort for nothing….*

"Hello, Lai," a familiar voice said. She turned her head and saw Jim Kassenbaum walking up to her. The former U.S. senator from Kansas had been one of Daniel's closest friends and had helped introduce LOA to the world in Lawrence the previous month. "How are you holding up?"

"I'm doing okay, Jim," she lied. "How are *you* doing?"

"Not one of my best days," he said sadly.

"I hear you. Thank you so much for being here today. You're coming up to Boston tomorrow, aren't you?"

"Of course," Kassenbaum said with a kind smile. "I wanted to offer my condolences to you, but I also wanted to tell you, your eulogy for Daniel at the service today was beautiful. I didn't realize you're such a gifted public speaker."

Lai chuckled softly. "Thanks, but I'm anything but that, Jim." She thought about what Daniel had told her before her interrupted speech in Honolulu. "But I got some advice from a dear friend who was a great public speaker. I guess some of it stuck." She'd been amazed that, despite the thousands of people at the National Cathedral, she'd felt no fear or anxiety as she'd stepped up to the microphone. She did what Daniel had suggested she do in Honolulu: she spoke from her heart. And she imagined she wasn't speaking to a huge crowd, but instead one-on-one to individuals among the mourners.

"Well, he was a great friend and public speaker," Kassenbaum said with a knowing smile.

Lai almost forgot about the duty for which she'd volunteered. "Would you like some coffee?"

"No, thanks—I've had more than enough already." He smiled again at Lai. "Quantum physicist, evangelist, orator, and now, White House coffee server. You're a very talented woman!"

"Aren't I, though?" she quipped. "I'm auditioning for my next career."

Kassenbaum laughed. "As if you're not busy enough with the LOA movement!" He noticed Lai's face wore an odd expression following his light-hearted remark. "And, about that ... you know I'll help you any way I can, in Kansas and anywhere else you may need me."

"Thank you, Jim. I—I really appreciate it," she said with a subdued smile. *I don't have the heart to tell him LOA is dead. I just can't do it without Daniel.*

Kassenbaum reached out to clasp her hands in his. "I need to go back to the hotel and pack, then head for the airport. I'll see you tomorrow in Boston."

"Okay—see you then, Jim. Safe travels." He headed for the main exit as Lai took a gulp of lukewarm coffee. She was about to top off her cup with decaf when she saw two familiar faces approaching: President Héctor Ramirez and NASA Director José de la Cruz. *It's a good thing Kapono stayed in Boston,* she realized when she saw de la Cruz.

"Buenas tardes, Lai," de la Cruz said. "It is good to see you again, albeit under difficult circumstances. My sincere condolences for your loss."

"Thank you, Director," she replied politely, but with an undercurrent of tension. The last time she'd been face-to-face with de la Cruz, he'd orally ripped her apart during a Prometheus Project hearing, after which she'd been dismissed as the project's chief scientist.

"Have you ever met President Ramirez?" de la Cruz asked Lai.

"I haven't had that pleasure," she said as her face brightened and she extended her right hand. "It's an honor to meet you, Mr. President."

"Thank you, Dr. Shen. I'm so glad to finally meet you." Ramirez was well into his second term as president, having been first elected in 2048 and reelected in 2052. He'd approved the Top Secret Prometheus Project but did not sign off on a replacement for the uncrewed spacecraft that exploded during a test flight in late 2053. Lai realized months later the disaster had actually been a blessing in disguise. If a rescue ship had been available for her failed mission to the wormhole the previous March, she wouldn't have been critically injured … and wouldn't have dreamed about the future.

Ramirez lowered his voice to a near-whisper. "José has told me so many good things about your work, and your bravery, on Prometheus."

Lai was flabbergasted but managed to keep her shock from showing on her face. *De la Cruz is talking me up to the president? What a hypocrite!*

"And, I've closely followed your work on the Love One Another movement. It is truly inspiring. I hope you will continue your efforts. Our country and the world need more emphasis on love and forgiveness."

"Yes, sir, they do. Thank you." *He has no idea how essential Daniel was to LOA.* "And, thank you for your tribute to President Bennett at the service today."

"I was honored to do it. He was a great public servant—a great man. I'm so sorry for your loss," Ramirez said sadly.

"Thank you, Mr. President. A loss for all of us."

"Yes, indeed." He glanced at de la Cruz, then turned back to Lai. "I apologize; I must get to a meeting with Israel's prime minister." The prime minister had traveled to Washington for the funeral. "It was so good to meet you, Dr. Shen. I wish you continued success with your crusade."

"Mr. President, there is something I need to discuss with Dr. Shen," de la Cruz said.

Ramirez nodded, "Director, Dr. Shen." He turned to join his chief of staff, who had been hovering a few feet away with two Secret Service agents, and they all walked toward the exit.

"How can I help you, Director?" Lai said stonily. "Would you like some coffee?"

"No, gracias. And please, call me José."

"All right." The chill in her voice lingered.

"Lai, last June, at the Prometheus hearing, what I did to you … it was despicable, and inexcusable. It was nothing personal against you. I have the highest regard for you. I was pressured to ensure you would be removed from the project." Lai nodded slowly; Katherine Etter had told her how Senator Irene Wilkes had used her influence over NASA's appropriations to force de la Cruz to do her bidding over the years—including helping her block Katherine from getting a job in the astroscience industry following the termination of the Prometheus Project. "I do not know if you can ever forgive me for what I did to you that day."

She looked into his hazel eyes. *He has kind eyes,* she noticed for the first time. "I forgive you, José. Would you please forgive me for how I acted then?" Her lips formed an embarrassed smile. "You've probably never heard so many F-bombs at a government hearing, huh?"

He returned her smile. "Gracias, Lai. And, of course I forgive you. But I believe your words—and the emphatic way you delivered them—were quite appropriate, given the circumstances."

She laughed for the first time in several days. *It's been a long time since I used some of those words.*

De la Cruz reached out with his arms, and she accepted his embrace. "All the best to you with your vital work on Love One Another. Be well, Lai."

"Thanks, José. You, too." As he walked away, Lai noticed her headache had almost disappeared. Then she saw Morgan walking quickly toward her.

"I'm sorry I was gone so long, Dr. Shen," he apologized. "I got into some conversations with folks I hadn't seen in many years."

"No problem. I'm afraid I didn't sell much coffee, though."

Morgan smiled appreciatively. "Thank you. And, thank you for what you're doing on the LOA movement. I'm really excited to see where that goes."

Lai's eyebrows raised in surprise. "You know about that?"

"Oh, yes! I've been following it since your first event in Kansas a couple of months ago." His face fell. "It was a damned shame—if you'll forgive the expression, ma'am—about what happened in Hawai'i."

"Yes …." she agreed quietly. "Morgan, I … I'm not sure I can continue the LOA movement. Daniel—President Bennett—was such a big part of it. I don't think I can keep it going by myself."

Morgan's eyes opened wide in dismay. "Dr. Shen, you *have* to keep it going! So many people in America, and around the world, are counting on it!"

"What do you mean?" she asked, bewildered. "There's only been the presentations in Lawrence and Minneapolis, and the little bit I said before the shooting in Honolulu."

"I watch a lot of news, and I'm on social media way more than I should be. *Everybody* is talking about LOA! Not just in the U.S.A., but across the world! People are longing for what you and Mr. B said about love and forgiveness, and how they can bring people together. The world desperately needs that. It needs *you*, Dr. Shen."

Daniel and Dr. King were right—love IS the greatest force in the universe, Lai thought. She made a decision.

"All right, Morgan … I'll 'finish the race,' as President Bennett liked to say. Besides," she added with a smile, "I don't think I would've made it in food service, anyway. I'll leave that in your capable hands."

"Yes, ma'am. Thank you."

"Thank *you*, Morgan. And, it's Lai."

"Okay, Lai. You take care, now."

"You, too." She started walking away from the coffee table and spotted Ben and Hannah about five meters away. She waved to them, Hannah returned the wave, and she joined them.

"You were at the coffee table for a long time. Are you doing coffee duty now?" Hannah kidded.

"Yeah, I finally found the perfect job!" Lai rejoined. Then she realized the next day might be the last time she'd see the two Secret Service agents—they would soon be reassigned. "I'm really going to miss you guys," she said sadly.

"Same here," Hannah replied. "I mean, who will I go running with?" she joked.

"Well, at least you'll be able to run at full speed now!" Hannah, a former Olympic champion swimmer, was a foot taller than Lai. Then Lai turned serious. She asked both of them, "Do you know where you'll be posted next?"

"I don't know," Ben replied first. "But that won't happen for a while. I have several weeks of vacation time saved up. I'm going to take a few weeks off, visit my extended family in Kenya, and decide what to do."

"That's great!" Lai exclaimed. "How about you, Hannah?"

"Well, I was thinking …. You're going to need security coverage for your LOA events. And you should have someone to coordinate that team, like Ben did for Mr. B."

"That makes sense," Lai agreed, then she winked at Hannah. "Can you recommend anyone?"

"I'd like to apply for the job," Hannah said. "I have over two years' experience with the Secret Service, and—"

"You're hired!" Lai said with a laugh, and she hugged her friend—and new chief of security.

But I'll need a lot more help to pull this off, Lai thought. *After tomorrow, I need to start interviewing the candidates Daniel had lined up for LOA. For sure, I need an expert in project management.* Then she smiled as she thought of the perfect person for that job.

| **18** |

July 15, 2055

"**H**ow many?!" Lai asked Katherine Etter, incredulous about the figure the Love One Another movement's project director had just given her over the phone. Lai was laying on the bed in her compact room at the Herbert Hotel in San Francisco, resting her aching back from the extra weight she'd been carrying for several months. She'd chosen the old, modest accommodations to save the LOA movement's funds, but also because of its quaint, homey ambiance and its close proximity to Moscone Center, where an LOA rally was to be held that evening.

"We've topped 18,000 registration requests already!" Katherine's excited voice confirmed. "Moscone West can hold only a little over 6,000 people. We need to move the event, Lai, or a lot of people are going to be disappointed."

"But, can we change venues that fast? It starts at seven tonight!"

"Ordinarily, no, but we got lucky. A concert that was scheduled at Chase Center for tonight was just postponed until tomorrow. I checked with the center's events coordinator. The arena is already set up for its maximum capacity of about 19,500 people. And because of the cancellation, we can get the arena for tonight at a *very* reasonable cost. We'll have to pay a cancellation fee to Moscone Center, but I think we should do this. What do you think, Lai?"

She considered Katherine's recommendation. The rally would be the first LOA event on the West Coast; it was to be followed by a rally later that week in Los Angeles. *I'd hate to turn away all those people,* she thought. *And with Daniel's generous bequest to the movement plus other donations, I think we can afford it.* "Let's do it!"

"Great! I'll confirm with Chase Center and send an alert out to everyone who's already registered, and I'll get word to all the media outlets. We can still start at seven. Can you let Hannah and Kaleo know?" Governor Peleke had flown in from Honolulu to support the two rallies on the West Coast.

"You bet," Lai replied. "I'll do that right now."

"Thanks, Lai. I need to call Chase Center now. I'll see you all at five for dinner and our final review for tonight, then we can ride together to the event, okay?"

"Sounds good. Thanks, Katherine—see you tonight." After Katherine had hung up, Lai messaged Hannah and Kaleo about the change in plans, then she said, "Sirai, call Kai Mililani—voice only." She used his alias in her contacts list in case anyone saw his name on her phone.

"Hi, sweetie!" Kapono's voice came from Lai's phone. "How's San Francisco?"

"Good! I hadn't been downtown since I left Lawrence Livermore for the Prometheus Project. Doesn't seem to have changed much."

"How are you feeling?"

She looked down at her enormous belly and rubbed it with her left hand. "Big. *Hella* big." She knew that doing a rally so close to her due date was a bit risky, but her doctor had told her it would probably be a couple of weeks before Yinuo arrived. She planned to fly home to Boston immediately after the rally in Los Angeles. "Ohhh," she moaned.

"What's wrong?"

"My back is killing me today—probably a flare-up from the crash-landing last year. The extra weight doesn't help any, I'm sure."

"Take it slow and easy," Kapono said gently. "I'm flying out to be with you. I'm at Logan now. I'll be there by the time the rally is over. I'll come to your hotel, okay?"

"Really? That's great! But, why are you coming now? I'll be home in a few days."

I wouldn't miss this night for the world. "I miss you. You've been on the road a lot for LOA the past few months."

"I miss you, too, my love. I'm glad you're coming. Be careful."

"Always. I wish I could see you at the rally. You're going to do great tonight."

"Thanks. Oh—we're moving the rally from Moscone to Chase Center. Katherine says over 18,000 people have registered already! Isn't that something?"

"That's fantastic! That's where the Warriors play, right?"

"Yeah, I guess." Lai didn't follow professional sports. The only sport she followed closely was women's gymnastics; she'd participated in it up until college.

"I'd better get to my gate. I'll see you soon, sweetie. I love you—aloha!"

"I love you, too. Have a good flight! Bye."

Lai laid her hPhone on the bed as another sharp pain shot across her lower back, making her wince. *Ugggh! I hope my back settles down before the rally.*

* * *

Lai was awestruck as her eyes swept the Chase Center arena. It was two minutes to show time, and it appeared the huge facility was filled to the rafters. "This is incredible!" she exclaimed to Katherine, who was checking something on a pad. "What was the final registration number?"

"Just over 20,000," the red-haired project director replied, raising her voice over the crowd noise. "Standing room only. The events coordinator told me we broke the old attendance record."

"No kidding! What was that?"

"I don't recall the number, but it was for a Taylor Swift concert back in '32."

Taylor Swift? "Holy shit! I was *at* that concert, Katherine, with my mom! It was a surprise for my 13th birthday!" The memories from what was one of the highlights of her life washed across her mind, and she closed her eyes. *I need to focus now.*

Katherine looked at Lai with a kind smile. "Doesn't that beat all? You're a rock star, Lai."

"Yeah, right!"

She put her hand on Lai's shoulder. "It's time. Are you ready?"

"Absolutely. Let's go!"

Katherine signaled to the control booth, and Lai's opening song, *Forgiveness and Love*, started playing over the arena's state-of-the-art sound system. Lai walked slowly toward the bulletproof transparent aluminum podium stand at center stage, smiling and waving as 20,000 people clapped and cheered. When she reached the stand, she gripped its top, caught her breath, and looked all around the pulsating arena. Then the music stopped and the crowd settled down.

Lai's face glowed in the bright spotlights; she looked around the packed arena and beamed. "Oh, wow!" she said in a near-whisper. The crowd applauded and cheered. Her heart was pounding—not from fear, but exhilaration.

"This is so amazing! Thank you so much for being here tonight. My name is Lai Shen, and I ... uhm ...." She felt a slight letting-go *pop* in her lower abdomen. "I'm so grateful and happy to be able to ... oh!" She felt warm liquid trickle slowly down her inner thighs. "I ... uh ...." She looked over at Katherine, Hannah, and Kaleo, who were standing just off stage. "I think I'm going to have a baby!"

There were *oooohs* and screams of delight from the crowd, accompanied by flashes from thousands of phone cameras. Lai's three friends rushed to the podium.

"I think it's time!" Lai told them.

"Go have that baby!" Kaleo said. "Don't worry—I've got this."

"Okay, thanks, Kaleo!"

Katherine and Hannah supported Lai's arms as they helped her off the stage. They heard Kaleo say, "Aloha, everyone! My name is Kaleo

Peleke, and I'm one of Lai's biggest fans. Some of you may know me as the governor of Hawai'i ...."

"What happened, Lai?" Hannah asked as they left the stage.

"My water broke."

"Have you had any labor pains?" Katherine asked.

"I don't think so. I've been having lower-back spasms on and off all day, though."

Uh-oh, Katherine thought warily. "How far apart are these spasms?"

"About every three or four minutes, I guess." Then Lai realized *why* Katherine had asked that question and remembered something from her Lamaze classes. "Shit. Back labor."

"Uh-huh," Katherine nodded. "Let's get you to the hospital—the sooner, the better."

Hannah had already checked on nearby hospitals. "Betty Irene Moore Women's Hospital is only a block away. I'll call their labor and delivery line to let them know what the situation is and that we're on our way."

"Perfect. I can take Lai there, if you want to stay here with Kaleo," Katherine told Hannah.

Hannah considered what to do. Lai was her primary responsibility, but the hospital was a relatively safe place compared to the arena. "Okay. I'll come as soon as we're done here. It's before nine so you can go to the main entrance. Take good care of my girl—my *girls*," she told Katherine.

"You can count on it." Katherine looked at Lai. "Are you okay to walk?"

"I'm good. It'll be more like a waddle than a walk, though."

Katherine laughed, then she helped Lai to the backstage exit.

* * *

Lai looked around the luxurious private labor and delivery suite as she lay on the birthing bed. "This is pretty plush, huh?" she remarked to Katherine. The room had a spa tub, a holographic fireplace, a media wall with a huge TV, and a beverage bar. She could see the deep blue and orange evening sky from a large window overlooking a garden court. "Nicest hospital room I've ever seen." *This even beats the hospital from 2153, from my dream.*

"It's great! You and your baby deserve the best."

Just then, a woman with blond hair tied up into a messy bun and wearing a white doctor's coat came into the room. "Good evening!" she said cheerfully as she stepped to the side of the bed. "I'm Rebecca Cardle, and I'll be delivering your baby tonight. Well, I hope it's tonight!"

"Me, too," Lai replied with a pained smile. "Hi, Doctor." She glanced toward Katherine. "This is my friend, Katherine Etter." Katherine and the doctor exchanged greetings.

Cardle glanced at the pad she was holding. "Oh, I see it's *Doctor* Shen."

"PhD—physics," Lai explained. "But please, just Lai."

"Okay, Lai." The doctor studied Lai's face. "Are you by chance the Lai Shen from Love One Another?"

"That's me," Lai confirmed.

"Oh, my gosh!" Cardle exclaimed. "It's so great to meet you! I wanted to go to the rally tonight, but I pulled the night shift."

Lai chuckled. "I wanted to go to the rally, too." She patted her enormous midsection. "My baby had other plans."

"I'm glad I'm here for you both." She looked at Katherine. "And thank you for being here for your friend." She turned back to Lai. "Will the father be able to join us?"

What do I tell her? Lai wondered. *Well, this worked once before.* "He's, uh, in a better place now."

"I'm so sorry," the doctor said sadly, and she grasped Lai's right hand. "With Katherine's help, we'll take good care of you and your baby." She glanced at her pad again. "Did your nurse go over the process, medication options, and so forth?"

"Yes, he did," Lai replied, then she gasped from a wave of pain from another contraction. "And, that epidural sounded *great.*"

"It makes things a lot easier," Cardle agreed. She looked at her pad. "Just checking your medical record from your home clinic …. I see you were in an accident in March of last year and suffered severe injuries, including a traumatic spinal injury and some brain lesions." She looked up with a regretful expression. "I'm sorry, Lai, but I strongly recommend against an epidural under those circumstances."

"Well, fuck *that!*" Lai's cheeks turned a deeper shade of red. "I'm really sorry!"

"Oh no, you're fine," Katherine said in her Midwestern accent. *I haven't heard her say that word in a long time. But I bet it won't be the last time she says it tonight.*

"If you need help with the pain, we have other options," the doctor explained. "Nitrous oxide is quite popular. I don't see any contraindications on your chart, and it's safe for both you and your baby. You'd have to use a mask to administer it, of course."

Laughing gas? "It won't make me laugh hysterically, will it?"

Cardle smiled and shook her head. "No, that's a misnomer. You might feel a bit giggly, though. It won't *eliminate* the pain, but it will dull it, lessen your anxiety, and give you a sense of well-being—even euphoria. And, it's self-administered—you choose when to use it. You'll be able to walk around during labor, and it wears off quickly so you can breastfeed after delivery."

"Assuming I *want* to walk around during labor," Lai rejoined. "Actually, that sounds pretty good, Doctor."

"All right, I'll order that for you," Cardle said as she tapped a few times on her pad. "The nurse will come back to be with you until it's time for the Big Event. I'll go get my catcher's mitt," she winked.

"Huh?"

"Sorry—just an obstetrician's joke. See you in a little while."

"Thanks, Doctor," Katherine said as Cardle went out the door. She reached into her purse for her hPhone.

"Who're you going to call?" Lai asked.

"Nobody. I'm going to make a video of you when you're all giggly," Katherine teased.

"Don't you dare!"

* * *

Lai lay exhausted on the birthing bed; strands of her damp black hair were plastered across her forehead, and her face glistened from her exertion over the past three hours. But as she looked down at the small, warm bundle on her chest, she had trouble remembering the pain. She remembered only her immeasurable joy when Dr. Cardle handed her daughter to her and she held her close.

"Isn't she the most beautiful thing you've ever seen?" Lai whispered to Katherine. Hannah was just outside the room; she'd made it to the hospital in time for the delivery. Kaleo was at the hospital also, but he had to jump on a holoconference call regarding an urgent situation back in Hawai'i.

"Absolutely," Katherine replied with a smile.

"Can you say hello to your Auntie Katie, Yinuo?" Lai said as the tiny fingers of her daughter's right hand wrapped around her little finger. Since Lai had no immediate family, Katherine had gladly accepted the role of honorary aunt.

"I think she has Kapono's eyes and nose," Katherine observed. *It's so sad he's not here. He'll never meet his daughter, and she'll never know him.* Lai had told Katherine several months ago that Kapono was Yinuo's father.

"I think you're right."

Hannah came into the room. "How's mom and daughter doing?" she said softly.

"I think we're both ready for a nap." Lai looked down at Yinuo. "But maybe she's hungry. How about it, cutie?" But Yinuo didn't seem to be interested just then. "Maybe a little later, huh?"

Hannah turned to Katherine. "How about you, Katherine? You've been here a long time. Do you need a break?"

Katherine stood up and stretched her back. "Now that you mention it, I am kind of hungry. I'm going to take a walk down to the self-service cafeteria. Do you want anything?"

"No, thanks," Hannah replied as she sat down in the chair Katherine had vacated. "I'll just feast my eyes on this little girl."

"Okay. I'll be back in a bit. I might check out the garden court—it looks like a beautiful evening out there."

"Take your time, 'Auntie Katie,'" Hannah said with a wink as Katherine went out the door.

"Could you hand me my phone, please?" Lai asked Hannah.

"Sure." *She just had a baby, and she can't stay off her phone*, Hannah thought in wonder. She picked up Lai's phone from the side table and handed it to her.

Lai keyed a one-word message to Kapono: *NOW*. Earlier, she'd texted him that Katherine was with her, so he'd have to wait to come to the room. He was waiting on the second floor, one floor below the birthing center. She locked the screen and handed the phone back to Hannah. "Thanks."

"No problem," Hannah replied as she set the phone back on the side table. *What was that about?*

After a couple of minutes, Kapono opened the door and came into the room.

"Kai!" Lai said in mock surprise. "What're you doing here?"

"I was at the rally and saw what happened. I figured you went to the closest hospital, and the front desk confirmed you were admitted tonight. I hope it's okay?"

"Of course," Lai replied. "Come and see Yinuo!" She felt like crying with joy that Kapono was able to meet their newborn daughter, but she managed to control her tears.

This is weird, Hannah thought. *It's after regular visiting hours, so only family should be allowed. I wonder how he got up here ....* What Hannah didn't know is that Kapono had taken his Hawai'i driver's license with him on *Chronos 3* as a joke, and he'd used it at the front desk to prove he was Yinuo's father, Kapono Ailana.

Kapono sat down at Lai's right side and gazed at his daughter. "She's amazing," he whispered as he beamed.

"Isn't she? Would you like to hold her?"

WTF? Hannah felt a hot tingling sensation in the back of her neck. *He must be a really close friend!*

"Could I?" He gently lifted Yinuo off Lai's chest and held her close. "Hello, Yinuo," he whispered. "I'm a friend of your mother's. You're one very lucky girl. She loves you very much. Maybe you'll be a physicist like her when you grow up." He grinned at Lai.

"A Nobel Prize-winning physicist, no doubt!" Lai added.

"No doubt." *Except there are no Nobel Prizes in the future.* He gazed for a couple of minutes into his daughter's face, rocking her slowly in his arms, then he looked up at Lai. "How are you doing, sw—Lai?"

"I'm doing okay. I'm really wiped. But, that nitrous is wonderful stuff." She looked at Hannah. "I highly recommend it."

Hannah chuckled, "I'll keep that in mind!"

Kapono carefully handed Yinuo back to Lai. "I have to get going."

"So soon?" Lai asked, although she was thinking, *Yeah, get the heck out of here! Katherine might come back at any minute!*

"Yeah, I have an early flight in the morning, back to Hawai'i. But I'm glad I got to see you and Yinuo. And," he turned to Hannah, "it was good to see you again, Hannah."

"Likewise, Kai," Hannah replied. *Wait—how does he know my name? I guess Lai must have told him about me after I saw him leave the chapel in Honolulu.* "Safe travels."

"Mahalo." He leaned over and kissed Lai lightly on her forehead. "I'll call you tomorrow and see how you're doing, okay?"

"Great, thanks. And, thanks for taking the time to come tonight."

"I wouldn't have missed it. Aloha," he said as he opened the door and left the room.

"That's one good friend," Hannah remarked.

"Isn't he? A hella kind man."

"Obviously." Hannah stood up, "Now, I'm going to check out your private bathroom."

"Be my guest!"

Soon after Hannah had closed the bathroom door, Katherine came back into the room, holding a small carton of apple juice. "*That* was strange," she told Lai as she sat down in the chair to the left of Lai's bed.

"What was strange?"

"As I was approaching your room, I saw a man walk down the hall, toward the stairway. He had a little gray in his hair, but otherwise … I could *swear* it was Kapono—or his twin." She shook her head. "It couldn't have been him, of course." She looked sorrowfully at Lai. "I guess it was because I was thinking of him tonight."

"Yeah, that must have been it," Lai replied as casually as she could as she thought, *Holy shit! That was way too close for comfort!*

| 19 |

November 17, 2055

Yinuo's brown eyes looked into Kapono's as he cradled her in his left arm. He was sitting on the sofa in Lai's apartment in Boston. Yinuo sucked hungrily on the bottle Kapono held to her lips. Although he'd been doing most of his daughter's feedings since Lai returned to working on the LOA movement in early October, he was still amazed at how much and how often she could eat.

This is going to get tricky, Kapono thought as he looked at his daughter. He knew from reading Lai's diary that Yinuo would interact with Katherine—a.k.a. Auntie Katie—and Hannah several times over the next two years and might refer to him as *Daddy* at some point. He and Lai had already devised a story for that circumstance: Kai Mililani was Yinuo's honorary father, just as Katherine was her honorary aunt. Kapono hoped Katherine and Hannah would accept that explanation in the short term. *In two years, it won't matter,* Kapono thought sadly. *Still, I need to avoid any further contact with Hannah, and especially with Katherine.*

His hPhone buzzed, and he saw *Lai* on its screen. "Accept call," he told Sirai. Lai's holographic image appeared and hovered a few inches over his phone. It looked like she was sitting up on her hotel bed. She was in Atlanta for the first LOA rally in Georgia.

"Aloha and good morning!" Kapono said. "Yinuo would say hello, but she's busy right now."

"I can see that!" Lai said as she laughed. "How are you both doing? You look so cute sitting there together on the sofa."

"She's doing great—eating like the stroker of a Hawaiian outrigger," he said as he watched his daughter continue to drain the bottle. "Dad, however, may be taking a mid-morning nap."

Lai laughed again. "I know that feeling! You'll be glad to hear I got eight hours of blissful, uninterrupted sleep last night. It was wonderful."

"I *am* glad to hear that." *At least she can catch up some on her sleep when she's on the road.* "How are things in Atlanta?"

"Good! Katherine just told me we're getting close to maxing out Mercedes-Benz Stadium for tonight's rally. Kapono, that's over 80,000 people!" Lai said in wide-eyed astonishment.

"That's fantastic!"

"Yeah—almost unbelievable. And you know, it was all your idea, my love."

Kapono shook his head. "I only planted a tiny seed. LOA's success is all because of you and your hard work—and Daniel, of course."

"Yes, if it weren't for him ...." She paused for a few seconds. "And I've had a lot of other help, too, from Katherine, Kaleo, and Jim Kassenbaum especially. Jim is here in Atlanta for tonight's rally."

"He's been a big help to you, hasn't he?" Kapono already knew all these details from Lai's diary, but he loved hearing her excitement as she shared them with him in real time.

"He sure has. Oh, speaking of Katherine, guess what? She has a girlfriend!"

"Really? That's great. I'm happy for her." Kapono knew Katherine had deprioritized her personal life for her career and thus had never married, nor had she seriously dated anyone for many years.

"Me, too. I haven't met Patience yet; Katherine met her back home in Kansas City."

You'll get to meet Patience someday soon, Kapono thought.

"Hey, love, I need to get going—I'm meeting Katherine, Jim, and Hannah at the stadium in about an hour to prep for the rally tonight.

Give our little girl a kiss for me. I'll see you both tomorrow. I love you."

"We love you, too. Good luck tonight, sweetie. Aloha," Kapono said as Lai's hologram vanished.

Kapono noticed Yinuo had emptied her bottle. He set the bottle on the coffee table, relayed her mother's kiss, then held the four-month-old infant against his shoulder as he patted her gently on her back.

I'm so lucky to have Lai back in my life, he thought. *And not only that, but I'm lucky to be part of Yinuo's life as she's growing up, and eventually I'll do the same with An. And I'll get to know Yinuo's husband and meet Linda many years earlier.*

His smile disappeared. *That is, if I don't mess this up somehow*, he thought uneasily.

| 20 |

April 25, 2056

"What do you think of this?" Lai asked Kapono as she held a bronze-colored, sleeveless boat-neck midi cocktail dress in front of her. Kapono, sitting on the bed, shook his head.

"You aren't going to a birthday party—even though it *is* your birthday," he opined.

"Yeah, you're right—a bit much," she agreed. She hung the dress back in the closet and pulled out the black cashmere dress she'd worn at Daniel Bennett's funeral. "How about this?"

"You aren't going to a funeral, either."

"Right. Hmm …." She returned the black dress to the closet and rummaged through it for a minute. "Ah-ha!" she exclaimed as she grabbed a short-sleeved dark green dress and held it up for Kapono's appraisal. It was the dress she'd worn for her first meeting with Governor Peleke in Honolulu 18 months ago.

"Perfect," he said as he signaled thumbs-up.

"Good!" She sighed with relief. She'd been obsessing about not only what she should wear for her meeting with Pope Francis II later that day, but how she should act and what she should say. She could still hardly believe the Bishop of Rome had asked to meet with her during his visit to Boston and other North American cities; he'd been an ardent supporter of the Love One Another movement.

"Relax, honey," Kapono said gently as she slipped on the green dress. "I've read that the pope is a down-to-earth fellow."

"Easy for you to say," she countered. "You get to stay here with Yinuo."

"I'd love to be able to go with you," he said regretfully. *No way THAT would work.* "But, I have a birthday cake to bake," he winked. She turned her back to him, and he zipped up her dress. Then she turned around and struck a dramatic pose, and Kapono looked her up and down. "*Dahling,*" he joked in a silly accent, "I have to tell you something. And, I don't say this to everybody. You look *mahvelous!*"

Lai laughed, "Cut that out!"

He stood up and wrapped his arms around her. "He's going to love you. Just be yourself." He paused for a second, then added with mock concern, "Maybe watch the F-bombs."

She laughed again. "Ya think?"

* * *

Lai climbed out of the back seat of the driverless rideshare car at the main entrance to the Residence Inn Boston Back Bay, which was close to Fenway Park. The pope would be saying Mass at the venerable stadium that evening. She walked through the front entry's 3D security scanner and into the lobby. She saw a tall, thin man in a black suit and the white collar of Catholic clergy and recognized him as Cardinal Secretary of State Mateo Villalba. He saw Lai in the lobby and stepped forward to greet her.

"Dr. Shen, thank you for coming!" he said as he smiled welcomingly and extended his hands to her.

"I'm honored, Your Eminence," Lai replied as she grasped his hands. *I think that's right,* she thought. She'd researched etiquette for addressing members of the Catholic clergy.

"If you would please come with me, the Holy Father is looking forward to meeting you."

Lai followed the cardinal to an elevator bank, and he pushed the call button. *Not the kind of place I expected the pope to stay at,* she thought as she looked around the nondescript hotel. Two men dressed in black suits and dark ties were standing near the elevator. Although they never looked at her directly, she could tell they were watching her every move.

The elevator doors opened, and Cardinal Villalba motioned with his hand for Lai to enter ahead of him. They rode up the elevator to the fifth floor, then the cardinal led her down the hall, past two serious-looking men she assumed were security guards, to room 505. He knocked gently on the door and opened it.

Lai followed the cardinal into the hotel room. A middle-aged man, dressed in a simple white cassock and wearing a small wooden crucifix around his neck, stood up from the living room sofa and approached them, wearing a placid smile.

"Holy Father, Dr. Lai Shen," the cardinal introduced Lai as he moved to one side and she stepped forward to greet the pontiff.

Am I supposed to kiss his ring, or ...? she tried to remember. But the pope took Lai's hands in his as he smiled at her.

"It's so good to meet you at last, Dr. Shen," the man in white said in a deep, melodious voice with a thick accent.

"I'm so honored to meet *you*, Holy Father," she replied. She thought she'd be nervous, but the pope's tranquil manner put her immediately at ease.

"Thank you so much, Mateo," the pope said to his secretary of state.

"Holy Father," the cardinal replied, bowed his head, and left the hotel room.

"Please, Dr. Shen, come sit and be comfortable," the pope said as he motioned to the sofa.

"Thank you, Holy Father. Would you please call me Lai?"

"Certainly, Lai. And you may call me Francis."

"Uh, okay ... Francis." *Wow,* Lai thought with surprise, *Kapono wasn't kidding about his being down-to-earth!* She sat down at one end of the tan faux-leather sofa, and Francis sat down at the other end.

"Pardon my manners," Francis apologized. "Would you like anything to drink, or eat?" He looked at the small table between the living room and kitchenette. It was loaded with a variety of fruits, pastries, and beverages, including a coffee pot.

"No, thank you, Holy—Francis."

He looked around the small one-bedroom suite. "Isn't this nice? I asked to stay at a rectory in a local parish, but Mateo vetoed that idea. He was concerned about my safety." He smiled and looked at Lai. "He looks out for me, sometimes to the extreme."

Lai smiled also. "I have a friend like that," she said as she thought about Hannah. She considered the man sitting next to her. *He's not at all what I expected!* She knew he was a native of Ghana and was the first African to lead the Roman Catholic Church in over 1,500 years.

"I'm uncomfortable living in such luxury, when so many brothers and sisters have no roof over their heads and not enough to eat," he said quietly.

A Residence Inn is luxurious to him? Lai thought in amazement. Then she recalled how Francis had pushed for the Vatican to sell off most of its assets during his seven years as pope, using the proceeds to help homeless and hungry people around the world.

"My family shared an Atta Kwame—a mud hut—with another family when I was growing up in Ghana," he continued. "Because of the efforts of the Church, the Peace Corps, and many other generous people, conditions have improved in Ghana and elsewhere in the world since then." He looked sorrowfully at Lai. "But there is still great need." Lai closed her eyes and nodded. "The Lord's work is unfinished. And, that brings us to why I asked to meet with you, Lai."

For the next half-hour, Lai and Francis talked about the LOA movement: how it started; its foundation in faith traditions such as Buddhism, Christianity, Islam, and Judaism, and also in ho'oponopono; and its objective of encouraging love and forgiveness to foster peace and unity around the world. After that discussion, Francis leaned back on the sofa and looked at Lai.

"It's fascinating to me that this worldwide movement that espouses Christ's message of love and forgiveness is led by—and please, I mean no offence, Lai—a scientist and atheist."

She smiled ironically, and nodded. "Pretty weird, isn't it?"

Francis returned her smile. "God works in mysterious ways."

Lai had wanted to ask Francis about something; she thought it was as good a time as any. "Francis, is it true Catholic priests have the power to forgive sins?"

"Only God has the power to forgive sins, Lai." She started to interject, but Francis continued. "A priest's authority to convey forgiveness of sins does not come from himself. It comes from Jesus Christ. By the power of the Holy Spirit, the priest stands in the place of Christ to declare the sinner forgiven. Does that make sense?"

"I think so. I know a lot more about quantum mechanics than I do about theology," she admitted.

"But you clearly know much about love, and the power of forgiveness," Francis said with an understanding expression. "Catholic Christians believe that forgiveness of sins is a great gift—a sacrament—from God. We believe that the peace of mind and soul that this sacrament imparts to us is one for which there is no substitute. It is a peace that flows from a certainty, rather than from an unsure hope, that our sins have been forgiven and that we are right with God."

"I do believe in the power of forgiveness," Lai replied. She thought about how her own experiences with forgiveness with Daniel, Klement, Tony, Jared, and others, had transformed her. *But there's things I've done—horrible things—I've never confessed to anyone ... not even Kapono.*

"Francis, I, uh, I was wondering ... would you hear my confession? Is that the right way to say it?"

"The sacrament of Reconciliation," Francis replied, "is where the priest, acting as the person of Christ, forgives sins when the sinner is heartily sorry for them, sincerely confesses them, and is willing to make satisfaction for them." He looked into Lai's eyes. "Have you been Baptized, Lai?"

"No, I haven't."

"Then I regret that I cannot celebrate the sacrament of Reconciliation with you," Francis said sadly.

Her face fell. "Oh … okay …."

"However," Francis added with a gracious smile, "God listens to all who ask for His help. I would be glad to talk with you about what is troubling you, counsel you, and pray for you, if you would like me to do that."

"Thank you … I'd like that," she said gratefully. *But I'm venturing into unfamiliar territory here.* "Is there something in particular I should say?"

"Just say what's in your heart, Lai."

Lai thought of what Daniel had told her in Honolulu, right before he died. "A dear friend gave me that advice once—former President Daniel Bennett."

"I met him when he was vice president. He visited the Vatican with President Pendamai many years ago, when I was a monsignor and was on assignment there. He was a good man. I am saddened he was taken from us."

"You know, he sacrificed his life for me," she explained as her voice broke.

Francis reached out to hold Lai's left hand, which was resting on the sofa. "'No one has greater love than this, to lay down one's life for one's friends.'"

She nodded, her eyes glistening. "Yes, I've read that."

"You know the New Testament?" Francis asked, surprised.

Lai smiled modestly, "A little bit."

* * *

After Lai and Francis finished talking, Lai wiped her eyes and looked at the pontiff. "Thank you, Francis. I really appreciate that. Those were things I'd been holding inside me for a long time."

"I'm glad to have been of some help to you, Lai." He sat forward on the sofa. "Now, I have a favour to ask of you."

What could I possibly do for him? "How can I help you?"

"I am saying Mass tonight at Fenway Park. In my homily, I am going to mention the Love One Another movement and ask my brothers and sisters in Christ to prayerfully consider supporting it." *That's great!* Lai thought. "I would greatly appreciate it if you could come there tonight and say a few words about the movement."

Lai was momentarily speechless. "I—I would be honored to do that, Francis."

* * *

Lai burst into her apartment. "Kapono!" she called out as she went into the kitchen and found him putting a cake into the oven. Yinuo was supervising his efforts from a baby bouncer on the kitchen table.

"How did it go with the pope?" he asked as he straightened up and kissed her.

"Amazing! But, I'm sorry to tell you, the birthday party will have to wait. I need to go somewhere tonight."

"Where?"

"Fenway Park!"

| 21 |

May 19, 2057

The opening notes of Pachelbel's *Canon in D Major* wafted from the grand piano at the front of the small, old church in Kansas City. Lai and everyone else in the church turned around as Katherine and Patience started walking slowly down the center aisle together, holding hands. *They both look so beautiful, and so happy*, Lai thought as they passed through rainbows of light streaming from the church's stained-glass windows. Katherine wore a white off-shoulder puff-sleeve lace gown, and Patience a mint green, floor-length, lace chiffon dress that Lai thought matched up perfectly with the bride's blue hair.

Katherine and Patience stopped when they reached the front pews. Katherine's mother and father and Patience's mother stood up and hugged their daughters. Then the couple stepped forward to stand with their maids of honor—Katherine with Lai, and Patience with her sister Laura. The four women turned to face the officiant as the last notes of the canon faded away.

"Please be seated," the officiant said to the congregation. "Welcome friends, family, and loved ones. We are gathered together today in the sight of God and each other as witnesses to celebrate the marriage of Katherine and Patience. We hold them up to each other as a family, and a community of loved ones, to christen this step on their journey toward what we pray will be a long, happy, and healthy life together."

The officiant asked the congregation to join in a blessing for the couple. Then she spoke about the institution of marriage, saying in part, "In the book of First Corinthians, the Apostle Paul provides us with a beautiful description of the kind of love that a marriage needs. He writes, 'Love is patient. Love is kind. It does not envy, it does not boast, it is not proud. It does not dishonor others, it is not self-seeking, it is not easily angered, it keeps no record of wrongs. Love does not delight in evil but rejoices with the truth. It always protects, always trusts, always hopes, always perseveres. Love never fails.'"

She looked at Katherine and Patience. "I want to urge you to hold to that vision of your love for one another, because even though all of us here support you, life throws us challenges, and in the midst of those challenges, it's the kind of love Paul was describing that is going to get you through it."

Then it was time for the exchange of vows. At the officiant's invitation, Katherine turned to Patience, and they held hands.

"I, Katherine, take you, Patience, to be my wife, and these things I promise you: I will be faithful to you and honest with you; I will respect, trust, help, and care for you; I will share my life with you; I will forgive you as we have been forgiven; and I will try with you to better understand ourselves, the world, and God, through the best and worst of what is to come, for as long as we live."

Patience repeated the same vows to Katherine, and then it was time for the exchange of rings. Lai handed Patience's ring to Katherine, and she slipped it on Patience's ring finger.

"With this ring, I thee wed," Katherine said softly to Patience.

After Patience gave Katherine her ring, the officiant said, "Katherine, Patience, having proclaimed your love for and commitment to one another in the sight of God and these witnesses, it is my pleasure to pronounce you, by the power vested in me by the Church and the State of Kansas, married!" She smiled at the happy couple. "You may now kiss your spouse!"

Katherine and Patience kissed, and the congregation applauded as a violinist began to play Vivaldi's *Spring*.

* * *

"Miro!" Lai cried as she hugged the former commissary manager of the Prometheus Project. "It's so great to see you again! It seems like forever since the project ended."

Miro Bottura embraced the woman he'd considered his favorite customer at the Prometheus base. "It does! It's so good to see you and all of my Prometheus friends again," he replied in his Italian accent.

The Prometheus team hadn't been together since the project was terminated in October 2054, right after Kapono disappeared in *Chronos 3* when the Wagamese Wormhole was destroyed. Many of Lai and Miro's teammates were able to attend the wedding: Chief Engineer Meira Friedman, Flight Director Haruto Hirano, Chief Medical Officer Alma Åhrberg, Chief of Security Major James Goebel and his wife Susan, and AI Research Scientist Asnee Shinawatra, among others. Also, many of Katherine's teammates from LOA were there, including Hannah and Jim Kassenbaum.

Lai and Miro noticed a group of people had gathered by the cake table and went to join them. The wedding couple was standing with a circle of friends and family members, including Patience's sister Laura, Hannah, Haruto, Meira, Alma, and the Goebels. Katherine was chatting with Major Goebel and his wife. Everyone was holding champagne flutes. A waiter offered champagne to Lai and Miro as they approached the gathering.

"Thanks," Lai said as she and Miro each took a glass from the waiter's tray.

"Lai and Miro, great timing!" Haruto exclaimed as they joined their friends. "I was just about to offer a toast." Everyone raised their flutes. "To Katherine and Patience—may they have many years of happiness," Haruto said, beaming.

"And may I add," Meira said with a grin, "Mazel tov!" The others echoed Meira's sentiment.

"Toda rabah," Patience replied. "Thank you, all. Katie's told me so much about you—well, not *everything*," she corrected herself with a chuckle. Patience knew the Prometheus Project was Top Secret.

"There's some stories we can tell you about Katherine," Meira said to Patience with a wink. "But we'll need more champagne first." Everyone laughed.

Haruto's expression became more solemn. "I'd like to make one more toast: to absent friends." He was, of course, referring to Kapono. Everyone nodded and followed Haruto's lead in raising their glasses.

"To absent friends," everyone repeated together.

"Thank you for that," Lai said gratefully. "Kapono wanted to—" *Shit!* she thought with alarm as she realized what she'd said. "I mean, I know he would have loved to have been here." She glanced around the circle of people. It appeared no one had caught her misstep—no one except Haruto. He was looking at her with an odd expression: a blend of bewilderment and suspicion.

Dammit, I've got to be more careful! Lai chastised herself.

* * *

"How was the wedding?" Kapono asked Lai as she entered their hotel room. He was sitting on the sofa with Yinuo, who was drinking from a sippy cup.

"Hi, sweetie!" Lai said to Yinuo as she kissed her on her cheek. Then she sat down on the sofa and set her daughter on her lap. "The wedding was great! There's a video of the ceremony, and I took some videos at the reception if you want to see those later."

"Thanks, I'd like that."

"Patience is a gem. And lots of people from Prometheus were there! It was so much fun seeing them again."

"I bet that was fun," Kapono said. "If only I could have come with you."

"Yeah ...." Lai agreed in a subdued voice. She looked at Kapono. "I, uh, I messed up, Kapono."

"How do you mean?"

"Haruto raised a toast to 'absent friends'—meaning you. I started saying how you wanted to be there." Kapono's eyebrows shot up. "I caught myself, and I don't think anyone except Haruto noticed it."

"Did he say anything about it?"

"No. But he had a strange look on his face."

"Well … I don't think there was any harm done."

"Probably not," Lai agreed. "It got me thinking, though … maybe you shouldn't come with me on any of my upcoming trips for LOA. And if you do go someplace with me, we should fly separately. There's cameras in airports—all over, really."

Kapono nodded. "You're right. I guess it was kind of risky coming to Kansas City with you." He reached out and held her left hand. "I love taking care of Yinuo. But I really miss you."

"I miss you, too, my love," Lai replied as she squeezed his hand. "But at least I get to be with you *sometimes*."

"Yes, at least we have that." *That's why I returned to the past. I knew I wouldn't be able to be with her all the time.* Then he started thinking about the wedding Lai had just attended, and he looked at her with love. "You know, I was thinking … maybe it's time to make an honest man out of me."

"What do you mean by that?" she asked, both bewildered and concerned. "You're not thinking of coming out of hiding, are you?"

"No, of course not." He reached out to hold both of her hands. "I mean, maybe it's time we got married."

"Oh!" she exclaimed in relief. "I would love that." *But he has no idea what kind of person he'd be marrying,* she thought sadly as she remembered her talk with Pope Francis II the previous year. "I'm wondering, though, if that would be a good idea. There's government red tape we'd have to work through, and that could expose you to extra scrutiny."

Kapono considered that problem. "Yes, that's true. Maybe it's not a good idea right now."

Right now? Lai wondered. *When would it be a good idea? He's going to have to conceal his true identity for the rest of his life!*

* * *

Jack Doohan scrolled through the seemingly endless list of low-priority security alerts from Kansas City International Airport from the past two days. Although the alerts had already been filtered by a Homeland Security AI algorithm, there were still hundreds of them for his second-level review. The agent in the Kansas City FBI field office was looking for any signs of possible criminal activity or terroristic threats—but there were none. *All quiet at KCI*, he sighed with relief as he reached for his coffee cup.

Then his head jerked forward as he saw something on his pad that made him stop scrolling. He clicked on an entry from 3:42 p.m. on May 18. It was a facial recognition alert from a video camera in Concourse B, near Gate B63. He read the alert description and AI analysis, then watched the video.

Hmmm, he thought as the video started. *That's interesting ... that's VERY interesting.* The recording ended, and he leaned back in his swivel chair and stroked his chin. *In fact, it's pert near impossible.*

| 22 |

May 21, 2057

"**S**irai, call José de la Cruz on a secure channel," Irene Wilkes said as she sat at the desk in her office in the Hart Senate Office Building in Washington.

"Calling," Sirai replied in an unaccented male voice. Soon de la Cruz's hologram appeared over the holopad on Wilkes' desk. He appeared to be sitting at his desk in his Independence Square office in Washington.

"Buenos días, Senator," the NASA director said pleasantly. "How may I help you this fine day?"

"Good morning, José. I just had a *very* interesting call from Todd Skinner, the FBI's executive assistant director for intelligence. It was regarding some video footage taken by a Homeland Security camera at Kansas City International on May 18."

"Why did Assistant Director Skinner contact you about a video from that airport?"

"Because he's aware I was the chair of the Prometheus Oversight Committee," Wilkes said impatiently. "The video clearly shows Lai Shen. She's carrying a young girl, whom I assume is her daughter."

Wilkes noticed de la Cruz's look of surprise. "Why are we interested in Dr. Shen's whereabouts?" he said indignantly. "I expect she travels frequently for the Love One Another movement she leads."

"Yes, I know that," Wilkes said with irritation. "But there was a man with her. It's not a clear image, but AI enhancement revealed it might be one of two people: someone named Kai Mililani, or ... Kapono Ailana."

De la Cruz's look of surprise morphed to one of total shock. "But, Senator, you know it is *impossible* the man was Dr. Ailana. There was no sign of his spacecraft for several days after the Wagamese Wormhole was destroyed. And, even if he made it safely to the future, there is no way for him to return to the present. Is the FBI certain about this?"

"They checked the other identity," Wilkes replied. "Other than what little is in the U.S. Customs and TSA databases about him, plus a few charges on a credit card registered to him but linked to Lai Shen's account, the FBI found nothing on this Kai Mililani."

"Interesting," de la Cruz said as he nodded slowly. "Senator, I am not a quantum physicist, but I know of no other way to travel through time except via a traversable wormhole such as the Wagamese Wormhole—not with current science, at least."

"What about science 100 years from now?" she posed.

He thought for a few seconds. "That is a valid point. And, Dr. Ailana was a brilliant quantum physicist. Thus, we cannot discount the possibility that he could have returned to this time, somehow. But, if he did—why would he keep his return a secret?"

"Why, indeed." Wilkes stared directly into the eyes of de la Cruz's hologram. "I told Skinner to put Miss Shen under 24-hour surveillance, as a matter of national security." Skinner had balked at her demand, but she was able to argue successfully that, under the American Security Act of 2036, surveillance of a child of Chinese nationals who had at one time been suspected of espionage would likely be upheld by the courts.

"But, Senator ...!" de la Cruz began to protest. Wilkes raised her right hand in a *stop* signal.

"Also, to put surveillance on Kapono Ailana's father in Maui, in case he tries to contact him." She folded her hands on top of her desk and looked at de la Cruz's hologram with a determined stare. "We need to find out if that man at KCI really was Kapono Ailana. And if so, we need to find out what he knows about the future … and *why* he didn't come forth with it."

| 23 |

November 7, 2057

Lai picked up a slender glass tumbler of orange liquid from the tray on the credenza in Kaleo Peleke's office in Honolulu. "Orange juice?" she asked Kaleo's press secretary.

"*Lilikoi,*" Thomas replied. "Also known as passion fruit."

"I thought it would be appropriate to celebrate with a native Hawaiian beverage," Kaleo explained. "And, appropriate in another way, too." He smiled appreciatively at Lai. "It was your passion, and your faith and hope, that led to yesterday's accomplishment."

Lai's cheeks flushed. "Thanks, Kaleo, but it wouldn't have happened without the efforts of everyone in this room—and many others."

She looked around the large office at the people who'd been instrumental in shepherding the ballot measure that had been put to a statewide vote the previous day: Kaleo, Thomas, Hannah, Lieutenant Governor Jeanné Kapela, Senate President Brandon Elefante, and House Speaker Lisa Kitagawa. The referendum on whether to change Hawai'i's constitution to embed the theme of "love one another" into the law had resoundingly passed, with 82 percent of voters approving the measure.

Kaleo raised his glass, and everyone in the room followed suit. "*Ho'omaika'i 'ana!*" he said as his eyes swept the room. "Congratulations to all of you, and the people of Hawai'i, for taking this first step toward a new approach to law, and law enforcement—one based on love and forgiveness."

"Thank you, all of you," Lai added, "for your hard work over the past three years. And thank you for your faith in this idea that a lot of people thought was just a crazy dream."

"I have to admit," Elefante confided, "I was one of those people who thought LOA was a crazy dream. But you, Lai, and the people of Hawai'i, proved me wrong. And this is one of those times I'm glad I was wrong."

"You weren't the only one in this room who thought the idea was crazy, Brandon," Lai confessed with a wry smile. She thought about her discussion three years ago with Kapono, over pizza in her quarters at the Prometheus base. *Like Brandon, I was wrong, too.*

"And now the *real* work begins," Kitagawa said. Everyone nodded and voiced their agreement as she smiled enthusiastically. "But, I think it's going to be a lot of fun."

"I'm looking forward to it," Kaleo said with mixed feelings. His second and final term as governor was to end in thirteen months. He'd offered to lead the LOA effort in Hawai'i after he left the governor's mansion, and Lai had gratefully accepted. "Now I must apologize, but I have a meeting in 15 minutes." The government officials and Thomas said their farewells and left the office; only Kaleo, Lai, and Hannah remained.

"I'll let you get back to work," Lai said to Kaleo as she set her glass on the tray. "If it's okay with you, I'd like to return the week after Thanksgiving to help with discussions on implementing LOA."

"That would be great, Lai—thank you." He looked at her face and noticed she looked utterly exhausted. "Maybe you could come back here with Yinuo and stay for a while—take some time off. You deserve a break. I know the weather here is a lot nicer than in Boston this time of year."

"It absolutely is," Lai affirmed. "And I *do* need some time off." Her last hiatus from LOA had been right after Yinuo was born, over two years ago. "Yinuo and I are going to spend a couple of weeks at my cabin in Minnesota. We haven't been up there in a long time. It's so peaceful there, especially at this time of year."

"That's a great idea," Kaleo said with a smile. He turned to Hannah, "How about you, Hannah?"

Hannah grinned. "I'm going to take your advice, Governor, and take advantage of this great November weather in Hawai'i." She looked at Lai, "Assuming that's okay with you, boss?"

"I insist!" She knew Hannah had taken hardly any time off since she'd joined Daniel Bennett's Secret Service detail over five years ago. "We can meet up when I'm back here after Thanksgiving, okay?"

"Sounds good to me!" Hannah said happily.

"I was wondering how Benjamin is doing," Kaleo asked Hannah. "Have you heard from him recently?"

"Yes, I talked with Ben last week. He said his security startup in Arlington is doing really well. He sends his regards."

"I'm glad to hear that," Kaleo said.

"Okay, now we *really* need to let you get back to work, Kaleo," Lai said as she noticed the time on his ornamental desk clock. "I need to get to the airport, anyway. I'm headed to Kansas City to pick up Yinuo at her Auntie Katie's." *I don't know what I would have done without Katherine these past two and a half years.*

"All right," Kaleo replied. "Hannah, aloha. It's always good to see you. I hope you enjoy your vacation here on the islands."

"Thank you, Governor. I'm sure I will!"

Kaleo turned to Lai. "Aloha, Lai," he said with a warm smile, then he hugged her and added, "*a hui hou.*"

"Goodbye, Kaleo. What does *a hui hou* mean?"

"Until we meet again."

* * *

I really hate deceiving Lai, Kapono thought as the driverless rideshare car turned into the short driveway of the small, one-story home. *But I don't know how I'd explain this trip to Maui to her without telling her more than I should about the future.*

After Lai flew to Honolulu for the LOA referendum, Kapono took a separate flight to Maui. He'd suggested to her that she drop Yinuo off with Katherine and Patience in Kansas City on her way to Hawai'i as it had been a long time since Yinuo had seen her Auntie Katie, and Lai agreed. *And I'm glad Yinuo can see Katherine one last time,* he thought sorrowfully.

He climbed out of the car and looked over the creamy-beige house with white and sage trim. *It looks the same as I remember. The palm trees are taller than the last time I saw them, though.* He stopped just before stepping onto the lanai. He heard only a muted *woof* from the back yard. *Was that Akela?* He thought his old golden lab would have dashed to the front yard to greet him.

He walked across the lanai and through the open French doors into the house. "Dad?" he called out as he looked around. Then he saw a familiar figure through the open back door—his father Keone was hoeing the garden. Akela lay in the native *nehe* ground cover next to the garden.

As Kapono stepped off the back lanai into the yard, Keone looked up and saw him approaching. He froze in total shock and dropped his hoe; he stared at his son as if seeing a ghost.

"Hello, Dad," Kapono said softly. Akela barked once, struggled to get up, and moved slowly toward Kapono, tail wagging.

"Kapono!" Keone cried, tears welling in his eyes as he rushed to embrace his son. "How can you possibly be here?!" They hugged each other for several seconds; neither of them wanted to let go.

"That's kind of a long story, Dad. How about we go inside?" Keone nodded, and Kapono put his arm around his father's shoulders as they went into the house, with Akela following slowly behind them.

"I need to wash my hands; it'll just take a minute," Keone said as he headed for the kitchen. "Would you like anything to drink?"

"Not right now, Dad—thanks."

Kapono sat down on the small sofa in the living area and looked around the tidy home. *Looks pretty much the same*, he thought. Then he looked up and saw his surfboard hanging on the wall in the loft that was his personal space when he lived there. *Lai must have shipped it back here*, he realized as he smiled gratefully.

Keone came back into the living area from the kitchen and sat down on a cushioned chest next to the sofa. In a strained but happy voice, he said, "I still can't believe you're here! I feared the worst when you were declared missing and presumed dead three years ago. You look well, Son." But Keone noticed Kapono looked considerably more than three years older. "Where have you been all this time?"

More like eight years, for me, Kapono thought. "Reports of my demise were greatly exaggerated," he said with a slight smile, then he leaned forward. "You know that the project I was working on was Top Secret." Keone nodded. "So, I can't tell you everything about what happened." He paused, thinking about how much he *could* tell his father. He decided that, at this point, he didn't need to be too careful about what he shared. "But my mission was to travel through a wormhole. And when I did, I found myself 87 years in the future."

Keone's look of shock almost matched his expression when he'd first seen Kapono a few minutes earlier. "That's … incredible," Keone finally whispered. "It must have been an amazing experience for you."

"It was. And I wish I could tell you all about it, Dad. But I can't. I hope you understand."

"I do, Kapono. I realize that knowledge of the future, in the wrong hands, could be very dangerous."

"That's right."

"I'm so glad you made it back to the present!" Keone said with a bright smile. "And I know Dr. Etter and Lai must have been happy to see you again."

"Dad, Dr. Etter doesn't know I've returned from the future. Only Lai knows—and now, you."

"Why is that, Son? Why haven't you told others?"

"Because of what you just said about the dangers of knowing about the future." He looked directly at his father. "Dad, I came back so I could be with Lai. You know I love her very much." Keone smiled and nodded. "With Lai, and with our daughter, Yinuo." Keone's smile expanded. "She's nearly two-and-a-half years old now." Kapono pulled out his phone and showed Keone a picture of Yinuo.

"She's beautiful, Kapono! I'm so happy for you and Lai!" Keone exclaimed with joy. He looked at the photo again. "How about that—I'm a grandfather." He looked up at Kapono. "Have you been back here for a while?"

"Nearly three years." Kapono saw his father's face fall in disappointment—perhaps even resentment. "Dad, I'm sorry I didn't come to see you sooner. I didn't think it would be a good idea, since I need to be careful to not change history. I hope you understand."

"I, uh, I guess I understand," he said quietly. "I've missed you these past three years, is all. You know I wouldn't have told anyone."

"I missed you, too, Dad. And yes, I know I can trust you."

"So, why did you come to see me *now*?" Keone asked with a puzzled expression.

"Because … I'm not sure I'll be able to see you again. I wanted to, uh, say goodbye."

Keone sat immobilized, a blank stare on his face, as he realized what his son had just said, and what he'd left unspoken. "Oh. I see. I … I suppose you know how and when I'll die." Kapono began to reply, but Keone raised his hand. "I don't want to know. And, I don't want you to say or do anything that would change my fate. I know you can't do that, even if you wanted to."

Keone stood up from the bench and sat down next to his son on the sofa. "I've had a good life, Kapono. But … I wouldn't mind seeing your mother again." Keone's wife Kealoha had died in the Maui fire of 2023.

A tear ran down Kapono's right cheek. "I'd like to see her again, too, Dad."

Keone looked down at Kapono's left hand; he saw no ring. "Are you and Lai married?"

"No—not yet."

"There's something I want you to have." He stood up, went into his bedroom, and after a minute returned and sat back down on the sofa. He placed a small gray box with a flocked cover into Kapono's left palm. "It was your mother's."

Kapono opened the box and saw a gold wedding ring with a round, pale-green peridot gemstone—*Hawaiian diamond*, Kapono thought as he remembered seeing the ring on his mother's hand when he was a boy.

"And also …." Keone removed his gold wedding band and handed it Kapono. "It would make me very happy if you'd take this, too."

"Thanks, Dad."

Keone looked out the back door and realized the Sun would set soon. "How long can you stay?"

"I need to leave tomorrow," Kapono said reluctantly. He was to meet Lai and Yinuo in Minneapolis on November 9 and drive with them up to Lai's cabin in northern Minnesota.

"I'll make dinner for us. And, while I do that," he looked at Akela, snoozing on the floor next to the sofa, "why don't you take Akela down to the beach? I think he'd really like that."

"I'd like that, too." Kapono looked down at the old lab and petted him gently. "How's he been doing?"

"He has trouble getting around, lately. You know, he's nearly 17 years old." He looked up at his son. "I think he's been waiting for you to come home. You may have to carry him down to the beach."

"No worries." He rubbed Akela's head. "Do you want to go to the beach, fella?"

Akela raised his head and answered by wagging his tail.

* * *

As the setting Sun painted the dark blue sky with streaks of orange and yellow, Kapono carried Akela down to the sandy shoreline of Kaanapali Beach. He gently placed the lab in the dry sand and sat down beside him. Akela rested his head on Kapono's right leg as they both gazed at and listened to the waves roaring toward the shore, fading away, and finally, dying.

Kapono rubbed Akela's head and thought about the decision he'd be forced to make in a few days—a decision that would affect every person, every living thing, on Earth. He thought especially about his friends and loved ones who'd be impacted by that decision: his father; Katherine and all of his other Prometheus teammates; and of course, Lai and Yinuo. And also, people who were yet to be born, including his grandson An, An's wife Linda, and his friend—and aspiring lover—Aroha.

He stared out at the indigo ocean waves and shook his head. *Who am I to make this choice for the entire world?*

As Kapono sat with Akela on the beach, he didn't see or hear the small drone floating about 100 yards down the beach. The remote pilot, an FBI agent sitting in her surveillance van near Keone's home, realized the light was probably getting too low for usable photos.

I think I have enough pics, anyway, the agent thought as she scrolled on her pad through the images she'd taken that afternoon. They included several shots from the beach, plus photos of Kapono arriving at Keone's home in the rideshare car and leaving for the beach in Keone's old Honda hatchback. *Time to wrap this up and send a report to Assistant Director Skinner.*

| 24 |

November 13, 2057

"Thank you for coming, Assistant Director," Irene Wilkes said as Todd Skinner stepped into her Senate office and closed the door behind him.

"No problem, Senator," the balding FBI leader with wire-rimmed glasses replied as he walked up to Wilkes's old, ornate walnut desk. "Good morning, Director," he said as he nodded toward José de la Cruz, who was sitting in a chair in front of Wilkes's desk. Skinner sat down in a chair next to de la Cruz.

"Buenos días, Assistant Director," de la Cruz replied cordially.

"So … you have news about Kapono Ailana?" Wilkes asked expectantly.

"Yes, I do." Skinner lifted a pad out of his black leather attaché case and looked at the screen for the retina scan. Then he tapped a few times on the screen. "The agent who was performing surveillance in Maui on Dr. Ailana's father captured photos that show with high confidence that Dr. Ailana visited his father on November 7 and 8."

"Excellent!" Wilkes exclaimed jubilantly.

Skinner glanced at his pad. "We tracked Dr. Ailana back to the mainland, first to LAX on November 8, then to MSP on November 9. He checked into the InterContinental Hotel at MSP that same day." Wilkes and de la Cruz were following his account in rapt attention. "That afternoon, Dr. Shen arrived at MSP from KCI and checked into the same hotel. Her daughter was with her."

"Do you know where they are now?" de la Cruz asked.

"Yes. Two days ago, Ailana, Shen and the child left the hotel in a 2028 Prius registered to Dr. Shen." Lai had inherited Kapono's old plug-in hybrid car after he'd been declared missing and presumed dead in October 2054. "They headed north on U.S. Highway 169. They were tracked to a lake cabin owned by Dr. Shen, near Blackduck, Minnesota. We believe with high confidence they're still there."

"Good work, Assistant Director," Wilkes said with satisfaction. "Now we'll find out *why* Kapono Ailana kept his return from the future a secret."

"Assuming he will talk with us," de la Cruz interjected. "He is under no compulsion to do so."

Wilkes's expression hardened. "I don't know about that. It was his duty, on a DoD-funded project, to return to the past if he could, and report what he'd learned about the future. He didn't do that." She looked at Skinner. "He could be charged with dereliction of duty—correct?"

Skinner shook his head. "No, Senator. Dr. Ailana is not a member of the military. Thus, a dereliction charge doesn't apply."

"That's unfortunate," she said with disappointment.

"However," Skinner continued, "Dr. Ailana is traveling under an alias—Kai Mililani. Thus he's probably committed passport fraud. That's a federal felony, with stiff penalties."

"Wonderful!" Wilkes said excitedly. "Would that be sufficient grounds to arrest him, and detain him for questioning?"

"Yes," Skinner confirmed, "he could be detained for 48 hours, at least. That's the limit in Minnesota."

"And, Miss Shen—she could be arrested and detained also, yes? She's obviously aided and abetted a felony," Wilkes said with relish.

"Most likely, yes," Skinner replied.

"But, Dr. Shen is not the person who traveled to the future!" de la Cruz protested. "It is Dr. Ailana with whom we need to speak."

"Miss Shen should've known better than to help him commit felony fraud," Wilkes snapped. *Looks like you might be getting re-ac-*

quainted with FCI Dublin, you little Chinese bitch. She looked at Skinner. "Assistant Director, this is a sensitive matter, regarding a Top Secret project. Since you have that clearance, I'd greatly appreciate it if you would personally supervise the arrests of Ailana and Shen."

"I can do that, Senator. I'll fly to MSP this afternoon and enlist a Twin Cities FBI agent to drive me up north tomorrow morning. I'll probably have an agent from the Bemidji office join us for the arrest."

"Perfect! Thank you, Assistant Director," Wilkes said as she got up from her desk. "Please let me know when you have them in custody. I'd like to be involved in their interr—their questioning."

Skinner stood up. "Understood, Senator."

* * *

"'Goodnight air,'" Kapono said softly as Yinuo lay still in her bed, listening to her father read the end of her favorite bedtime story. "'Goodnight noises everywhere.'" He closed the small book.

"Please, read it again, Daddy!" Yinuo pleaded.

"Not tonight, honey. You've had a big day, and it's past your bedtime." He leaned over and kissed her on her forehead, then checked her blankets to make sure she and her toy panda bear Qing Bao were securely tucked in.

She looked at Qing Bao. "Goodnight, panda bear. Goodnight—"

"*Goodnight,* sweetie," Kapono said in such a way that Yinuo knew her procrastinations were useless in delaying the inevitable. "Sweet dreams." *Probably the last sweet dreams she'll have for a long time,* he thought sadly as he switched off the light on her nightstand. He stepped out of the bedroom, closing the door quietly behind him.

Lai was in the living room of the cabin, wearing the floral silk robe her mother had given her or her 25th birthday—the last birthday gift she'd ever received from her parents. She turned on the holographic fireplace as Kapono walked from the hallway into the living room.

"Is she asleep?" Lai asked.

"I think so," he replied as he gave her a hug. "How's your back?"

"Better, thanks." While Kapono had put Yinuo to bed, Lai had taken a hot bath to ease the pain in her back. She'd injured it when *Chronos 2* crash-landed in March 2054, and it flared up occasionally. "But," her mouth gaped open in a huge yawn, "now I'm *really* sleepy. I'm going to crash in that recliner for a while. Want to join me by the fireplace?"

I'd love to, he thought. *But it's probably better if I don't.* "I think I'll sit with Yinuo for a while."

Darn, I thought he'd offer to rub my back, like he usually does when it hurts. "Okay, love." She kissed him on his cheek. "Wake me up for bed if I fall asleep here."

"I will." *Something will, anyway.* He walked back into Yinuo's bedroom and closed the door.

Lai moved slowly over to the old, overstuffed leather recliner. She saw a pad sitting on the side table. Thinking it was hers, she picked it up to move it to the wireless charger. As the screen flicked on, she realized with a start, *This is Kapono's! Why didn't he lock the screen?* She glanced down at the screen and saw her diary entry about that day. *I shouldn't read this*, she realized. *But ... the day is almost over. It'd be fun to see what I wrote about it—will write about it. What harm could that cause?* She started reading the diary.

Kapono was sitting in the rocking chair in Yinuo's room, absorbed in thoughts about what was about to happen, and how the lives of Lai, Yinuo, and everyone else on Earth would be forever changed. Then he jerked upright. *Where did I leave my pad? And, did I lock the screen?* He looked around the room—it wasn't there. He got up from the chair and quietly but quickly went out of the bedroom and down the hall to the living room.

Lai was standing by the recliner, holding Kapono's pad in quivering hands. She looked up at him with an expression of utter devastation; tears streamed down her red cheeks. "*No!*" she cried out in an anguished whisper. "*Tell me it's not true!*"

He gently took the pad from her hands and held her. "I'm so sorry ...." he started to say as he lambasted himself for his recklessness.

She pushed back from his embrace; her look of devastation had changed to anger. "You could have stopped it! *Why didn't you?*"

Kapono kept holding her arms gently. "Lai, remember, we talked about this—about the dangers of changing the future."

"But, who's to say which future is the right one?!"

"*You* did, Lai—many years from now."

Lai's anger was swept away by her shock over what Kapono had just said. *That's the first time he's told me anything about my future.*

Before she could reply, her phone buzzed. She saw *Katherine* on caller ID. She looked up at Kapono; he could see in her eyes what she wanted to ask.

"You can't help her—it's too late," he said quietly, sorrowfully.

Lai hesitated for a second, then she picked up the phone. "Hi, sweetie," she said in an unsteady voice.

"Hi, how are you?" Katherine's voice carried an undercurrent of concern. "Is everything all right?"

"Oh, uh, yeah, I'm okay." Lai fought to keep her voice under control. "I'm ... I'm just really tired. We made it up to the cabin—Yinuo and me, I mean."

"I bet you're tired, zipping all over the world for the last three years! I know you worked very hard to make the referendum in Hawai'i successful. And I know how much it meant to you."

Hawai'i! Lai thought with alarm, remembering its strategic military importance. *Hannah ... Kaleo ....* She looked up at Kapono, who was standing close to her. *Your father!* Tears started running down her face again, and she brushed them away with her free hand.

"Thanks, sweetie. You've, uh, been such a huge help to me, not just on LOA, but with Yinuo. She loves you so much. And, I love you, Katherine."

"I love you, too, Lai. Are you *sure* you're okay? It sounds like you're crying."

Lai wiped her nose with her sleeve and cleared her throat. "Yeah. How—how are you and Patience doing?"

"We're doing great! We're in downtown Minneapolis for my astroscience conference. She's a huge hockey fan. We're going to see her Blues play the Wild tomorrow night in Saint Paul." Lai heard a voice in the background say *Hey, Lai!* "Patience says 'Hi'! Oh, guess what? I finally got an astroscience job!"

"That's, uhm, that's great, Katherine .... Tell me about it."

"It's with InfiniTrek. I'm the new program director for the development of the Voyageur V spacecraft for the Europa mission!"

Lai heard over her phone's speaker what sounded like a siren wailing in the background. *Oh my god, there isn't much time!* "I'm really proud of you, sweetie ... uhm, could you do something for me?"

"Of course." Katherine seemed puzzled by Lai's halfhearted reaction to her good news.

"Could you give Patience a big hug ... for me?"

"Sure, I'll do that. But you'll never guess how I got the job—I got some unexpected help!"

"That's—that's good ...." The seconds ticked away in Lai's head, as if there were a countdown timer in it. "Could you give Patience that hug *now* ... please?"

"Well, okay. Just a minute." There was a pause as Katherine set her phone down and went over to her wife. "This is from Lai," Lai heard Katherine say. Then she heard Patience say, *Thanks, L—*

Patience's voice suddenly cut off. Lai looked at her phone and saw *Call Disconnected.* She dropped the phone on the recliner and collapsed, sobbing, into Kapono's arms.

As Kapono held Lai tightly and comforted her as best he could, he saw faint slivers of light poking through gaps in the blinds covering the living room window. He realized the light came from a gigantic fireball 200 miles away.

After a couple of minutes, Lai had composed herself. Then she realized, *Kapono can't tell me what we need to do. It's up to me.* She wiped the tears off her face and picked up her phone—phone service was still active, albeit at a greatly reduced bandwidth. And, the power was still on. She quickly plugged her phone into the nearest charging outlet and set Kapono's pad on a wireless charger. *My pad's charged up,* she thought, *and we filled up the car this afternoon, and it's plugged in.* "Is your phone charged?" she asked Kapono.

"Yes, it's in our bedroom." He smiled inwardly at how Lai had taken charge during what was the worst night of her life.

She started browsing on her phone, giving Kapono a running commentary. "The usual news feeds seem to be down, but I'm getting bits and pieces from people all over the world." She looked up at him with a grim expression. "It *is* World War III, Kapono. It looks like the whole world's been impacted, especially the nuclear powers and the Northern Hemisphere."

"Yes," he said solemnly. "What do you think we should do?"

She thought for a few seconds. "This part of the country wasn't hit directly, so we're safe here for a little while." She recalled what she'd read about the aftermath of a nuclear holocaust. "But there'll be a nuclear winter—probably a really bad one, based on what I saw about the extent of the attacks. We'd better not be in northern Minnesota when *that* starts."

"I agree. Where do you think we should go?"

"Let's see … maybe South America—not as many targets down there." She thought for a few more seconds, then shook her head. "No, that's probably not a good idea. It's a long way down to South America. We'd have to drive through the center of the U.S.; there'll be a lot of bomb damage and radiation. The main highways may not be drivable."

She paced in front of the fireplace, deep in thought. "A better bet would be New Zealand, or maybe Australia. But, how to get there? It's November, and the nuclear winter will start soon. And we'll need a ship, of course. I doubt any long-range passenger planes are still flying. I wonder …."

She searched on her phone until she found a road map of the U.S. and Canada. She saved the map to her phone and zoomed in on northern Minnesota and south-central Canada. "What if we headed west through southern Canada, to avoid bomb damage and radiation, then zigzagged southwest toward the Pacific Coast?" She looked up at Kapono. "Am I on the right track?"

"Yes," he confirmed with an encouraging smile.

"You know, it would be a *lot* easier if you'd just *tell* me how Yinuo and I got to New Zealand, or wherever!" she said with irritation. Kapono started to reply. "I know—you can't tell me about the future. I'll figure it out, somehow. I did before, right?"

"You did," he said with admiration and love.

Suddenly, Lai realized she'd forgotten something—some*one*. She looked at Kapono, "Do you remember Anong Wagamese?"

"Of course—the young man who discovered the wormhole named after him."

"I met him and his mother a few years ago. They live less than 50 kilometers west of here." She went over to Kapono. "I want to ask them if they want to come with us."

"Absolutely," he agreed. "It's the right thing to do."

"Okay." The lights flickered. "Right now, we'd better get packing! First, let's dig out the battery lanterns, flashlights, and candles."

| 25 |

November 14, 2057

The Red Lake Nation Tribal Council listened intently as Anong and Lai explained what the impending nuclear winter would mean for the tribe. Anong, his mother Minwaadizi and Uncle Bizaan, Lai, Yinuo, and Kapono (under his alias Kai Mililani) had arrived at Red Lake High School's fallout shelter very early that morning. Although the shelter was extremely crowded and had only minimal light and heat provided by a generator, everyone was grateful to be alive and together, and they were intent on making the best of the nightmarish situation.

After giving a sobering summary of the effects of a nuclear winter, Anong asked the council members, "Are there any questions?"

"From what you told us, the biggest impact will be from extreme cold, about 20 degrees below average. Is that right?" Vernelle asked.

"Yes," Anong replied. "Although for several weeks at least, the drop in temperature could be as much as 35 to 70 degrees Fahrenheit due to up to 99 percent of sunlight being blocked."

"After that," Lai added, "the average drop in temperature could be over two degrees Fahrenheit for 10 years or more. That may not seem like much, but during the so-called Little Ice Age in the 1800s, the average temperature drop was less than *one* degree." She forced a thin smile. "Ironically, global climate change will help us, there. The significant warming of the Earth's climate over the past 80-some years will mitigate to some extent the impact of the colder temperatures."

Her smile disappeared. "It's still going to be brutal, though—especially in places like northern Minnesota."

"Growing crops will be difficult at best, yes?" Robert asked.

"Extremely difficult, even impossible in the short term," Anong replied solemnly, "due not only to the cold and lack of sunlight, but precipitation will be significantly reduced. And, of course, there's the danger from radiation, especially in the near term."

"The tribe has been able to amass a lot of food here in the shelter," Samuel, the tribal chairman, said. "Our initial estimate is that we have at least a two-year supply."

"That's great!" Lai exclaimed. But she worried, *I hope that's enough.*

"Are there any other questions?" Samuel asked as he looked at the other council members. There were none. He stood up. "Anong and Lai, *miigwech aapiji.* Thank you for increasing our understanding of the nuclear winter and how it will affect the tribe. The council will ensure everyone has this information. It will be invaluable as we look to the future."

"I'm glad I could be of help," Lai replied. "And, thank all of you for sharing your shelter with us."

"I hope you and Kai and your daughter will stay with us for a while," Minwaadizi said.

"That's really kind, Minwaadizi, but if we have any chance of reaching the West Coast before the nuclear winter hits, we need to leave right away." Lai looked at Anong, then his mother. "Have you thought any more about coming with us? Bizaan can come, too." *Although that'll be pretty tight in the Prius....*

"Yes," Minwaadizi replied. "And my brother and I appreciate your offer. But we've decided to stay here, with the tribe."

"Then I'm staying, too," Anong said.

Minwaadizi turned to her son. "If that is your will, so be it. But I ask that you reconsider, Anong. The new world will need people with your knowledge and wisdom." Following Anong's discovery as a high school senior of the wormhole that was to be named after him, NASA and Harvard had awarded him a full scholarship; he'd earned bachelor's and doctorate degrees in astrophysics at that university.

"But I want to stay with you, Mom, and Uncle Bizaan. I could help you, and everyone, here."

"I know you could, Anong. But you have been given a great gift. You can better share that gift in a place like New Zealand or Australia than here on the reservation." She turned to Lai and Kapono with a hint of a smile. "And, I doubt Lai and Kai have driven much in the winter—am I right?"

Kapono chuckled, "Not in Maui!"

"Just a little," Lai replied. *And nothing like what we're likely to face soon.*

Minwaadizi turned back to her son. "They need your help, too. Your uncle and I have the entire tribe to help us."

Anong closed his eyes and nodded. "All right. I'll go with them." He looked at his mother. "I'll come back as soon as I can."

"We'll be here," Minwaadizi said.

"Minwaadizi, are you sure?" Lai asked.

"Yes."

"Thank you for your sacrifice. We'll make sure he's safe." Lai reached out to embrace Minwaadizi, and they hugged. Then Lai hugged Bizaan.

"I was wondering, what type of tires are on that Prius? All-season?" Bizaan asked.

"Yes," Kapono replied, "the low-rolling-resistance type."

"Not the best tires for where you're going. I own a garage. I think I have some winter tires that'll fit that car. Let's go there and check."

"That's so kind of you, Bizaan. But I have no way to pay you for them," Lai said. With the devastation of the United States and most other developed nations, the world's financial systems were in ruin, and U.S. currency was worthless.

"It's my gift to you." He grinned, "Besides, I wouldn't want my nephew to drive on crappy tires!"

"I think we're ready to load-and-go," Kapono told Lai. He turned to Minwaadizi. "In Hawai'i, *aloha* is both a greeting and a farewell. And sometimes we add *a hui hou*, which means, 'until we meet again.' Aloha, Minwaadizi—*a hui hou.*" He hugged her, and then Anong hugged his mother and his uncle.

"We have no word for *goodbye*," Minwaadizi explained.

"Why is that?" Lai asked.

"Because we will all see each other in the afterlife. And, perhaps because there's a spirit that follows each of us—the spirit that keeps us connected to the end of time."

Lai looked at Kapono and wondered if he was thinking what she was: *That sounds similar to ho'oponopono—everyone and everything are connected.*

"So, I will tell you *aangwaamaadaadizin*—I wish you a careful journey," Minwaadizi said.

| 26 |

November 15, 2057

Among strained to see out the Prius's large windshield as freezing rain pelted the car. The tiny gray ice pellets made seeing and driving bad enough by themselves. But the near-total darkness, even at nine in the morning, caused by the onset of nuclear winter made driving down the two-lane highway in rural Alberta even more challenging—and dangerous.

Kapono was sitting up front with Anong; Lai and Yinuo were in back. *It's nearly time to clean the filter*, Kapono thought. The hatchback's HEPA filter captured almost all the radioactive dust settling to the ground from the stratosphere before it entered the cabin, but they had to regularly clean the filter and brush off the car. *Or scrape the car off*, Kapono realized as the freezing rain continued to fall.

They'd made excellent progress since leaving the Red Lake Nation reservation the previous morning. Lai used the roadmap she'd downloaded to plot a course that took them from northern Minnesota into Manitoba on U.S. Highway 59. They then skirted the southern Canadian border to avoid the military installations in North Dakota and Montana, and large cities. They drove west across Manitoba on Highway 3, then took Highway 18 through Saskatchewan. They drove non-stop, except for short breaks every hour or so to clean the filter and car. Anong and Lai, the two people with winter driving experience, did the driving.

Anong checked the miles-per-gallon readout: *58.4*. The gas gauge read one-quarter full. They'd made it all the way into eastern Saskatchewan before the plug-in hybrid car needed gas. Luckily, they found a station in the small town of Griffin that had one functioning pump, powered by a storage battery. They traded food for just under 38 liters—10 gallons—of gas. *I don't know how we'll buy gas next time,* Anong worried—*assuming we can FIND gas.* They had barely enough food for the rest of their journey to the West Coast.

"How're you doing, Anong? Do you need a break?" Lai asked.

"I'm okay, but ice is beginning to build up on the road." The temperature had plunged rapidly since they'd left Minnesota. It was in the upper 50s Fahrenheit then; he glanced at the car's outdoor thermometer: *12° F.*

"Good thing you're driving, then!" Lai said gratefully. *And good thing Bizaan gave us those winter tires.* She looked at Yinuo, sitting beside her in a car seat. Lai had just given her breakfast, and she was asleep. Then Lai gazed out at the flat, dark landscape passing by her window. *Kind of reminds me of Kansas,* she thought. *But grayer ... and colder.*

They'd passed Medicine Hat, Alberta 30 minutes earlier and were driving west on Highway 3 toward Lethbridge. At that point, they planned to head south into far western Montana, then continue through northern Idaho and eastern Oregon toward Coos Bay, avoiding the highest elevations of the Rockies. Lai believed that small port would likely be undamaged and might have an oceangoing ship. If not, they'd continue south to Newport, and if necessary all the way to Eureka, California. Lai figured Eureka would be their best, but also their last, hope; all ports south of Eureka would probably have been destroyed.

Suddenly, Anong saw a large animal—*an elk?*—dash across the road in front of them. He decided in a split second that hitting it may not only injure or even kill it but seriously damage the car; he tweaked the steering wheel to avoid the animal. It just cleared the car's left front fender, but the car went into a spin on the icy highway.

"Hang on!" Anong shouted as he fought to regain control. Kapono and Lai braced themselves as the Prius crossed the shoulder and came to an abrupt stop in the shallow ditch beyond it.

"Is everyone okay?" Anong asked anxiously as he looked at his passengers.

Kapono and Lai replied they were unhurt. Yinuo started crying, and Lai comforted her while she checked her over. "It's okay, honey," she whispered soothingly to her daughter. "I think she's just scared," she told Anong and Kapono.

"That was lucky!" Anong said as he tried to move the car. The front tires spun, but the car didn't move. "Okay—maybe not so lucky. I think we're hung up on the berm." The car was resting on the sidewall of the ditch, its front end pointing upward. "I don't think we can get it out ourselves."

"No, I don't think so, either," Kapono agreed.

"When was the last time you saw another car on this road?" Lai asked.

"Not since we passed Medicine Hat," Anong replied. "That was over 45 kilometers ago."

Kapono wouldn't have let me route us this way if he knew it wouldn't work out, Lai thought. Then a chill shot down her spine, and not from the cold: *What if this didn't happen before?*

Anong was staring at something through his side window. "Kai, Lai—do you see that? Is that a house?"

Lai leaned toward the driver's side back window and peered through the darkness. She saw a black shape that could be a house, and next to it a larger building with a pitched roof. *A barn?* she wondered. They appeared to her to be about 500 meters away. "If it's a house, I don't see any lights. Maybe they have no power—or no one's home."

"It could be shelter for us, at least," Anong suggested. He looked at Kapono. "How about we check it out?"

Kapono looked uncertain. "Uh, maybe you and Lai should take a look. I'll stay with Yinuo."

Lai noticed Anong's look of surprise. She was surprised, too, until she realized, *Kapono isn't supposed to be here. He's right—I need to do it.* "I need to stretch my legs, anyway," she said with a smile. "Let's go, Anong. It isn't far." She kissed Yinuo on her cheek. "I'll be right back, sweetie. Daddy will be here with you."

Anong and Lai zipped up their winter parkas and put on their gloves, ski goggles, and N99 masks. Lai had found her mother's and father's winter gear in a cedar chest at the cabin, and Anong's tribe shared some masks with them. Her father's parka was a tight fit on Kapono, but he was grateful to have it. They climbed gingerly out of the disabled car and frozen ditch and headed across a desolate field toward the two dark shapes.

After crossing the field, they confirmed the two buildings were in fact a house and a barn. Both were completely dark. They went up to the front door of the house, and Lai took off her right glove and knocked. Ten seconds passed … nothing. She looked at Anong, then knocked again, harder. After another 10 seconds, she thought, *I wonder…?* and tried the door knob. It turned, and the door opened. "Let's see if anyone's home."

They stepped into what appeared to be the living room of a tidy, rustic home. A few dim lights were on, and the house was agreeably warm. There were metal shutters covering the windows. Anong closed the door, and he and Lai removed their parka hoods and goggles but kept their masks on.

"Hello?" Anong called out. There was no response. "Someone obviously lives here," he said quietly. "But, where are they?" They looked around the living room. It adjoined a combination kitchen and dining area. There was a closed door at each end of the living space. They stepped into the kitchen, and Lai peeked through the window of the oven.

"Someone's doing some baking," she surmised.

They heard a *click* behind them. Anong recognized it as the sound of a gun being cocked, and he froze.

"Don't move a muscle," a gruff male voice said from behind them. "Put your hands on top of your heads and kneel on the floor—*now!*"

Lai and Anong complied. "I'm sorry, we just—" Lai started to explain.

"*Shut up!*" the man ordered. "Now, take off those parkas and set them in front of you—nice and slow!" Anong and Lai followed his directions. "Put your hands back on your heads!" Then he said in a quieter voice, "Search them, Miriam."

Lai felt and saw a woman's hands searching her, then she saw the woman do the same to Anong.

"They're clean," Miriam said. She picked the two parkas up off the floor, placed them into a metal box sitting against a wall, and closed the lid of the box.

"All right—stand up nice and slow, turn around, and take off your masks," the man demanded. Anong and Lai got to their feet and turned toward the voice. They saw a 50-something man and woman; the man was holding a rifle, pointed directly at them. "Who are you, and what're you doing here?"

"I'm Lai, this is Anong," Lai began in as calm a voice as she could manage. "I'm so sorry about intruding into your home. Our car ran off the road and got hung up in the ditch, and we saw your house. We didn't think anyone was here."

"Well, there *is* someone here!" the man replied roughly. He stared at Lai's face. "You're Chinese, aren't you?"

"I'm American, sir—I was born in California. My ancestry is Chinese."

The man sniffed and looked at Anong. "What tribe are you from?"

"I'm Ojibwe, sir, from the Red Lake Band of Chippewa Indians in Minnesota."

Miriam smiled faintly. "I'm one-sixteenth Ojibwe." She turned toward the man, "Jonah, put down that blasted gun! They mean us no harm." Jonah lowered the rifle but kept it in his hands.

"Thank you," Lai said as she exhaled with relief. "We were hoping maybe you could help us get our car out of the ditch?"

Jonah rubbed his chin. "Yeah, I guess I could hook it up to my tractor. How bad is it damaged?"

That's a good question! Anong thought. *With the angle it took going into the ditch, I'd be surprised if the front suspension isn't mangled pretty badly.* "I don't know, sir. It may not be drivable. Is there a garage nearby?"

Jonah scoffed, "The nearest garage is over 40 kilometers away. And I doubt they're open for business right now."

"Where were you headed?" Miriam asked.

"The West Coast of the United States—Oregon, maybe as far as California," Lai replied. "Eventually we hope to get to New Zealand or Australia."

Jonah laughed contemptuously. "Are you *crazy?* You'll *never* make it that far during this nuclear winter, not even if your car wasn't hung up in a ditch! Whose fool idea was *that?*"

"Mine," Lai said with a small, embarrassed smile.

"Figures," Jonah said under his breath.

Miriam looked at Jonah. "They could stay with us until the weather improves and they get their car fixed."

"Now *you're* the crazy one, Miriam! It won't be safe to make that trip until spring—more likely summer!"

"We have enough food for the two of them. They can stay in Joshua's room," Miriam said. She looked at Lai and Anong. "Joshua's our son. He ... he was visiting friends in central Toronto when the war hit. We haven't been able to reach him. But we heard that Toronto is ... uhm ... it's gone," she said quietly as her eyes began to fill with tears.

"I'm so sorry!" Lai said sorrowfully as she reached out to Miriam. Jonah lifted the rifle barrel.

"Just stay where you are," he warned. Lai quickly lowered her arms and stepped back.

"That's hella kind of you, ma'am," Lai said. "But, there's four of us—two are still in the car. One is—"

"That'll never work!" Jonah exploded. "Four more people, for six months or more?!"

"We have our own food," Anong offered. *I don't think it'll be enough for six months, though.* "We won't be any trouble."

"Who else is in the car?" Miriam asked Lai.

"My two-year-old daughter, and her father."

"We can't turn them away, Jonah!" Miriam burst out. "Two years old! Remember what our Lord said: 'For I was hungry and you gave Me food; I was thirsty and you gave Me drink; I was a stranger and you took Me in.'" She noticed Lai nodding and smiling slightly. She stared at Lai's face, as if in recognition. "What's your last name?"

"Shen."

Miriam's eyes opened wide. "Are you the Lai Shen from the Love One Another movement?"

"I am! You've heard of it?"

"Oh, yes! We've heard you on the radio, haven't we, Jonah?" Jonah nodded, and the scowl on his face subsided. "You've done so much good." She paused, and her face fell. "Well, I guess you *did* a lot of good. That's all gone now, isn't it?"

Lai nodded sadly. "Yeah … I guess it is."

"That settles it," Miriam said with finality as she shot Jonah a sideways glance, then she smiled at Lai. "Go get your little girl and your husband."

"We're not married," Lai clarified.

Jonah muttered something, and Miriam glared at him disapprovingly. "'Judge not, that you be not judged.'" She turned back to Lai. "Jonah can help get your car out of the ditch later. You're welcome in our home, Lai Shen."

"Thank you, Miriam and Jonah!" Lai said gratefully. *But I just had the shit scared out of me! I'm going to get you for that, Kapono.*

| 27 |

March 21, 2058

The near-constant darkness and bone-chilling cold of the nuclear winter had eased. Instead of daytime temperatures struggling to reach 40 below zero Fahrenheit in Alberta, they'd occasionally soared to as high as 10 below in recent weeks. Lai and Kapono had never experienced anything like it. Anong had lived through a few cold winters in northern Minnesota as a boy, but climate change had taken much of the sting out of Minnesota winters in the past few decades.

Soar is relative, Lai thought as she sat at the kitchen table, bundled up in two thick wool sweaters borrowed from Miriam. She was sipping from a cup of hot ersatz coffee; their hosts' real coffee had run out three months ago. But she didn't mind. The hot black liquid warmed her up, and she and her loved ones were safe.

Lai, Anong, and Kapono had learned Miriam and Jonah were not only Christian fundamentalists, but survivalists. They'd carefully prepared for a cataclysm such as had occurred the previous November. Their house had two-foot-thick walls, a reinforced roof, and metal shutters on its windows. Its HVAC system filtered out radioactive dust. Electricity was provided by solar power, with a geothermal backup. Because of the nuclear winter, they relied almost entirely on geothermal electricity and heat. Water came from a deep well. And, they'd provisioned enough food to last a family of three for five years.

Kapono was in the second bedroom reading to Yinuo before she went down for a nap. Anong was with them, re-watching one of the movies Lai had saved on her holopad. The small bedroom had only one twin bed. Lai and Yinuo slept there, and Kapono and Anong slept on the floor in sleeping bags provided by Miriam and Jonah. They never complained. "Better than the Four Seasons Resort in Maui!" Kapono had told Lai with a cheerful smile.

Miriam came into the kitchen from the main bedroom, poured herself a cup of coffee, and sat down across from Lai. She was a few years younger than Lai's mother would have been, had she and Lai's father not died tragically in 2045. Over the past four months, the two women had developed a close bond. They often talked late into the night. Miriam shared stories about her life on the Alberta prairie and her Christian faith, and Lai talked about growing up as a child of Buddhist parents in California, her turbulent college years, and her three years leading the LOA movement.

After exchanging pleasantries, Miriam said, "It's clear you and Kai love each other very much."

Lai nodded, "Yes, we do." *If only she knew what that man did for me, for love….*

"So, why aren't you two married?"

"Good question. I guess it's because too many things, like the war, got in the way. But, we will someday. Maybe when we get to New Zealand."

"Good." Miriam took another sip of coffee. Then she leaned forward on the kitchen table and said more quietly, "Jonah and I need to do some chores in the barn. It'll probably take us a couple of hours, at least. And," she shared as she looked toward the main bedroom, "I just made up our bed. I was thinking, if you and Kai are tired and want to take a nap in our room while we're in the barn, that would be fine. The door locks from the inside, so no one will disturb you."

A perceptive smile spread slowly across Lai's face as she realized what Miriam was telling her. She reached out and grasped Miriam's hands. "Thank you, Miriam."

* * *

"I have some news," Jonah said as he came out of the main bedroom into the kitchen. Lai was helping Miriam clean up from dinner; Yinuo sat mesmerized at the kitchen table watching Anong and Kapono play chess. The two chess players looked up at Jonah.

"Is it *good* news?" Anong asked with a hopeful expression.

"Maybe," Jonah replied. "On the shortwave just now, I found out there's a ship making runs between Auckland and Eureka every so often, taking folks from California to New Zealand." Anong's and Lai's faces instantly broke into excited grins.

"That's great!" Lai exclaimed happily. "Were you able to get any details?"

"Some. They're planning on returning to Eureka sometime in late July, maybe August—the exact date isn't set yet. That's the good news."

"What's the not-so-good news?" Anong asked apprehensively.

"I found out how much they're charging per person for a one-way trip to Auckland." Jonah's expression darkened. "Ten ounces of 24-carat gold, or $50,000 Australian dollars—$55,000 in New Zealand dollars."

"Well, we sure don't have any of those," Anong said dejectedly.

Lai glanced at Kapono, but his expression was indiscernible. Then she saw Miriam staring at Jonah, with what seemed like pleading in her eyes. Jonah noticed his wife's gaze. He looked down at the floor for a few seconds, then he looked up at Lai.

"We have some gold," he said quietly. "Enough to pay for your trips to New Zealand, and then some." Lai noticed Miriam's eyes filling with tears. "You'll need some gold to get your car fixed, too, whenever the garage opens up again, and for gas. We're not going anywhere, and we'll still have enough to get by. You need it more than we do."

Lai was speechless for a few moments; tears ran down her cheeks. "I don't know how to thank you!" she cried as she hugged Jonah. To her surprise, he hugged her back.

"Your little girl—all of you—deserve a better life than this," he said.

Anong looked at Jonah and Miriam. "Why don't you come with us?" he asked.

"Thanks for the offer, son," Miriam replied. She'd started referring to Anong as *son* several weeks ago; he was about the same age as her son Joshua. "But Jonah and I, we've lived in Alberta all our lives. It's what we know." She looked at her husband, and he closed his eyes and nodded. "We'll ride it out. There's better days ahead ... for all of us."

| 28 |

July 20, 2058

"Anytime this century would be great," Lai said with mock irritation. She'd been waiting for over 15 minutes for Kapono to make his next chess move. He looked up from the board and smiled.

"It takes time to figure out a mate in seven," he replied with a wink.

"In your dreams," she teased. "On the bright side, I guess I have plenty of time to get more coffee." She got up from the kitchen table and headed for the coffee maker on the countertop behind her. "And maybe read a book, too."

Just then, Miriam came in the front door. She'd been working on something in the barn with Jonah.

"Grab your coats and come out to the barn with me," she told both of them.

"What's up?" Kapono asked as he stood up from the table.

"It's a surprise," Miriam said with a smile. It was an odd smile, Kapono noticed—it didn't involve her eyes.

"Should Yinuo and Anong come, too?" he asked as he and Lai grabbed their parkas from hooks by the front door. Anong was reading to Yinuo in the second bedroom.

"No, this surprise is only for the two of you."

I wonder what it could be? Kapono thought as he slipped on his parka and headed out the front door with Miriam and Lai.

The still-frozen ground crunched under their shoes as the three of them walked the short distance to the barn in the dim late-afternoon sunlight of the easing but persistent nuclear winter. Temperatures had moderated in recent weeks and had begun to creep above freezing during the day. Miriam opened the large barn door for them, and they stepped inside the big red building.

As the door swung shut behind them, Kapono noticed there was almost no light inside the barn—only one overhead lamp by the door. Thus he couldn't see more than a few feet in front of him. *Miriam's doing a good job keeping us in suspense about this surprise!* he thought.

Then he heard footsteps as someone approached from the darkness. As they stepped into the cone of light, Kapono could finally see the person's face. And what he saw made his mouth and eyes open wide in shock.

"*Haruto!*" Kapono exclaimed with surprise and joy. Against all odds, Haruto Hirano, the Prometheus Project's flight director, was standing two feet in front of him.

"Oh my god!" Lai burst out as she rushed to hug Haruto. "I can't believe it's really you!" But he didn't return her embrace. She stepped back and looked up at his face, which showed no sign of emotion. "I'm … I'm really glad to see you."

I wonder what's wrong, Kapono thought. *Well, no matter—he's alive, and he's here.* "I'm so glad you made it through the war!" Kapono said happily. "Lai and I didn't know which of our teammates survived."

"Y'all are glad, huh?" Haruto finally said in his Texas drawl. "I'll bet you are. But the thing is," he continued in a flat, cold voice, "I didn't make it."

"None of us did," a female voice said from the shadows. Kapono and Lai looked in the direction of the voice and saw two shapes emerge from the darkness into the small pool of light—a woman and a man.

It can't be! Kapono thought in utter amazement as he recognized the two people: Senator Irene Wilkes and NASA Director José de la Cruz. *How could they possibly be here? What in hell is going on?!*

"You seem confused, Dr. Ailana," de la Cruz said. He looked at Lai, "And you also, Dr. Shen. Allow me to shed some light on your bewilderment. Lights."

A few overhead lights came on. Kapono looked around the barn and saw, standing motionless all around them and filling the barn, who he estimated to be several hundred people. The light was too faint for him to make out individual faces, but he shivered as he had the feeling, *I think know these people!*

"Yes, Dr. Ailana—you *do* know all of these people," Wilkes said grimly. "These are all the people you know who did not survive World War III … all of the family, friends, and colleagues you *murdered*."

Kapono was speechless. Before he could respond, de la Cruz added, "Four hundred seventy-six of the seven billion people you killed through your arrogance, and your inaction."

"But, *I* didn't kill them!" Kapono protested. "World War III wasn't my fault! It was a mistake—a miscalculation!"

"No, you did not *cause* World War III," de la Cruz agreed, his voice emotionless and cold. "But you could have avoided it. Instead, you chose to play God with the lives of everyone on Earth. And thus, our blood and the blood of seven billion others is on your hands."

"Please, listen to me!" Kapono pleaded. "I wanted to stop the war. I would have done anything to save all of you, and all the others who died! But there was too great a risk that an alternate future would be even worse!"

"You don't know that, Kapono," a familiar female voice with a Midwestern accent said. As two women approached Kapono and Lai, they were able to make out their faces. Kapono gasped when he realized who they were.

"Katherine! Patience!" he exclaimed. He'd become familiar with Patience through the videos of Katherine and Patience's wedding that Lai had shared with him.

Katherine looked at Lai. "Hello, Lai," she said in a lifeless voice, without even a hint of kindness. Then she looked at Kapono. "You couldn't know what would've happened had you averted the war last

November. Perhaps Lai's Love One Another efforts would have prevented the disastrous future predicted by the RAND study, and the others."

Patience added in a harsh voice, "One thing's for sure: you let Katie and me be incinerated in that hotel in Minneapolis, when you could've easily warned us. You just didn't give a damn, about us or anyone else, did you?"

"Not even your father," Keone Ailana said sorrowfully as he stepped forward from the crowd of people. "After all the pain you suffered when your mother died, I couldn't believe it when you let me die."

Kapono was anguished by overwhelming grief. "Dad, I—I would have given anything to save you!" Tears streamed down his face as he looked at all the people standing before him. "All of you! But it was too great a risk! You have to believe me!"

"Ah, *now* you shed tears for us," Wilkes said as her dark gray eyes bored into Kapono's. "It's a little late for that."

"But not too late for atonement," Miriam added. Kapono noticed that her son Joshua, whom he recognized from photos Miriam had shared, was standing beside her.

"I'd do anything to make right what I did to all of you!" Kapono cried. "But I'm afraid it is much too late for that."

"Maybe not," Katherine mused. "Perhaps, if you could be made to feel what we felt ...."

"Yes ... yes, that is an excellent idea, Katherine," de la Cruz said. "There may be a way for Dr. Ailana to atone for his sin." He looked at the barn door as Jonah stepped through it. He was wearing some sort of large backpack; attached to the backpack was a hose that had a nozzle at its end.

Kapono had an idea what the contraption on Jonah's back was, but he hoped he was wrong. "What is that?" he asked Jonah cautiously.

"This here is my brush clearer," he said with a dry smile. "Most folks would probably call it a flamethrower." Kapono's eyebrows shot up in alarm.

"To adequately atone for what you did to us and billions of others, you need to feel the pain we felt," de la Cruz explained.

"And our greatest pain wasn't suffering our own deaths," Katherine elaborated, and she looked at Patience. "It was watching those we love die. *That* is how you can make right what you did, Kapono."

"What do you mean?" Kapono asked warily. In response, Haruto and de la Cruz stepped to either side of Lai and grasped her arms tightly.

Wilkes said in a low, dangerous voice, "You will watch the person you love more than anyone else in the world, your *ku'uipo*, die ..."

"God, no!" Kapono shouted as he felt two massive arms grab him and hold him. He turned his head around and saw it was Ben Abwao restraining him.

"... by incineration, in the same way hundreds of millions of people died because of you."

"*Kapono!*" Lai cried out desperately. Haruto and de la Cruz dragged her to the center of the barn and lashed her arms behind a post as she fought to free herself. Jonah ignited the flamethrower; a tongue of blue flame sprouted from the nozzle.

"A fitting and just end for a non-believer," Miriam said with a look of righteous satisfaction. "As it is written in the Book of Revelation: 'And anyone not found written in the Book of Life was cast into the lake of fire.'"

"*Kapono, help me!*" Lai screamed.

"*Lai!*" Kapono shouted as he tried to break away from Ben's steel grip. "Let her go—take me instead!" he pleaded.

The corners of Jonah's mouth turned up slowly and deliberately as he pointed the nozzle of the flamethrower at Lai. He pulled the trigger, and a torrent of blue and orange flame exploded from the nozzle.

"Kapono!"

He opened his eyes and saw Lai's concerned face close to his. "Lai? What ...?"

"You were having a bad dream, honey," she whispered. She was kneeling beside his sleeping bag on the floor of Miriam and Jonah's second bedroom. He looked to his left and was relieved to see that Anong was fast asleep. *If he'd heard Lai call me Kapono ....*

"Mommy, where are you?" Yinuo asked in a worried voice from the bed she shared with her mother.

"I'm talking with your daddy for a minute, sweetheart," Lai replied in a soft, soothing voice. "I'll be right there. Go back to sleep." She turned back to Kapono and gently caressed his head. "Are you all right?"

There were beads of sweat on his forehead. "Yeah, I'm, uh, I'm okay now. It ... it was that same dream." For several weeks, Kapono had been tormented by a recurring nightmare. The details were mostly the same each time, although occasionally both Lai and Yinuo were to be incinerated while he was forced to watch.

Lai lay down next to Kapono, wrapped her right arm around him, and held him tightly. She thought about the horrible nightmares she'd suffered for many years after she was raped by her senior prom date and, two years later, abused repeatedly in prison. Her roommates at Stanford, Rahmah and Maribel, had comforted her after her rape nightmares, but there was no one to help her after her nightmares about prison. She was glad she could be there to comfort Kapono.

"I know how awful these can be, my love," she said gently. "I wish there were some way I could help make them go away."

He looked at her and kissed her on her forehead. "You *are* helping, sweetie," he whispered as he wrapped his arms around her. "I don't know what I'd do without you."

He recited the ho'oponopono mantra—*I'm sorry, please forgive me, thank you, I love you*—several times in his mind; that usually helped calm him after a nightmare. He knew he wasn't adept at interpreting dreams, but he couldn't escape the thought, *Maybe there's something to this dream. Maybe not trying to prevent World War III was a huge mistake....*

Then he looked at Lai's peaceful face snuggled on his shoulder and had another thought: *Maybe I shouldn't have traveled back in time at all.*

| **29** |

August 7, 2058

"We *will* make it," Lai said with guarded optimism as she drove the old, patched-up Prius at high speed down U.S. Highway 101 through the center of Eureka, California. She glanced at Kapono, who was sitting in the front passenger seat. "Right?"

"If you don't kill us with your driving first," he deadpanned.

"Very funny," Lai muttered. They were headed for the large pier in Humboldt Bay once known as Chevron Pier, where the ship they were hoping to take to New Zealand was to depart in less than one hour. *After all we've been through over the past nine months, we ARE going to get on that ship!*

As she sped through Eureka, she saw only a few vehicles on its streets and highways. Although the city hadn't been bombed in World War III, its businesses and historic Victorian houses appeared to be run down and mostly deserted. *The nuclear winter must've taken its toll here*, Lai thought sadly, *just as it did from Alberta all the way to the West Coast.*

By the end of July, the nuclear winter and ambient radiation had eased to the point that highway travel was possible. As soon as a garage in Taber reopened, Lai, Anong, Kapono, and Yinuo bid farewell to the generous couple who'd shared their home—and much more—with them, had the Prius towed to Taber for makeshift repairs, and set out on August 4 for Eureka.

Lai took a sharp right onto the pier's access road. As they approached the pier, she realized with alarm, *Holy shit, there's a lot of people here!* A large crowd had gathered on the pier by the pocket freighter S.S. *Centaurus.* She pulled into a parking space and shut off the car. "Let's go!'"

With Kapono carrying Yinuo, the four refugees dashed toward the boarding ramp of the small freighter. Lai noticed several people standing along the side railing of the ship. They were holding semi-automatic rifles and keeping close tabs on the crowd on the pier below. "Looks like 'love one another' goes only so far," she remarked sardonically to Kapono.

A middle-aged man with a weathered face, full salt-and-pepper beard, and thick Scottish brogue was barking directions. *He must be the captain,* Lai surmised based on his authoritative manner and jaunty white nautical cap. She was about to call out to him when she heard a familiar voice.

"Lai! What the hell are you doing here?!"

I don't believe it! she thought, both shocked and joyful to see the familiar face. "I'm so glad to see you, Jared!" The 40-something man with black hair and beard weaved through the crowd to Lai, and they hugged each other. "I'd hoped you made it through the war!"

Jared Levine had been a senior at Stanford when Lai was a sophomore there. She helped him organize an on-campus protest against the American Security Act. But, unbeknownst to her, he and others planted a firebomb in Hoover Tower. Lai was charged with 32 federal felony counts, which her attorney was able to plead down to a class A misdemeanor. She served 60 days at FCI Dublin—two hellish months that altered the course of her life. She forgave Jared over four years ago. When he was released from prison in 2055, she helped him complete his political science degree, then hired him to lead California's LOA organization.

"Are you going to Auckland, too?" Jared asked Lai.

"We're trying to!" She quickly introduced "Kai" and Anong to Jared; he'd met Yinuo before the war.

"Better hurry, then—I think they're almost full-up," Jared said. "We can catch up later. It's so great to see you!"

"You, too!" She stepped closer to the man she'd assumed was the ship's captain. "Sir," she called out to him over the noise from the crowd, "do you still have room for more passengers?" Jonah had found out that passage on the *Centaurus* was first-come, first-served.

The captain looked down at Lai from his perch on the boarding ramp. "Aye, lass, I do—if ye dinnae mind bein' in close quarters. I have one wee cabin wi' two bunks. And I've got enough provisions for two."

"But, there's four of us!"

"Hmm …. Is one of them the bairn?" he asked, nodding toward Yinuo.

"Yes, sir," Lai confirmed.

"Well, if ye dinnae mind sharin' a bunk, and yer food, wi' the lassie, I can take three, includin' the bairn. That's all."

Lai's favorite expletive almost made it out of her mouth, but she swallowed it when Jared called to the captain, "I've decided not to go. They can have my spot."

She grabbed Jared's arms. "Jared, what the hell are you doing?!"

He looked at her with a half-smile. "I get seasick taking a bath. Puking my guts out all the way to New Zealand doesn't seem like it'd be much fun. Besides, I may not like it there—I've heard there isn't much night life, and it's really expensive."

Kapono was listening to Lai and Jared when he suddenly remembered something from Lai's diary: *Jared was on that ship!* He didn't know details of Jared's future, but he didn't want to risk changing history. *Besides,* he thought, *I can't let him give up his ticket out of here for us. Who knows what will happen to him if he does?*

"Hold on a minute," he told Lai, then he jumped over the gate blocking the crowd from the boarding ramp and went up to the captain as one of the guards kept her rifle trained on him. "Captain, could I talk with you for a minute? It's urgent."

"All right," the captain agreed gruffly, looking at his watch. "One minute." He nodded once to the guard and stepped up a few feet higher on the ramp; Kapono followed him.

"My name is Kai Mililani," Kapono said.

"Fearghas MacKenzie."

"Captain, I'm that little girl's father. The young man with us and Mr. Levine are close friends of ours. We need to stay together. If you'll let all four of us *and* Mr. Levine on your ship, I won't eat any of your food—we have some of our own. And, I won't take up a bunk—I'll sleep on the deck."

MacKenzie looked at Kapono for a couple of seconds. "The bairn's father, are ye? Well, I winnae break up a family—not if I can help it." He extended his right hand. "I agree te yer proposal, Mr. Mililani."

"Thank you, Captain!" Kapono said gratefully as he shook MacKenzie's hand.

"For the usual fare, of course," MacKenzie added.

"Of course," Kapono nodded.

"Kai—that's a Welsh name. Are ye from Wales?"

"No, sir—I'm Hawaiian."

MacKenzie's eyebrows lifted up. "Hawai'i …." he said softly. "My sincere condolences te ye, Mr. Mililani."

"Thank you, Captain."

"I best start the boarding. See the purser for yer tickets," he said as he motioned toward a man standing behind a portable table on the pier and started walking up the boarding ramp.

"I'll do that—thanks, Captain." Kapono climbed down to join Lai and the others on the pier. "We're all set," he told the group. "We're *all* getting on that ship." He looked at Jared and smiled. "Thank you for offering to help us. But it looks like you'll have to deal with some discomfort for the next few weeks."

Jared returned Kapono's smile. "I'll manage."

"Speaking of discomfort," Kapono said to Lai and Anong, "there'll be four of us in a tiny cabin with two bunks."

"Kind of like in Alberta," Lai replied. *Actually, more like FCI Dublin,* she thought with a shudder. *But with much nicer people, at least.*

"I call dibs on that prime deck space for sleeping!" Anong said.

"Oh, no, you don't," Kapono countered. "I already got the captain's okay for that."

"Dang, I was looking forward to it," Anong said facetiously. "Would you be willing to take turns?"

Kapono smiled gratefully and nodded. "I could go for that. Thanks, Anong."

* * *

Anong, Kapono, Lai, and Yinuo stood with several other passengers at the stern railing of the *Centaurus* as she sailed between the two jetties forming the entrance to Humboldt Bay, out into the Pacific Ocean. The late-night sky was cloudless; some of the brightest stars and planets were visible as faint orange dots through the haze of the nuclear winter. A dirty-orange, nearly-full Moon was rising over the hills just beyond the bay.

They kept their thoughts at that moment to themselves. Anong was thinking about his mother, uncle, and friends on the Red Lake Nation reservation, hoping they were safe and wondering if he'd ever see them again. Lai was saying a silent farewell to everyone she was leaving behind in the freighter's wake—those she hoped were still alive, and those who had passed from earthly existence to … she didn't know what. She only knew she dearly missed all of them.

Kapono was somewhat amazed they'd gotten to this point in their long, perilous journey without changing history—not in any obvious way, at least. There had been the tense moment at the pier; he breathed a belated sigh of relief that it had been resolved fairly easily. He wondered when and where the next twist in time would happen, and whether it would be sorted out as easily—if at all.

He shivered in the cold night air. *Early August in California isn't anything like it used to be,* he thought.

"Daddy, do you know you can never get away from people?" Yinuo asked her father as she looked up at him with her big brown eyes.

"Why is that, sweetheart?"

"Because you're a person, and you can never get away from yourself."

Kapono exchanged raised-eyebrow glances with Lai. *No wonder she'll be one of the world's top scientists someday.* He bent down and picked up his three-year-old daughter. "Time for bed, sweetie."

"But I want to see the dolphins!" she protested. Kapono had once read her a book about how dolphins tag along with ships. *She remembers everything!* he thought in wonder. *But she's not going to be able to see any dolphins—not tonight, nor for a very long time.*

"I think they're already asleep, honey."

"Okaaay," she said in a quiet, disappointed voice. As Kapono, Lai, and Anong turned away from the railing toward their cabin, Yinuo looked one more time at the faint orange orb growing steadily larger on the eastern horizon. "Goodnight, Moon!"

| 30 |

19 August 2058

After the *Centaurus* had crossed the equator into the South Pacific, temperatures warmed to the point Lai and her cabin mates wished their tiny cabin had air conditioning. The small freighter was approaching the Cook Islands. Traveling at an average speed of 15 knots, the old ship had made good progress since leaving Eureka 12 days ago. The voyage thus far had been uncomfortable, but uneventful.

Anong and Yinuo were in their cabin watching a movie on Lai's holopad while Lai and Kapono took an after-dinner stroll on deck. Radioactivity had dissipated in the Southern Hemisphere to the point that outdoor activity was generally safe. They were leaning against the starboard railing, looking out at the ocean passing slowly by. The Sun had almost disappeared on the western horizon; what remained of it cast an eerie scarlet glow in the sky and on the wavetops.

They were sharing stories from their nine·months with Miriam and Jonah in Alberta. Lai was telling Kapono about the time Miriam had asked her if they planned to get married.

"I told her we would someday—maybe when we get to New Zealand," Lai recounted.

Kapono put his right hand on top of Lai's left hand, which was resting on the railing. "Or ... how about now?"

"You mean, *right now?*" she said with surprise. "But, who would marry us?"

"Captain MacKenzie could do it."

"K, that's a nice thought, but I think that stuff in movies about ship's captains marrying people is a load of BS. Maybe if MacKenzie were captain of a cruise ship, but I don't think he has the authority to marry us."

"It just so happens," Kapono said with a smile, "I researched that question before the war. Ship's captains *can* legally marry people, under certain circumstances."

"Really? Like what?"

"Such as, if the captain is also a judge, justice of the peace, notary public, or minister."

"Captain MacKenzie doesn't seem to be a man-of-the-cloth type of guy," Lai opined. "As I should know, being such an expert in religion," she joked.

Kapono laughed. "I agree about his not being minister material. But it turns out, he *is* a notary. I asked him. And he said he'd be honored to marry us."

"No shit!" Lai exclaimed. "That's ..." her face suddenly became somber, "... that's great, Kapono."

"I thought you'd be happy about that," he said, bewildered by her reaction.

"I *am*. It's just ...." She looked into his eyes. "I think that, before you marry me, you should know what kind of person you'd be marrying."

He gently held her arms. "I'm pretty sure I know."

"I'm not so sure," she said so quietly Kapono almost didn't hear her over the sound of the waves. She bit her lower lip. "Remember right before your mission to the wormhole, I told you there was a lot of shit I'd done that I hadn't told you about?"

"Yes, I remember."

"Well, I need to tell you about that, before we get married."

"If you think you need to. But I don't think anything you tell me will make me change how I feel about you."

We'll see, Lai thought as she took a deep breath. "After I got my PhD at Cambridge, I got a job with the Harvard Center for Astrophysics."

"Yes, you've told me about your time there."

"I haven't told you *everything* about it." She looked out at the nearly dark sky and black ocean flecked with scarlet. "I didn't know anyone there at first, and I had a lot of free time. I got bored. So, I started seeing guys. I hadn't done that since I was raped in high school."

Kapono was confused. "That's good, that you started dating again—right?" Although he'd been open with Lai about his past relationships with other women, she'd never told him about the other men in her life—until just then. He assumed a woman like her would have had other suitors.

"You don't understand. I didn't date those guys—I *used* them. I used them … then I tossed them aside when I was finished with them."

"What do you mean, you 'used' them?"

Lai licked her lips. "For a few months, I slept with a different guy almost every night … all one-night stands. I stopped counting at 100." Kapono's eyebrows raised almost imperceptibly at the number, but otherwise his face was expressionless as he listened.

Her voice became quieter as she continued. "Some of them seemed like really nice guys. I didn't know them long enough to find out for sure. I didn't want to find out. A few of those guys told me they wanted to wait, to get to know each other better before we …. I didn't want to get to know them better. I only wanted what I wanted. Some of the guys told me '*No.*' I … I was insistent." She looked at Kapono, her eyes filled with guilt and regret. "Do you know what I'm saying, Kapono?"

"I think so," he replied softly.

"It didn't bother me at all at the time. I figured, payback's a bitch. But it's bothered me a *lot* since then."

Kapono held her arms again and looked into her eyes as he recalled what she'd shared with him a few years earlier about the abuse she'd suffered as a teenager and young adult. "You were a different person then, Lai."

"Yeah …. That doesn't wave it all magically away, though."

"Did you ever ask them to forgive you?"

"Not directly. I did indirectly, after you taught me about ho'opono-pono. I planned to reach out to those I could find after I moved to Boston in late '54, but then I got wrapped up in LOA and you returned, then Yinuo was born …. I told Francis about it when I met him in Boston."

"What did he say—if you don't mind telling me?"

"He asked me if I was heartily sorry for what I'd done and sincere in asking for forgiveness, and if I was willing to make amends. I told him I was, but I wasn't sure how to atone for what I'd done." She looked up at Kapono again. "He said my efforts on LOA more than made up for what I did 15 years ago."

"I agree." *And, she has no idea what impact her work on LOA will have in the future.* "Lai, you've demonstrated your love for others and for the Earth. You're the most grateful person I know. And you've accepted accountability for your actions and sought forgiveness for them. I think there's just one more thing you need to do."

"What's that?"

"You need to forgive *yourself.*"

"Yeah … I guess I can do that." She looked up at Kapono. "Can *you* forgive me?"

"I don't think there's anything for me to forgive. But, if you'd like me to … of course I forgive you—now, and to the end of time."

Lai hugged him tightly. "Thank you. I love you."

"I love you, too." He gently lifted her chin with his finger so he could look into her eyes. "So, can we get married now?"

"It won't change history, will it?"

"I don't think it will be a problem. You never married," he said gently.

"So I was an 'old maid,' huh?" Lai said with a twinkle in her eyes.

"Absolutely not. You're just really picky."

She looked up at Kapono and smiled winsomely. "Yeah, I am that." She raised up on her toes and kissed him. "Let's do it."

* * *

Captain MacKenzie rummaged through the drawers of the small desk in his cabin as Lai, Kapono, Yinuo, Anong, and Jared waited patiently.

"Beggin' yer pardon—I've never done this before," he apologized. "Ah, there 'tis," he said with relief as he took a small black book out of a drawer and turned to face the wedding party. "I assume ye'll be wantin' the abridged version?" he asked Lai and Kapono.

"That's fine, Captain," Lai replied. She looked down at her white blouse and black jeans, then glanced at Kapono's dark blue Hawaiian shirt. As a girl, she'd fantasized about having a huge wedding like she'd seen in movies and TV shows. *But, this is perfect*, she thought as she smiled sweetly at Kapono.

MacKenzie leafed through the book until he found the appropriate text. "All right, then, here we go." He cleared his throat. "Family and friends," he looked at Yinuo, Anong, and Jared, "thank ye for coming today te share in this wonderful occasion. We are here together te unite Lai and Kai in marriage." He looked up at them. "We all know that, dinnae we now? Let's get te the good part, shall we?" He flipped forward a few pages. "I've been divorced twice, so I'll spare ye my thoughts on how te ensure a long, happy marriage."

"Mahalo," Kapono said with a bemused smile.

"Here we are …." He looked at Kapono. "Do ye, Kai, take this woman te be yer lawfully wedded wife, te live together in matrimony, te love her, comfort her, honour and help her, in sickness and in health, in sorrow and in joy, te have and te hold, from this day forward, as long as ye both shall live?"

Kapono looked into Lai's eyes and smiled tenderly. "I do."

The captain turned to Lai. "Do ye, Lai, take this man te be yer lawfully wedded husband, te live together in matrimony, te love him, comfort him, honour and help him, in sickness and in health, in sorrow and in joy, te have and te hold, from this day forward, as long as ye both shall live?"

"I do," Lai vowed as she gazed with love at Kapono.

"Braw. Do ye have rings?"

Kapono nodded, crouched down to Yinuo, and held out his right hand. She grinned, pulled a gold ring with a pale-green peridot gemstone out of her pants pocket, and placed it into her father's palm. He stood up and took Lai's left hand in his hands.

"Please repeat the following," MacKenzie told Kapono. "Wi' this ring, I thee wed and pledge ye my love now and forever."

Kapono slipped the ring on Lai's ring finger as he repeated, "With this ring, I thee wed and pledge you my love now and forever."

She stared at the ring. "It's so beautiful!" she cried.

And it's perfect with her green eyes. "It was my mom's. My dad wanted you to have it."

"But I don't have a ring for you!" she lamented.

Kapono turned to Anong, who smiled and placed a gold wedding band into his hand. He handed it to Lai. "It was my dad's."

She slipped it onto Kapono's ring finger. It was very loose; he'd lost over 40 pounds during their stay in Alberta and their voyage on the *Centaurus*. "With this ring, I thee wed and pledge you my love now and forever."

"Fandabidozi!" MacKenzie exclaimed. "By the—" He was interrupted by a loud knock on the cabin door. "Och! Come!"

The door opened and the second mate stepped into the small room. "So sorry to intrude, Captain," he apologized, "but you're needed immediately on the bridge."

"What's amiss, Mr. Leslie?"

The young officer glanced at the others in the cabin, then said in a hushed tone, "Weather, sir."

Most of the color drained from MacKenzie's face; he realized he wasn't being summoned to the bridge for a mundane discussion about the weather. "I'll be wi' ye in a minute, lad."

"Thank you, sir." Leslie looked at Lai and Kapono, "Congratulations!" Then he stepped out of the cabin and shut the door behind him.

"Where were we, now? Aye …. By the authority vested in me by the Commonwealth of New Zealand, I now pronounce ye husband

and wife!" He set the little book on his desk. "Now, if ye'll please excuse me, I need te get te the bridge." He started for the door, then stopped and looked back at Kapono and Lai. "Carry on." Then he went out the door.

"You're supposed to kiss now!" Yinuo directed.

"Thanks, sweetie—I didn't realize that," Kapono said with a grin as Lai grabbed his head, pulled it down, and followed their daughter's behest.

* * *

"What do ye have, Mr. Akhtar?" MacKenzie asked his first mate as he stepped into the *Centaurus*'s cramped control room.

"Take a look, sir," Akhtar replied tensely as he motioned with his head to the radar screen.

MacKenzie stepped over to the radar station and looked down at the round, green screen. *Crivvens!* he thought with alarm as he saw a large blob across the top of the screen. "What do ye make of it?" The first mate had a meteorology degree from the University of Colorado at Boulder.

"Looks to me like a Cat 3 typhoon, sir, which means winds of 100 knots, give or take. Hard to tell for sure without satellite images." Most satellites had been disabled by electromagnetic pulses during World War III.

"Well, we dinnae want te go in there. Do ye think we can go around it?"

"I don't think so, sir. It's between us and the Cook Islands. And it's headed *for* us. I estimate the outer bands will be over us within 20 minutes."

MacKenzie realized the wind and waves of a Category 3 typhoon could cause significant, even catastrophic, damage to a ship as small as the *Centaurus*. He turned to the second mate. "Mr. Leslie, pass the word te the crew te batten down the hatches—prepare for a typhoon.

Check the lifeboats, and make sure everyone has a life jacket." *Not that those will be of much use in a Cat 3 typhoon.*

"Aye, Captain," Leslie replied as he started heading for the door. MacKenzie caught him by his arm.

"Don't alarm the passengers." *Not yet,* MacKenzie appended in his thoughts.

"Aye, sir." Leslie left the bridge, and MacKenzie picked up the microphone for the ship's PA system.

"Yer attention, please. This is the captain," he said as calmly as he could. "We'll be goin' through a wee bit of rough weather soon. All passengers must return te their cabins and remain there 'til further notice. Secure all personal belongings. As a standard precaution, the crew will distribute life jackets. Please put them on. Thank ye."

He hung up the microphone and looked again at the radar screen. The blob was larger and had inched closer to the center of the screen. He peered out the bridge's forward windows and saw an angry, charcoal-gray wall of clouds spanning the horizon, sporadically illuminated by flashes of lightning. *It'll be quite the memorable wedding night for ye, Lai and Kai.*

| 31 |

20 October 2059

"I just don't think it's possible to travel back in time," Makani asserted confidently, her arms crossed. "If it was, we'd already have been visited by people from the future."

Lai was taken aback by her favorite student's statement. *If she only knew,* she thought. Her upper-level science class was discussing black holes and wormholes—a topic she thought was particularly appropriate given it had been five years almost to the day since Kapono had leapt into the future through the Wagamese Wormhole. She'd just told her class about traversable Randall-Sundrum II model wormholes—which Anong's wormhole was—and shared that, theoretically at least, they could be used to travel through time.

"How do you know we haven't been visited by time travelers?" Lai countered.

Makani pondered her teacher's question for a few seconds. "They would've told us," the 13-year-old Ma'uke native replied with a clearly implied *duh*. "I mean, how could something like that be kept a secret?"

"Maybe they went back in time only to observe, unobtrusively," Lai suggested.

Makani didn't look convinced. "Why go to all that trouble just to take a look around? It doesn't make sense, Ms. Shen. They could've done something to help us, like—like stop World War III from happening!"

Oh, wow, Lai thought. *Out of the mouth of babes....* "Well, that could open a huge can of worms." She looked around the small classroom at her nine students. "Has anyone heard of the butterfly effect?" The teenagers responded with blank stares or by shaking their heads.

Then Lai noticed Anong standing in the open doorway to the classroom; he wore an expression that told her he had something urgent to tell her. She looked at the old analog clock on the wall—class was over for the day. "Okay, we'll discuss that tomorrow. Meanwhile, think about what could happen if someone *were* to go back in time and change history. See you tomorrow. Aloha!"

As the students left the classroom, Anong went up to Lai. "You'll never guess what happened!" he said excitedly.

"You and Kamea are engaged!" Lai guessed hopefully. Anong had met the 24-year-old island native over one year ago, and he'd fallen immediately and completely in love with her.

"No, not that," Anong said with a wistful smile. "Captain MacKenzie finally got a response to his pleas for a rescue ship! They'll be here later today!"

Ever since the *Centaurus* had been crippled by the typhoon 14 months ago and intentionally run aground on the coral reef surrounding Ma'uke in the Cook Islands, MacKenzie had been trying to arrange for transport for his passengers and crew to Auckland. But the few commercial and naval vessels that remained in the South Pacific in the post-war world had much higher priority tasks than to ferry 124 people who were safe and sound to New Zealand.

"That's—that's great, Anong." But Lai's voice and expression told him she didn't think the news was all that great.

"I thought you'd be happy about that, Lai," Anong said with bewilderment. "It's what you and Kai wanted, isn't it?"

It IS what we wanted, Lai thought. *But I love the life we've built here.* Then Lai thought about Anong and others who would be overjoyed at the prospect of finally reaching New Zealand. "Yes ... and I'm excited for you and Kamea, and everyone else!"

Anong grinned. "It's been a long time coming, hasn't it? I need to go tell Kamea the news. The ship is supposed to arrive at six tonight, off Taunganui Landing. Spread the word, okay?"

"I will." Kapono was on an offshore fishing expedition; Yinuo was just finishing her day in school.

"See you at the landing at six!" Anong yelled over his shoulder as he ran off toward his hut, on the road to the village of Oiretumu.

"Okay, thanks!" Lai called out after him. She collected the papers from her desk, put them into her knapsack, and started off down the road toward Yinuo's school.

This is our home now, she reflected. The residents of Ma'uke were surprised when the *Centaurus* ran aground on their reef and her passengers and crew struggled ashore, but they'd welcomed the refugees with open arms and hearts. They thought the arrival of 124 people to their island was a blessing. The atoll's population had dwindled steadily in the decades before World War III, and it had taken a big hit after the war due to lack of tourism and no market for the island's chief export: the *maire* plants used to make leis.

There were fewer than 100 people living on Ma'uke when the *Centaurus* arrived; many had migrated elsewhere within the Cook Islands. Suddenly, there were enough people to farm the rich volcanic soil, reopen schools, and maintain the island's infrastructure. There was plenty of abandoned housing available for the new arrivals, but many homes were in a sorry state of repair. The island's solar-powered electrical station also needed work, and the *Centaurus*'s chief engineer fixed it and kept it running.

As Lai walked down the dirt road on the warm spring afternoon, she thought about how carefree and happy she and Yinuo were, living on the island. There was sufficient food from the atoll's crops and from the sea life that had begun to recover from the war. The climate was moderate, albeit cooler than it had been before the war, thus the refugees' dearth of clothing wasn't an issue. Anong had become a farmer, Jared an assistant to the island's executive officer, Kapono a fisherman, and Lai taught science and math in the primary and secondary schools. Yinuo was thriving; the four-year-old was reading at an astonishing fifth-grade level and showed exceptional aptitude for the physical sciences—*not surprising*, Lai thought as her lips spread in a smile. The horrors of World War III had faded in her mind … faded, but not disappeared.

By the time Lai arrived at the primary school to pick up her daughter, she'd made up her mind about what she would tell Kapono about staying on Ma'uke Island when he returned from his fishing expedition.

* * *

Nearly everyone on Ma'uke had gathered at Taunganui Landing in anticipation of the arrival of the rescue ship. Lai and Yinuo found Anong and Kamea and waited with them on the beach; Jared was huddled with Ma'uke's mayor and executive officer about 50 meters away. Captain MacKenzie had announced the ship would arrive about six p.m. But he'd given no other details, leaving those for the captain of the rescue ship.

Lai checked the clock on her phone; it read *5:59*. Without phone service and Wi-Fi, *It's just a hella pricey clock, calendar, camera, and notepad*, she thought. She shielded her eyes with her hand from the setting Sun and peered out across the ocean. *Nothing out there.*

"We should be able to see the ship by now," she remarked to Anong.

"Yeah, if it's on time," he agreed.

Just as he finished replying to Lai, the surface of the ocean beyond the reef erupted, and a black tower emerged slowly from the sea, causing a commotion on the beach. There were three tall, narrow projections on top of the tower. After a few seconds, a sleek black hull and tail fin broke the surface.

"What is that, Mommy?" Yinuo asked as she pointed to the black shape resting on the ocean's surface.

"It's a submarine, sweetie," Lai replied with surprise. "A ship that travels under the sea."

"Like the *Nautilus!*" Yinuo shrieked with delight. She'd recently read the classic science-fiction novel *20,000 Leagues Under the Sea.*

"That's right, honey." *But THIS submarine is real.*

Everyone on the beach watched intently as a few crew members stepped out of the submarine's sail onto the deck and broke out a dingy. Four people climbed into the dingy and headed across the water toward one of the passages in Ma'uke's reef. After several minutes, the dingy reached the beach, and two uniformed men and one woman climbed out into the shallow water and made their way up the beach to where Captain MacKenzie was waiting for them. They all shook hands, then the woman handed one of the men a megaphone.

"Hello, everyone!" the man said, his voice amplified by the megaphone. "I'm Captain Peter Towers of the U.S.S. *Saint Paul.* We're here in response to Captain MacKenzie's request for help. I'm pleased to tell you we're prepared to transport up to 140 people to Sydney."

There was a collective gasp of surprise from the crowd. *Sydney?* Lai wondered. She looked at Anong; he obviously had the same question.

"I realize the *Centaurus* was headed for Auckland," Captain Towers continued. "I'll explain. The *Saint Paul* has been on continuous patrol since before the outbreak of the war."

Oh my god! Lai thought in amazement. *That's at least two years at sea in a submarine. And I thought our trek from Minnesota was rough!*

"Our nuclear fuel is nearly exhausted," Towers continued. "We need to reach Sydney to join the Royal Australian Navy. I'm sorry, but we don't have enough fuel for a stopover in Auckland. I've arranged for representatives of the Refugee Council of Australia to meet us when we arrive in Sydney. They'll help you find temporary housing. They can also help you get to Auckland, if you still wish to do that.

"As we can take only up to 140 of you, passengers and crew of the *Centaurus* will have preference. It will be cozy on board, to put it mildly. But it's only a five-day trip—plus we'll skip ahead one day when crossing the International Date Line. I ask that you bring only one backpack or suitcase per person—we simply don't have room for more than that. We will start boarding at 0600 tomorrow, and we'll depart at 0730. Please see Captain MacKenzie or one of his officers tonight if you wish to come with us to Sydney. Thank you for your attention; I'll see you tomorrow!"

As Towers handed the megaphone back to the female officer, there was a loud cheer with applause from most people in the crowd. Lai turned to ask Anong his thoughts, but he and Kamea had moved about 10 meters away; they were having an animated discussion. Lai couldn't hear what they were saying over the crowd noise and roar of the ocean, but neither one of them looked happy. She thought she could see tears on Kamea's face.

After a couple of minutes, Kamea grasped Anong's arms, kissed him, and walked slowly away through the sand. Anong didn't follow her, so Lai and Yinuo went to him.

"What happened, Anong?"

"Kamea doesn't want to go to Sydney. She wants to stay here, with her family."

"So, you're staying with her, right?" Selfishly, she hoped that Anong would stay on the island with her, Kapono, and Yinuo. She knew Anong and Kamea were inseparable—at least, that's what she believed.

Anong closed his eyes, then looked at Lai with sorrow she hadn't seen from him since the day most of the world was destroyed. "No. I'm going on that submarine."

"But, you love each other so much!" Lai said, in shock. "I thought you were happy here with her."

"I am happy," he said softly. "Happier than I've ever been. But I promised my mother I'd go to New Zealand or Australia to help the world recover from the war. I can't do that on this tiny island. I need to honor my promise to her … and to the Earth." He looked directly at Lai. "I need to look beyond myself, and what I might want."

As Lai listened to Anong, she became upset with herself about her selfishness. *If I went to Sydney, I could apply my scientific knowledge to help more than just a few students, as I'm doing here. And maybe I could even try to restart the LOA movement....* She smiled approvingly at him.

"I should've known that would be your decision—to think of others first, and honor your promise to your mother. I'm proud of you, Anong. But I'm sorry you need to make such a sacrifice. Someday, some lucky woman will find you—or you'll find her."

Anong half-smiled. "Yeah ... someday."

Lai hugged him. "Thank you."

"For what?"

"For slapping me upside my head." Anong looked at her with a puzzled expression. "Never mind." She took Yinuo's hand. "We'll see you bright and early tomorrow."

"Are we going on the submarine, Mommy?" Yinuo asked excitedly.

"Yes, we are, sweetie."

27 October 2059

Agueda Pereira sipped faux coffee as she sat on her living room couch and reviewed the latest refugee manifest from the *Saint Paul* on her pad. As the new deputy CEO of the Refugee Council of Australia, she was responsible for coordinating the council's resettlement efforts for the 117 people from Ma'uke Island who would be arriving in Sydney later that day.

She was ecstatic to have been named deputy CEO a few weeks earlier. She'd been working for the council since she herself became a refugee nearly two years ago. On the horrific day World War III devastated most of the world, she was representing Cal Berkeley at an international physics conference at the University of New South Wales Caringbah campus. When Berkeley was destroyed along with the rest of the San Francisco Bay Area, she was welcomed by the survivors of the nuclear attack on Sydney. She could think of no better way to repay them for their kindness and generosity than to help other refugees coming to Australia.

As she scrolled through the names, one caught her eye: Lai Shen. *Could it be ...?* she wondered. She tapped on the name to see Lai's profile. *Born 25 April 2019 ... that's about right,* she thought. *Bachelor's and doctorate degrees in quantum physics—I recall she did become a physicist, like her father.* She saw Lai was married and had a four-year-old daughter. She looked at all three photos and noticed Lai's rare green eyes. Then her eyes fixed on the photo of Lai's husband, Dr. Kai

Mililani. *The name isn't familiar,* she thought. *But he sure looks familiar, somehow....*

* * *

Lai lifted Yinuo up to Kapono, who was standing on the boat landing for the pier, then climbed out of the launch onto the landing. She looked out across Woolooware Bay at the *Saint Paul,* moored about one kilometer offshore. The submarine had disembarked its passengers at the pier in the southern Sydney suburb of Woolooware because Sydney Harbour had been obliterated in the war.

The family of three collected their bags and walked down the pier toward shore. At the end of the pier, Captain MacKenzie was saying farewell to the people he'd shepherded to safety. A few passengers and crew of the *Centaurus,* including its chief engineer, had decided to remain on Ma'uke Island. When Lai reached MacKenzie, she let go of her roller bag and hugged him.

"Thank you, Captain—for everything."

"Yer welcome, lass. 'Twas braw havin' ye all on board, and on the island afterwards. I'll not soon forget yer weddin' day, te be sure."

"Nor will we!" Kapono said as he shook the captain's hand. "Thank you, sir, for getting us here safely."

"Take good care of yer bonnie wife, and the bairn," MacKenzie said to Kapono as he patted Yinuo on her head. "And, dinnae ye dare follow my example for marriage!"

Kapono chuckled, "We won't. Aloha, Captain."

They reached the shore and stood in line for the welcome tables the Refugee Council had set up. Refugees were being checked in there and assigned to case workers. Lai noticed Anong and Jared talking with a case worker about 10 meters away, and she exchanged waves with them.

After several minutes, they reached the front of the line, and Lai said to the greeter, "Hello, I'm Lai Shen. This is my husband Kai Mililani and our daughter Yinuo Shen."

"G'day, welcome to Australia!" the young woman said with a bright smile. She checked the pad on the table in front of her. "Oh! You've been flagged for special handling."

"What does that mean?" Lai asked apprehensively.

"No worries! It only means someone other than a regular case worker will be assisting you. Just a moment, please." She picked up her phone and sent a short message to someone. "If you could please wait over there," she looked to the side of the table, "she'll be here straight away."

"Okay, thank you," Lai replied. The three of them stepped off to the side. After a couple of minutes, Lai saw a woman who looked to be in her mid-70s walking toward them, smiling broadly.

"Dr. Shen!" she exclaimed as she walked up to Lai with open arms. "My name is Agueda Pereira. I'm so glad to meet all of you and welcome you to Sydney!"

As Lai exchanged greetings with Agueda, Kapono was struggling to not let his face betray his discomfort and concern. *I hope she doesn't recognize me after all these years*, he worried. Agueda had been the dean of the physics department at Cal Berkeley when Kapono was a student there; she handed him his diploma at graduation. Because of Lai's diary, he'd known they'd meet Agueda when they arrived in Sydney. But he couldn't think of any way to avoid that encounter.

"And this is my husband, Kai Mililani," Lai said to Agueda.

"It's a pleasure to meet you, Dr. Mililani," the gray-haired woman said pleasantly. She stared intently at Kapono's face. "My apologies, but you look very familiar. Did you attend the University of California at Berkeley, by chance? You remind me of an exceptional physics student who was there 20 years ago."

Kapono decided he needed to lie. *One more lie on a mountain of lies*, he thought regretfully. "I went to MIT," he replied—not technically a lie, since he'd gotten his PhD there, but not the complete truth.

"Oh! Did you know Dean Akel there? He headed up the physics department."

"I did," Kapono said. *I wonder if he's in Sydney, too!*

"A fine man, and a good friend," Agueda said sorrowfully. "I fear he didn't survive the war."

"I'm very sorry to hear that," Kapono said with genuine sadness.

"Thank you," Agueda said. Then after greeting Yinuo, she turned back to Lai. "Dr. Shen …."

"Please, call me Lai."

Agueda nodded. "Lai, are you related to Ru Shen, former professor of physics at Cal Berkeley?"

"Yes, I'm his daughter. Why do you ask?"

"I was the dean of physics at Berkeley when your father taught there." Lai noticed her expression changing to one of great sadness, and regret. "I was the person who dismissed your father from his professorship 21 years ago. I didn't want to …. I didn't believe any of the things the FBI said he'd done. I was pressured to act. I should have stood up for him, even if it meant my job." She looked into Lai's eyes. "I didn't. And, I know what it did to him—and how it must have affected your mother, and you."

Memories of Lai's father and mother swept through her mind from 20 years and half a world away. "Dean Pereira," she said gently as she reached out to hold her hands, "my father never blamed you for what happened. He realized you were under a lot of pressure to take action. He told me once he considered his dismissal 'a blessing in disguise.'" *And perhaps it was,* she thought. *My life probably would've been much different if it hadn't happened.*

"Thank you for that, Lai," Agueda said, her eyes glistening. "This has been haunting me for over two decades." She paused. "You remind me a lot of your father."

"Thank you, Dean Pereira. That's one of the greatest compliments anyone's ever given me."

"Please, it's Agueda." She smiled graciously at the three of them. "I'd be honored if you'd stay with me until you're settled. My apartment isn't large, but you'll have your own room."

Lai glanced at Kapono, who assented with his eyes. "We'd be hella happy and grateful to stay with you, Agueda. Thank you for taking us into your home."

"Wonderful!" She bent down to Yinuo. "I bet you're tired after your long journey, yes?"

"Yeah, kind of," Yinuo replied. "But the submarine was really cool!" They all laughed.

"The light rail station is right over there," Agueda motioned with her right hand, "and it stops just a block from my place, in Miranda. Shall we head over there?" Lai and Kapono collected their bags and walked with Agueda and Yinuo toward the station.

As they started walking, Lai said, "Agueda, we came to Sydney with two friends, Anong Wagamese and Jared Levine. It looked like they were assigned to a case worker. Would it be possible to find out where they're staying?"

"Of course. I'll make sure you have each other's contact information. If you have phones, I'll get them connected to service for you. If not, I'll arrange for phones for you. They won't be the latest and greatest, but they'll work just fine."

"We have phones, thanks." *It's going to be so great to be able to use them again!*

They came to a two-way street. Lai looked to her left, saw no traffic, and started across. Kapono's left arm shot out and blocked her way as a car hummed by from their right.

"Careful! Remember, cars drive on the left here."

"Thanks!" she gulped as her heart settled back down from her throat.

As they continued toward the station, Agueda gave Lai and Kapono an overview of post-war Sydney and the world in general. "One of the most interesting aftereffects of the war is what's come to be known as the Newton Effect," she explained.

"What's that?" Lai asked.

"It's based on Newton's Third Law of Motion." *For every action there is an equal and opposite reaction*, Lai recalled. "It appears the immense shock of billions of deaths and worldwide devastation has triggered an equal and opposite reaction among the survivors." She stopped and looked at Lai and Kapono. "Believe it or not, until recently there was almost no crime anywhere in the world—at least, none we know about. Many areas of the world are unreachable. But unfortunately, the Newton Effect seems to be tapering off. Recently, there's been reports of theft, even some fighting and looting, in parts of Australia and New Zealand." She looked at Lai. "The Love One Another movement you led before the war had made great inroads in Australia, New Zealand, and other countries around the world. But that movement ended with the war, of course." She started walking toward the train station again.

"Yeah …. Could still make a difference?" Lai wondered aloud as she walked.

"I've discussed that question with sociologists from our local university," Agueda said. "They have no doubt LOA would have had a reinforcing, even amplifying, impact on the Newton Effect. And, I agree with them. But," she added with sadness in her voice, "that's an academic question now."

Maybe now, Lai thought as she glanced at Kapono. *But not for long, if I have anything to do about it!*

| 33 |

24 December 2061

Lai re-read the message that had arrived on her hPhone the day before. *I still can't believe it!* she thought. Australia's Secretary to the Department of the Prime Minister and Cabinet had invited her to meet with the prime ministers of Australia and New Zealand to discuss an idea she'd promoted during her recent LOA rallies: create a worldwide organization to help the nations that survived World War III rebuild and avoid future conflicts—like the United Nations, which had disbanded after the war, but better.

She leaned back in the cushioned wicker chair on the patio of the fourth floor flat, took another sip of engineered coffee from her mug, and gazed out at the apartment buildings and trees lining University Road. She closed her eyes as she thought about everything that had happened to her, Kapono, and Yinuo in the two-plus years since they'd arrived in Sydney on the *Saint Paul*.

Thanks to help from Agueda Pereira and others, they'd adjusted quickly to life in post-war Australia. Agueda helped them get jobs at the University of New South Wales Caringbah campus. To their good fortune, theoretical quantum physicists were in short supply in Australia. Lai became a part-time physics professor, and Kapono—Kai, as he was known to everyone except Lai—a physics research assistant. He was offered a much higher-level position, but he turned it down due to his need to stay in the background as much as possible. Agueda helped Anong and Jared find jobs, also. After living with the former

Cal Berkeley dean for two months, Lai, Kapono, and Yinuo moved to their own small apartment in Miranda.

Lai could teach only part time because she was focused on restarting the Love One Another movement. Remembering Daniel Bennett's advice from when he'd helped her launch LOA in 2054, she started small with a few online events and interviews in late 2059. The following year she led in-person rallies in north and south Sydney, Canberra, Newcastle, and Brisbane. In recent months, she travelled to Adelaide and Perth for rallies there, and then in late November she was finally able to arrange a flight to New Zealand for rallies in Auckland, Wellington, and Christchurch.

She was ecstatic about the enthusiastic reception LOA had received. But, sitting on the patio that warm summer morning, she had to admit she was more than ready for a break. She figured Kapono was, too. He'd been working hard at the university and helping with Yinuo when she wasn't in school.

As Lai thought about Kapono and Yinuo, she heard them come in the front door. "I'm out here!" she called through the open patio door. Yinuo ran to the patio and gave her mother a big hug. "Hi, sweetie! How was shopping?" Yinuo had gone to the supermarket with her father.

"Good. But we couldn't find any real coffee for you."

No surprise, Lai thought. Genuine coffee had been nearly impossible to find since the war. "No worries," she replied—she'd picked up a few Australian phrases over the past two years. "Maybe next time."

Kapono finished putting away the groceries, stepped onto the patio, and leaned down to kiss Lai. "I'm glad to see you're relaxing a bit," he said, then he noticed the phone in her hands. "Or not?"

"I *am* relaxing," she retorted. "Well, mostly." She pulled Yinuo up onto her lap. "But, I was thinking—we all deserve a break. You and your daddy are working hard in school, and I'm still recovering from my trip to New Zealand."

"What are you thinking?" Kapono asked. He hoped it was what Lai had written in her diary about that day.

"There's a 3D movie starting today at the Miranda cinema. I think we should go. Maybe Anong can come with us." Anong had been so busy with his job and volunteering with the Refugee Council that they hadn't seen him for several weeks.

"Yesss!" Yinuo exclaimed, imitating her father. "What movie, Mommy?"

Lai winked at her. "It's a surprise. But I think you're going to love it, honey. I'll check with Anong and make reservations for us for this afternoon."

Kapono let out a silent sigh of relief. *Even for as small a detail as going to a movie on a Saturday afternoon, history is tracking as it's supposed to.* There would, of course, be one small change to the excursion to the cinema that day: Kapono would be with Lai, Yinuo, and Anong.

* * *

As Lai, Yinuo, and Kapono walked down the sidewalk toward the cinema, Lai looked across the street and noticed a newly-opened toy store. She motioned to Kapono to bend down so she could whisper into his ear.

"I want to look in that store across the street for a koala. Yinuo would love it!" Qing Bao, Yinuo's cherished toy panda bear, had been a casualty of the typhoon. "We have time before the movie starts—it'll just take me a few minutes."

"Sure, we'll wait here for you." Kapono smiled slightly as he remembered that Lai's side trip to the toy store was in her diary, too. Just then, Anong walked up from behind them.

"Hi! It's great to see you again!" he said with a big smile. He hugged Lai and shook hands with Kapono, then he squatted down and asked Yinuo, "How's my favorite girl?"

"I'm very well, thank you, Anong. I can't wait to see the movie!"

Lai looked at her daughter. "I need to go across the street really quick, sweetie. I'll be right back." Then she stepped to the curb, looked right, waited for traffic to clear, and jaywalked across the street to the toy store.

As Kapono, Yinuo, and Anong waited outside the cinema, a monarch butterfly landed on Kapono's bare forearm and flittered its wings. Kapono brought his arm down close to Yinuo so she could better observe the beautiful butterfly.

"It's so pretty, Daddy!" she exclaimed in delight.

"Isn't it?" Kapono agreed. Then, after the butterfly had been on his arm for six seconds, it flew off.

"What's playing at the cinema?" Anong asked Kapono.

"The holographic remake of *The Lion King* from 2044 was recently found intact," Kapono replied. "As I recall, it's pretty spectacular. But I still remember seeing the original 2D version when I was Yinuo's age. That was the one with James Earl Jones."

"Who?"

"James Earl—" Kapono stopped, frozen by a sudden, intense feeling of *déjà vu*. Then he realized why he had that feeling. He remembered some dialogue from a video he'd seen years ago, from one of his favorite science-fiction shows:

> *My young man is taking me to a Clark Gable movie.*
> *A WHO movie?*
> *A Clark Gab—don't you know?*

He whirled around and looked across the street, searching for Lai.

"What's wrong, Kai?" Anong asked.

"Probably nothing," Kapono replied as he scanned the storefronts across the street one more time, then turned back to Anong and Yinuo.

Six seconds are infinitesimal when compared to the billions of years the universe has existed, or only the thousands of years of recorded history. But sometimes, six seconds can make all the difference in the world.

The butterfly that had entranced Yinuo flew across and down the street and landed on the sill of the open passenger window of a delivery truck stopped at a traffic light.

"G'day, mate," the driver said as he smiled happily at the alluring insect. "Where are you off to today?"

The butterfly flicked its wings twice in response. A horn beeped from behind the truck; the truck driver looked away from the butterfly and noticed the light had turned green.

"Keep your shirt on, mate," the driver muttered. Irritated by the other driver's impatience, he drove his truck through the intersection. To his horror, he saw a petite woman with black hair step into the street from in front of a car that had stopped at the curb a few seconds earlier. She was looking to her left and thus did not see the electric truck as it bore down on her.

"Blimey!" the driver shouted as the truck's pedestrian-avoidance AI activated and its brakes and tires squealed in protest. The woman turned her head just as the truck struck her with a sickening *thud*. She was flung 10 feet by the impact. After her body crumpled awkwardly to the pavement, she lay still. A paper bag containing a stuffed toy koala lay a few feet away from her.

"*No!*" Kapono cried out in disbelief and anguish from across the street. He glanced quickly at Anong.

"I've got her!" Anong assured Kapono as he picked Yinuo up and turned her away from the sight of her mother lying bleeding and motionless 20 feet away. As Kapono dashed to Lai's side, Anong pulled his phone out of his pocket and held it up to his face. "Call Triple Zero, and urgently request paramedics to this location!"

"Calling, and I've sent your urgent request to Emergency Services," his AI assistant replied.

The driver of the truck had also called Triple Zero, then he jumped out of the cab and crouched down next to Lai. "I'm sorry, I'm so sorry! I didn't see you!" he cried. A small crowd of people had encircled Lai, to protect her from traffic until help arrived.

Kapono heard sirens approaching as he knelt beside his unconscious wife and cradled her right hand, tears streaming down his face as he shook his head and thought, *Oh God, what have I done? WHAT HAVE I DONE?*

* * *

Kapono and Anong sat silently in Sutherland Hospital's emergency reception area. The lights of a small Christmas tree twinkled from across the room. But neither Kapono nor Anong was feeling any sense of joy from the holiday season. In fact, Kapono didn't feel anything at all except immense concern for Lai—and overwhelming regret for his selfishness.

Because there was no way to tell how long the wait would be, Anong had asked Agueda Pereira if she would look after Yinuo, and she gladly agreed to take care of the six-year-old girl who called her Nanna.

When news of the accident broke, Lai's colleagues and friends from the university and the LOA movement had sent messages of support and offers to donate blood or whatever else might be needed. Many of them had gathered outside the hospital for an early evening vigil, hoping and praying for Lai's recovery.

Kapono and Anong looked up as a man in a white doctor's coat came through the double doors from the critical care area and approached them. They both stood up.

"I'm Dr. Wang. I'm the lead neurosurgeon caring for your wife, Mr. Mililani," he told Kapono. "Please, have a seat," he requested as he sat down next to Kapono and Anong.

"How is she, Doctor?" Kapono asked. The doctor paused before responding, causing Kapono and Anong to fear the worst.

"She suffered severe brain trauma in addition to other injuries, including a lacerated kidney, a broken hip and femur, several broken ribs, and fractures of multiple vertebrae," Dr. Wang said softly but clearly. "Although those are very serious injuries, they're treatable.

However, she's not responding to treatment for her cerebral injuries as well as I'd hoped." He looked directly at Kapono. "Do you know if she's suffered brain trauma in the past?"

"Yes, at least twice. She was in an accident in March 2054 and suffered brain lesions and other severe injuries." Lai had almost died when *Chronos 2* crash-landed in Kansas. "She was in an induced coma for 11 weeks afterward. Also, she suffered a moderate concussion the following January," he added as he remembered how Daniel Bennett had saved Lai's life.

The doctor nodded, his expression grim. "I believe that explains why her condition is more critical than I would have expected. I must be honest with both of you—I'm not sure she will survive."

Kapono grabbed the doctor's arms as he cried, "She *has* to survive! *The future of the world depends on it!*" Dr. Wang looked at him with a bewildered expression, and Kapono released the doctor's arms as he realized he'd said too much. "I mean," he stumbled, "she's been working on some important initiatives, like the Love One Another movement."

The doctor nodded again. "Yes, I know about your wife's work there. She's very inspiring." He looked at Kapono, then at Anong with a determined expression. "I promise you that I and the rest of the team will do everything possible for her. But," he added solemnly, "I think you should prepare for the worst."

| 34 |

25 December 2061

Kapono focused on the faint but regular beeping sound coming from the monitors attached to Lai. He had the thought, as irrational as it was, that if he concentrated hard enough, he could make the beeping continue through the force of his will.

He was sitting beside Lai's bed in ICU, where he'd been since she'd been brought there from surgery the night before. He'd insisted that Anong go home to get some sleep. Yinuo was still at her honorary grandmother's apartment.

Lai was unconscious; her slow, labored breathing was aided by a nasal cannula. Kapono thought of the other time he'd kept vigil at her bedside: after she'd been critically injured in the crash-landing of *Chronos 2*. On that occasion, she'd awakened from a coma to the sound of his voice. He hoped, and prayed, that she would wake up as she had back then.

He knew she might be able to sense his presence, feel his touch, and hear him even in her unconscious state. Thus, he held her right hand gently in his hands and talked to her, hoping for some sign she could hear him.

"Lai, I'm so very sorry," he said in a soft, strained voice. "I should never have returned to the past. I told myself I was doing it for you—that you wanted and needed me to return. But I realize now, I did it mostly for myself." He looked at the monitors, then at her bruised but peaceful face—there was no change.

"You know I read your diaries. You and Yinuo had an amazing life without me. You made such a difference to so many people—to the whole world. I risked all that with my selfishness and arrogance. I'd do anything if I could reverse that, make things the way they were before I interfered in the past. I … I don't know if you can ever forgive me for what I've done to you and Yinuo, and all the people whose lives you touched—or will touch."

He thought he saw Lai's lips move. It was only the slightest of a quiver. "Lai? Can you hear me?"

Her eyes opened, albeit only as narrow slits. Through the slits, Kapono saw her look at him. At the same time, the corners of her mouth turned upward in the faintest of smiles.

"Love …." she said in a barely audible whisper.

He leaned forward, "What is it, sweetie?"

"Love … never fails."

Kapono's eyes filled with tears at the sound of Lai's voice, and her words. "No, it doesn't," he agreed as he nodded and squeezed her hand.

Then her eyes closed. A few seconds later, the rhythmic beeping from the monitor changed to a steady, high-pitched tone. Kapono's head jerked up, and he stared at the monitor. He saw only horizontal lines.

He heard a voice over the hospital's PA system, "Code Blue, ICU Four! Code Blue, ICU Four!" Almost immediately, two nurses and a doctor rushed into the room.

"Sir, I have to ask you to leave right now," the doctor said politely but urgently as he quickly moved to Lai's bedside and began treating her, assisted by the nurses. Kapono immediately stood up and backed away from the bed to give the three caregivers room.

"Of course," he replied as he headed for the door. Before he opened it, he turned to look one more time at his beloved *ku'uipo*. *Hang on, Lai*, he urged with all his might. *Please, hang on!*

* * *

Agueda opened the front door of her flat for Kapono. His devastated expression wasn't a surprise to her; he'd told her about Lai when he'd called about coming to bring Yinuo home.

"I'm so sorry," she said sorrowfully as she reached out to embrace him.

"Mahalo, Agueda. And thank you for taking care of Yinuo."

"I'm just glad I could help. That child is such a joy."

He stepped into the living area of the small apartment. "How is she doing?"

"She's in the guest bedroom, reading. She's worried about her mother, of course."

"I'd like to talk with her privately."

"I understand. Please let me know if there's anything I can do. I know a wonderful children's counselor, if you think it would be good for Yinuo to talk with her."

"That could be helpful. I'll let you know."

Kapono opened the bedroom door and saw his daughter sitting on the bed, reading *Harry Potter and the Sorcerer's Stone.* When she saw him at the door, she jumped off the bed and rushed over to him.

"Daddy!" she exclaimed as she wrapped her arms around his legs.

"Hi, honey." He hugged her around her shoulders, kissed her on her forehead, and closed the door. "How are you?"

"I'm okay," she said tentatively as she looked up at him. "Can we go see Mommy now?"

"Come sit with me, sweetie, and let's talk." He sat down on the foot of the bed, and Yinuo sat down next to him. He put his left arm gently around her shoulders.

"What's wrong, Daddy?"

"I have some sad news to tell you," Kapono began as he struggled to find words that no young child should ever have to hear. He remembered how difficult it had been for his father to tell him that his mother had died in the Maui fire of 2023, when he was one year younger than Yinuo. Keone's words had been gentle and kind, but also honest and direct.

"Your mommy was badly hurt. The doctors did everything they could to help her. But, her body stopped working, and she ... uhm ... she died." He tried to control his tears, but they started trickling down his cheeks.

She considered what her father had just told her. "So, I can't go see her now?"

"No, sweetheart. We won't be able to see her again."

Tears started flowing freely down her reddened cheeks. "Was it my fault?" she said in a small, anguished voice.

"No, of course not. Why do you say that?"

"Because she was buying a koala for me when the truck hit her. If she hadn't gone to the store …."

Kapono hugged her more tightly and looked directly into her eyes. "Sweetie, no—it *wasn't* your fault. It was an accident. It wasn't any-one's fault." *Except it was,* he realized. *It was MY fault. But how could I possibly explain that to her now? Maybe when she's much older….*

Yinuo wiped her nose with the back of her hand and looked up at her father. "Is she with the angels now?" Miriam had told Yinuo about heaven and angels during their nine months in Alberta.

"Do you think she is?"

"Yes," she said confidently.

He kissed her on the top of her head. "I think so, too."

| 35 |

28 December 2061

Kapono looked out at the hundreds of people who'd come to pay their last respects to Lai at her memorial service. Due to inclement weather, the service had been moved from Elouera Beach to the University of New South Wales's gymnasium. Anong had given a moving eulogy for his best friend, and several others, including Jared, Agueda, and some of Lai's students and fellow teachers, had offered ad-hoc testimonials to her impact on their lives. With the service nearing its conclusion, Kapono stood at the podium stand and addressed the mourners.

"Thank you all for coming on what is both a very sad day, but also a joyful day. We're sad because we'll miss Lai very much. Her loss has left a deep emptiness in our hearts. The world is a different place—a lesser place—without her. But we're filled with joy and gratitude for having known her and loved her. And I know she'd be so happy to see all of you here, expressing your love for her and for each other.

"As most of you know, Lai wasn't a religious person. But she studied several faith traditions, including Christianity. One of her favorite lines from the New Testament was from the Apostle Paul: 'Love never fails.'" He paused to collect himself. "In fact, those were her final words. It was her dream that all people would be able to put aside anger and hatred and love one another. And as you know, she worked tirelessly toward that goal. The best way we can honor her memory is to do whatever we can to achieve that dream—here in Australia, and around the world. That's what I'm going to do. And I ask all of you, Lai's friends and colleagues, to help me.

"I hope you'll stay for fellowship and refreshments in the foyer. There will, of course, be coffee." He noticed many knowing smiles in the crowd. "Mahalo, and aloha."

As Kapono stepped away from the podium, a man with a familiar face approached him. *He's the driver of the truck that hit Lai!* he realized.

"Mr. Mililani, I know I'm probably the last person you want to see right now," the man began in a quavering, sorrowful voice. "But I had to come here today and pay my respects, and to tell you how terribly sorry I am for what I did."

"Thank you for coming," Kapono replied. "I appreciate it. And, I want you to know it wasn't your fault." He'd refused to press charges.

"But I should have been more careful—"

Kapono reached out to put his hands on the man's upper arms. "It was *not* your fault. It was *my* fault."

The man looked at Kapono with bewilderment. "What—what do you mean, it was your fault? How could it be your fault?"

Kapono hesitated. "It's … complicated. But, please don't blame yourself. Lai wouldn't have wanted that."

"Well, all right. Thank you, Mr. Mililani. I wish I would have known your wife. She sounds like one in a million."

Kapono smiled softly. "She was. You take care."

He started heading for the foyer to join Agueda, Anong, and Yinuo when a middle-aged woman dressed in a black skirt suit walked up to him.

"Dr. Mililani, my name is Matilda Stewart," she said as she extended her right hand. "I'm Australia's minister of social services. The prime minister asked me to come today as her representative, as she had a prior commitment. I wish to convey the prime minister's most sincere condolences, and mine as well, for your loss."

Kapono shook Stewart's hand. "Thank you for coming, Minister Stewart. That was very kind of you, and the prime minister." Suddenly Kapono recalled what he'd just said about doing whatever was possible to achieve Lai's dream, and he realized what he had to do. "Minister, I have a favor to ask of you."

"What can I do for you?"

"Just before Lai died, the prime minister invited her to discuss the creation of an organization to help the world's nations recover from the war and avoid future conflicts. I would like to go ahead with that meeting, if that's acceptable to the prime minister. I'm very familiar with Lai's thoughts on that subject. Could you please ask her about that for me?"

"I'll be glad to do that, Dr. Mililani. I believe the prime minister will be open to it. I'll ask her assistant to get back to you as soon as possible."

"Thank you, Minister Stewart—I really appreciate it."

After Stewart had left the gymnasium, Kapono lingered near the podium, deep in thought. He decided what he must do to make up for Lai's tragic death and ensure history held to its intended course. He would follow in her footsteps and try to do everything she did to build the LOA movement and United Earth, and eventually become chief physicist for United Earth. And of course, he'd care for Yinuo and ensure she'd grow up into the exceptional woman she'd become. *With Lai's diary, I should be able to—*

A terrible thought flashed through his mind—he hadn't looked at Lai's diary since before she was hit by the truck. He quickly returned to his pad on the podium stand and tapped into the diary. He clicked on the entry for Christmas Eve, 2061. He could scarcely believe what he read:

24 December 2061 – 9:40 p.m.

What a great day! I thought Yinuo and I needed a break, so we went to the local cinema—it reopened only a few weeks ago. Anong came with us. When we arrived there, he stayed with Yinuo so I could dash across the street to buy her a koala, to replace Qing Bao. She loved

> *it! She said she has to think about the name. She loved the movie, too—the 3D remake of The Lion King from 2044. I think I enjoyed it almost as much as the original version I saw when I was a little girl.*
>
> *Then we walked down the street to have dinner at a new Vietnamese restaurant....*

Kapono stared at the pad for several seconds. *That ... that can't be!* he thought incredulously. *I wonder ....* He clicked on the date index, scrolled down to the last entry in the diary, and opened that entry:

> *23 December 2111 – 10:14 a.m.*
>
> *I asked Yinuo if she and An would help me make the video for Kapono today. She said we'll do it this afternoon. I shouldn't have waited so long. I get tired so quickly, and I hope I can say everything I want to tell him. How do you compress nearly 60 years into a few minutes?*
>
> *I need to tell him to not try to return to the past to stop World War III. I know he'll want to do that, but I have to agree with Yinuo that it would be a terrible idea to change the past. We have no idea how even a small change would affect the future....*

He stopped reading. *This is impossible!* he thought as he shook his head slowly. *Her diary entries should have stopped a few days ago. But instead, it's as if the accident never happened!* His mind sifted through everything he knew about physics for an answer. After several seconds deep in thought, his face broke into a knowing smile.

"He was right," Kapono whispered to himself. *That's the only possible answer—he was right! There's a future event that will restore history back to as it should be!* He skimmed through his memory of the future and quickly grasped what must happen—what he must do—to make things right again for Lai, Yinuo, and An … for the entire world. Then he smiled again as he reflected on the fact that *to make things right* is literally what ho'oponopono means, and he thought about his father. *Mahalo, Dad, for introducing me to ho'oponopono when I was 14.*

But he realized he wouldn't be able to set history right until many years in the future. The advice Aroha had given him came to his mind: to focus on the here and now.

That's what I need to do, until the day I'm able to undo what I've done. I need to help my family and friends, and all people of the world, as much as I'm able. I may not do as well as Lai did, but I'm going to try, with everything I've got.

| 36 |

11 January 2062

"Just how would this new organisation differ from the United Nations?" Australia's Prime Minister Elanora Gordon asked Kapono.

Kapono looked at Gordon and the other ministers as he considered how best to answer her important question. He was sitting at the conference table in the wood-paneled Cabinet Room of Canberra's Parliament House. Sitting with Kapono and Gordon in brown leather chairs at one end of the huge table were New Zealand's Prime Minister Noah Sullivan and Minister of Foreign Affairs Tauiti Potaka, and Australia's Minister for Foreign Affairs Mark Thistlethwaite and UN Ambassador Amanda Wong. Fortunately, Wong had been on a home visit when World War III struck; New Zealand's UN ambassador was in New York City then. That the Parliament House survived the war unscathed was something of a miracle; the missile aimed at Australia's capital city malfunctioned and struck 15 miles west of Canberra, sparing most of it.

"One big difference is, there would be no vetoes," Kapono replied. Some of the ministers, including Ambassador Wong, nodded.

"The five permanent members of the UN Security Council tended to use vetoes to defend their own interests and policies or to promote an issue of importance to them," Wong explained. "It was a useful tool—for those five nations. But it was also the most undemocratic element of the United Nations." She smiled slightly. "Let's can it."

"As a practical matter," Foreign Affairs Minister Potaka added, "the national governments of those five countries no longer exist." Kapono and the ministers closed their eyes or nodded solemnly.

"The other major difference with the United Nations is that I propose the new organization have only one governing body, rather than a Security Council and General Assembly," Kapono asserted.

Foreign Affairs Minister Thistlethwaite spoke up, "The Security Council played a key role in settling international disputes and maintaining peace and security."

"That's true, Mark," Kapono agreed. The participants had been on a first-name basis since the meeting began. *This meeting will take twice as long if we use everyone's titles*, Prime Minister Gordon had joked. "But there are so few nations left after World War III, why couldn't one body serve that purpose while representing all members?" Only 30 percent of the countries in existence before the war had still-functioning national governments.

"That's a good point," Prime Minister Sullivan conceded. "And it would certainly make the new organisation simpler and more nimble. What would this governing body be called?"

"Speaking of simplicity, how about just the Council?" Wong suggested. Everyone stated or nodded in agreement.

"I'd like to discuss the issue of enforcement," Thistlethwaite expressed. "That was a major problem for the United Nations, and it had access to far more resources than Earth has now. Australia's navy is probably the largest in the post-war world, including the ships adopted from the U.S. Navy, but it was decimated by the war, as was our air force. And our army is quite small."

"I've been thinking about that, Mark," Kapono replied. "The Earth today is much different than before the war, in many ways. One of the most significant differences is the impact of the Newton Effect, reinforced by the Love One Another movement my late wife Lai Shen led." Kapono saw the ministers nodding in agreement. "With everyone embracing love for one another, I believe that if they see the Council's actions as being in the best interests of all people of the world, with love as the motivation, there shouldn't be much if any opposition to them."

"But I recall many heated debates and disagreements among the UN's member states," Wong said. "Love wasn't always uppermost in their minds when deciding a course of action," she added with a wry smile.

Kapono's expression mirrored Wong's. "True." He looked around the table. "But Lai had an idea about that." He paused as he recalled his discussion with her late one night about her idea of forming a new organization to replace the United Nations. "I think you're aware the citizens of Hawai'i voted to embed the theme of love for others into their laws right before the war. While that was a well-intentioned idea, Lai realized in hindsight it would likely be impractical at a global level. But she thought, what if this new organization had in its charter a *guiding principle* of Love One Another? It would be a constant reminder for the Council to consider love for others in its decision-making and serve as a guidepost in case of an impasse. It would help ensure that love would indeed be a motivation for the Council's actions."

Wong nodded thoughtfully. "I think that might just work—it's a good idea."

"Here's a basic question," Sullivan interjected. "What should this new organisation be called? I don't think we want to recycle the United Nations name."

"I agree," Gordon concurred. "Not only would it be confusing, but we're talking about a significantly different body."

Kapono looked at Sullivan and Gordon, then at the other ministers sitting with him at one end of the long conference table. "The objective of the Love One Another movement is to encourage love and forgiveness to foster peace and unity around the world. And fostering peace and unity among all the people of Earth would be the primary mission of this new organization, would it not?" Everyone agreed. "So, what do you think about calling it United Earth?"

| 37 |

24 October 2065

Kapono and Yinuo looked out at the thousands of people gathered at Aotea Square in downtown Auckland. The crowd included representatives from many of the 59 signatory nations. Those unable to send delegations were participating in the ceremony via a worldwide telecommunications network that had been created in 2062 using three new geostationary satellites.

"This is so ripper, Dad!" Kapono's 10-year-old daughter exclaimed. She'd picked up Australian phrases and slang from her primary school classmates. *She's even developed a bit of an Australian accent*, Kapono realized as he smiled affectionately at her. They were sitting on folding chairs on a raised platform along with several other people who'd been instrumental in creating the organization to be established on the sunny, mild spring day.

Kapono's excitement about the event they were about to witness was tempered by sorrow. *Lai should be sitting on this stage with Yinuo, not me*, he thought sadly. He looked at his daughter, who was beaming as she was taking in the festive atmosphere, and leaned over to her. "Always remember, this was all made possible by your mother's vision and efforts."

Yinuo looked at her father. "I know Mum worked really hard for this day. And I know you wish she could be here with us. I wish that, too. But I also know everything you've done to bring the world closer together. And, I'm really proud of you, Dad."

Tears welled up in Kapono's eyes; he kissed Yinuo on her forehead. "Mahalo, sweetie. That means a lot to me."

Elanora Gordon stood up and stepped forward to the slim wooden podium stand at the front of the stage. "If I may ask for your attention, please," she said into the microphone. The crowd settled into silence as they focused on Australia's prime minister. "First, I wish to thank all of you for being here today for this auspicious occasion. I especially thank the representatives from other nations, who have travelled from Africa, Central and South America, and Asia-Pacific to be here with us in person." There was loud and lengthy applause. "I also welcome all who are joining us remotely from around the world, from as far away as Iceland." The crowd applauded appreciatively.

Gordon introduced the people on stage with her, highlighting each person's contributions. Then she briefly reviewed the philosophy and objectives of the organization that had emerged from the ashes of World War III. Finally, she introduced the first president of the new organization, former New Zealand Prime Minister Noah Sullivan, to read the Preamble of the organization's charter.

Sullivan stepped to the microphone to thunderous applause and cheers. After a couple of minutes, he motioned with his right hand for the crowd to settle down. When they had done so, he started reading from a pad on the podium stand.

"'WE THE PEOPLE OF THE PLANET EARTH,'" Sullivan read slowly and solemnly, "'to save future generations from the scourge of war, which has brought untold devastation to the Earth and to the human race, and to reaffirm faith in fundamental human rights, in the dignity and worth of each person, in the equal rights of all people in every nation, and to establish conditions under which justice and respect for the obligations arising from treaties and laws can be maintained, and to promote social progress including the end to homelessness and hunger ....'" Sullivan paused for a moment, then continued with the Preamble.

"'AND FOR THESE ENDS to practise tolerance and live together in peace with one another as good neighbours, establishing as our

Guiding Principle *To Love One Another*, to work together to maintain international peace and security, and to ensure, by the acceptance of principles and the institution of methods, that armed force shall never again be used, save in the common interest and as a last resort, and to employ international cooperation for the promotion of the economic and social advancement of all peoples, HAVE RESOLVED TO COMBINE OUR EFFORTS TO ACCOMPLISH THESE AIMS.'" Sullivan paused again and gazed out at the thousands of people standing shoulder to shoulder on the plaza before finishing the Preamble.

"'Accordingly, our respective Governments, through representatives assembled in the city of Auckland, who have exhibited their full powers found to be in good and due form, have agreed to this Charter and do hereby establish a worldwide organisation to be known as United Earth.'"

The crowd erupted into loud, joyous celebration as the new president turned to embrace and thank Prime Minister Gordon, Kapono, and the others on stage with them.

After Sullivan had thanked and congratulated Kapono, he gazed above the crowd, into the blue sky dotted with white, puffy cumulus clouds. *You did it, ku'uipo!*

| 38 |

10 November 2088

Kapono beamed as only a proud father can as he sat at a round banquet table in the event hall in Caringbah. He was watching Yinuo and her husband Liam hold each other close as they swayed slowly to *Unforgettable* during the bride and groom's traditional first dance. *They look so happy together*, Kapono thought. *And I couldn't ask for a better son-in-law.*

Watching his radiant 33-year-old daughter glide over the dance floor in her white bateau-neck, low-back trumpet gown resurfaced memories of another beautiful bride, who wore a white blouse and black jeans as she stood beside him in Captain MacKenzie's cabin. *It's hard to believe that was over 30 years ago*, he thought wistfully as he reflected on how quickly time had passed. *It seems like it was just yesterday that Yinuo was 12 years old and graduating from primary school....*

After secondary school, she'd earned a bachelor's degree in physics from the University of New South Wales. She wanted to continue in her parents' footsteps and get a PhD in quantum physics, but the only such program available in Asia-Pacific was at the Australian National University in Canberra, and there was a long waiting list. She assisted her father with the Love One Another movement and in his role as United Earth's chief physicist until finally starting her graduate studies in 2084. She met Liam Martin in Canberra two years later. *It's something of a miracle Yinuo met Liam when she was supposed to and they got married on the same day Lai wrote about in her diary.*

Yinuo was right—Liam and I did hit it off, Kapono thought as he recalled what his daughter had told him when he arrived in the future through the Wagamese Wormhole. He and Yinuo's *ku'uipo* shared a love of the ocean. Although Kapono's days of riding the biggest waves were over, he loved going surfing with the slender, brown-haired Australian at Crescent Head and other beaches near Sydney.

The song ended, and Yinuo and Liam kissed to applause from the guests. Kapono got up from the table and approached the couple, extending his left hand to his daughter.

"May I have this dance, honey?" he asked her. Liam flashed a smile and walked off the dance floor. Yinuo took her father's hand and placed her left hand on his shoulder while looking into his eyes.

"Absolutely!" she said in a way that reminded Kapono of Lai.

The music began, and they started dancing. Kapono recognized the song Yinuo had selected for their dance: *Father and Daughter*.

"That's perfect," he told her as he listened to the lyrics.

"Thanks, Dad. I thought so."

"Not quite like your mother's and my wedding, is it?"

"Well, no, but there was no way we were going to top a ceremony at sea replete with a typhoon, so Liam and I decided to go a more traditional route," she said with smiling brown eyes.

"Good call," Kapono replied with a wink.

"Dad, I … I just want to thank you for everything—for always being there for me. I know it couldn't have been easy for you as a single dad, juggling your more-than-full-time chief physicist job with your efforts on LOA and helping United Earth get started. I always felt that you put me first. I'm not sure how you managed that, but you did. And I …" her voice broke, "… I think you're the best dad in the world."

Yinuo's heartfelt words were tearing Kapono up inside. "Mahalo, sweetie. I appreciate your saying that. I love you." But he was thinking, *If she only knew how I stole her mother from her for most of her life …. Lai should be here right now, celebrating this day with her daughter—just as she should have been there for all the past and future events in Yinuo's life.*

But, now's not the time to say anything—not on one of the happiest days of her life.

"I love you, too, Dad." She noticed his sorrowful expression. "Are you okay?"

"Yeah, I'm good." He forced the sorrow from his face and smiled lovingly at his newlywed daughter. "I'm so happy for you and Liam. You're going to have a great life together." *Until he gets sick*, Kapono thought sadly. He quickly pushed that thought out of his mind and refocused on the present. "He's a great guy—and one very lucky man."

"He's bewdy bonza, isn't he? I wish Mum could've ...." She was unable to finish her thought.

"I know, sweetheart. I wish that, too."

The last guitar notes of the song faded away, and Kapono hugged his daughter as the guests applauded and moved toward the dance floor. Kapono and Yinuo had turned to head back to their table when Anong walked up to them, smiling broadly.

"May I have this dance?" he asked Yinuo.

"I would be delighted, Dr. Wagamese," she replied with a bright smile as she took Anong's proffered hand.

As the music began and they started dancing, Yinuo looked up and down at Anong in his gray tuxedo. "You look very debonair, Anong."

"Thank you," he said appreciatively as he gazed at Yinuo's beautiful wedding gown. "We both clean up pretty well, huh?" he joked, thinking of their 14 months wearing minimal, threadbare clothing on Ma'uke Island.

She laughed, "Fair dinkum!"

"Yinnie, I wanted you to be one of the first to know—I'll be leaving Australia soon. I've joined the Peace Corps." United Earth's Peace Corps, which had been founded the previous month, was modeled after the United States' organization that hadn't survived World War III.

"Really?! That's great, Anong!" she said with genuine excitement, but also some sadness at the thought of the man who'd been like an uncle to her moving far away. "Where are you going?"

"I volunteered for the first mission to North America, in south-central Canada," he grinned, "and northern Minnesota."

Yinuo forgot her disappointment about Anong's leaving. "Oh my God! That's ripper, Anong!"

"Isn't it? I'll be returning to the Red Lake Nation reservation to help the survivors. They had a rough time during the nuclear winter, and they're just now starting to rebuild."

"Have you had any news about your mum and your uncle?"

"No, not yet," he said softly. "Communications with that part of the world are tenuous at best." He smiled, "But, I'm hopeful. And, I'm glad I can return there after all these years." *As I promised Mom I would.*

The music stopped, and Yinuo hugged her lifelong friend. "I'm so proud of you, and happy for you." She broke the embrace and looked into his eyes. "Be careful in Minnesota, okay? I want to hear all about your good work there when you return to Australia."

"I'll be careful," Anong promised. *But I'm not sure about coming back here. Maybe it's time I went back home to stay.*

| **39** |

24 October 2090

"I wonder what *that* is?" Yinuo asked her father as they walked with Liam from the light rail station toward the new United Earth headquarters tower at Aotea Square in central Auckland. Kapono, 77 years old with thinning gray hair, was walking slowly due to a flare-up from an old surfing mishap. His daughter pointed at a large shape covered by a tarpaulin in the center of the plaza next to the building's main entrance.

"I don't know, honey," Kapono replied. "But I guess we'll find out pretty soon."

He knew what *would* have been under the dark blue tarpaulin, if he hadn't changed history 29 years earlier. *But it won't be that,* he thought sorrowfully.

He'd been invited by United Earth President Amanda Wong to be a guest of honor at the ceremony celebrating the 25th anniversary of the founding of United Earth. Kapono and other guests of honor, including United Earth's first president, Noah Sullivan, would be sitting with Wong on a temporary stage next to the mysterious shrouded shape.

Yinuo, Liam, and their six-month-old son An had reserved, front-row seats in the audience. Yinuo had taken time off from her job as professor of physics at the University of New South Wales, and Liam had arranged a few days' leave from the United Earth Navy, in which he served as a lieutenant. Liam, who was carrying An, was concerned

208

his son might cause a fuss during the ceremony. But Kapono had reassured him, "An's name means *peace*. There's no way he'll be any trouble."

As Yinuo and Liam took their seats in the audience with An, Kapono stepped gingerly onto the stage, found his chair, and exchanged greetings with Sullivan and the other honored guests.

"Do you know what's under the tarp?" Kapono asked the elderly former president.

"Haven't a clue," Sullivan replied. But Kapono thought he saw a twinkle in his friend's eyes.

After a few minutes, President Wong stepped onto the stage to applause from the audience, greeted the guests of honor, and approached the transparent aluminum podium stand with the blue and white United Earth emblem on its front. "President Sullivan, honoured guests, ladies and gentlemen," she began. "Thank you all for being here today or joining us remotely to celebrate the 25th anniversary of United Earth."

After a fairly long program—*longer than it needed to be*, Kapono thought—that included a re-enactment of Sullivan reading the Preamble of United Earth's charter and the first public performance of the recently-commissioned United Earth anthem, Wong stepped up to the podium stand once more.

"And now," she announced, "it is time to honour and thank someone without whom United Earth would likely not exist." As she continued her tribute, Kapono thought apprehensively, *Oh no—it can't be!* When Wong told the audience, "In addition to playing a crucial role in the formation of United Earth, this individual has worked tirelessly to encourage the people of the world to love one another while serving as United Earth's chief physicist," his fears were realized.

In the audience, Yinuo listened to the president with increasing interest, then excitement, as the subject of her tribute became clear. She looked at her father sitting on the stage and beamed with pride.

"It gives me great pleasure to unveil this statue in honour of one of Australia and United Earth's finest citizens, Dr. Kai Mililani." Immediately after Wong said those words, the dark blue tarpaulin slipped to the ground, revealing a bronze statue of Kapono.

Oh God, no, he thought in dismay. *That should be Lai's statue!*

* * *

When the ceremony was finally finished, Yinuo, Liam, and An went up to Kapono, and Yinuo threw her arms around her father. "That is so bloody fantastic, Dad! And no one is more deserving!" Liam added his congratulations; even An looked happy about the statue as he gazed up in wonder at the tall bronze sculpture.

"Mahalo, both of you," Kapono said politely, without enthusiasm. "But you know, there were many others responsible for the creation of United Earth: President Wong, former President Sullivan, Tauiti Potaka, Mark Thistlethwaite—"

"Sure, Dad, I know that," Yinuo replied. "But you helped with that while leading the Love One Another movement, *and* you've worked your tail off as United Earth's chief physicist." She looked at her father with love. "I'd say that deserves a statue, at the least."

"If you say so," Kapono relented. He studied the bronze figure and frowned. "That's not my favorite Hawaiian shirt pattern," he critiqued. "And, I was *never* that buff. And the chin is—"

"It's great, Dad." Yinuo turned to her husband, "Isn't it, Liam?"

"I think it's ripper—and well-deserved. Except," he added with a waggish smile, "they should've put a surfboard on it."

Liam's joke pulled Kapono partially out of his funk. "Fair dinkum," he chuckled.

Yinuo walked up to the Hinuera stone base of the statue and read the inscription on the large plaque affixed to it:

Kai Mililani, PhD
United Earth Founder and Chief Physicist
"I'm sorry – Please forgive me – Thank you – I love you"

She looked at her father and smiled with satisfaction. *It's perfect.*

A middle-aged man and a boy of about 10, both Māori, walked up to Kapono. "Excuse me, Dr. Mililani," the man said. "My name is Ariki Ngata; this is my son, Witi."

I've got to be careful, here! Kapono thought. He extended his hand to the man. "I'm pleased to meet you, Mr. Ngata," he said as they shook hands, then he looked down at the boy. "And I'm glad to meet you also, Witi." *Although I already met you, over 50 years from now.*

"I'm sorry to interrupt you and your family," Ariki apologized, "but I wanted to congratulate you on your honour, and personally thank you for everything you've done for New Zealand, and for the entire world."

"Thank you, that's very kind of you, sir," Kapono replied humbly.

"Witi very much wanted to meet you." He put his right hand on his son's shoulder. "You're his hero. He's told me he wants to serve his country, perhaps the entire world, when he grows up—just like you."

Oh wow, Kapono thought as he fought to hide his shock. *What a temporal paradox that could be ... or, is it a paradox?* He recalled United Earth President Witi Ngata telling him in 2141 that he'd first met Lai when he was 10 years old, and she'd inspired him to enter public service.

He bent over to shake Witi's hand. "That's a very commendable goal, Witi. What are you thinking you'd like to do to help your country and the Earth?"

"Someday, I'm going to be president of United Earth," Witi said without hesitation.

Witi's father smiled proudly at his son and looked at Kapono. "He has some big dreams, Dr. Mililani."

Kapono remembered another dream—Lai's dream. He returned Ariki's smile, then looked at Witi. "Our dreams create the future, Witi."

| 40 |

12 June 2106

Yinuo entered the soft-blue-walled bedroom. Winter sunlight streamed through a large window framed by bright-colored curtains. "All finished?" she cheerfully asked her father. She stepped to the side of his bed and looked at the half-full soup bowl on the overbed table. "You didn't eat much, Dad." She'd made the saimin soup—his favorite—from scratch, not trusting her new food replicator to do it justice.

"I'm sorry, honey. It was delicious, and I appreciate your making it for me. I'm just not very hungry right now," Kapono replied in a strained, tired voice. He was sitting up in a hospital-style bed. His health had been failing for several months, and Yinuo and Liam were caring for him in their home. His doctors ascribed the cause to the long-term effects of post-war radiation exposure, but there was a contributory cause they could never have imagined: the shielding on Kapono's time machine hadn't fully protected him from the radiation emitted by its matter/antimatter reactor.

"No worries. I can save it for later, if you'd like," she said as she picked up the lunch tray from the table. "Do you feel like eating anything else? I made some haupia. I think it came out all right. Would you like some for dessert?"

"That sounds good," Kapono replied with a thankful smile. He hadn't enjoyed the fragrant Hawaiian pudding for many years. "Maybe a little later." He closed his eyes as he thought, *I need to do this NOW.*

I've put it off long enough. He opened his eyes and looked at his 50-year-old daughter. "But right now, we need to talk about something—something important. Please, sit with me," he said as he patted the right side of the mattress.

"Sure, Dad." She set the lunch tray on top of a dresser and sat down on the edge of his bed. "What do you want to talk about?"

"Something I should've told you a long time ago, but I couldn't bring myself to do it. I need to do it now … while I still have time."

She brushed strands of her father's wispy white hair off his forehead. "I don't want to hear any talk like that."

You're not going to want to hear this, either, he thought sullenly. "I don't know how to tell you this, so I'm just going to come out with it." He looked directly into her eyes. "My name isn't Kai Mililani."

Yinuo's expression froze, as if her father had said something in a foreign language she didn't understand. "Uh … *what* did you say?"

"My name is not Kai Mililani," he said slowly. "It's Kapono Ailana."

She was too stunned to respond. She knew who Dr. Kapono Ailana was—at least, she *thought* she knew. Her mother had told her he was a physicist she'd worked with who attempted to travel to the future through the Wagamese Wormhole in 2054. Her eyes carried a mixture of shock and barely-contained anger.

"If this is some sort of a sick joke …." she blurted out as her eyes started filling with tears.

"No, sweetie," Kapono said sadly as he reached out to hold her hand. She pulled it back.

"So, you're not my father?!" she said painfully as tears started running down her cheeks.

"*Yes*, I'm your father. I'm so sorry to hit you with this after all these years. Please, let me explain what happened," he pleaded.

Yinuo wiped her eyes with her hands and composed herself. "All right. Go ahead—I'm listening," she said without emotion.

Kapono told his daughter about how he and Lai had fallen in love before his mission to the Wagamese Wormhole, and how he'd leapt 87 years into the future and met an older version of their daughter and grandson there. Then he explained why he decided to return to the past to be with the love of his life, using her diaries and calendars to ensure history followed its course. He didn't share the details of *how* he returned to the past. Instead, he focused on what he thought was important for Yinuo to know: how he used an alias to avoid detection, and how he managed to avoid changing the past—until that awful day in December 2061. As he recounted what had happened then, he could no longer hold back his own tears.

"Your mother shouldn't have been hit by that truck. She'd be alive today, if it wasn't for me," he said sorrowfully as Yinuo struggled to fully understand what her father was telling her. "I took all those years with her away from you. There's nothing I can say or do to make that up to you."

He saw his daughter's lips start to tremble; she looked as if she were going to start sobbing. "*But ...* I know how to make things right—how to set history back on course, so your mother does *not* die in 2061 but instead has a long, full life, as she was meant to."

"How ... how will you do that?"

Kapono picked up his pad from the overbed table and tapped its screen a few times with his fingers. Then he offered the pad to Yinuo. "Take a look at this—it's your mother's diary entry from Christmas Eve, 2061."

She took the pad from her father and read what was on the screen. As she did, her face showed the same shock Kapono's had, when he'd read the same entry after Lai's memorial service.

"*How can this be?* It doesn't mention anything about the accident!" She looked again at the pad. "And there's entries *after* that one—for many years into the future!"

"Yes. I believe what this means is, Novikov was right—the laws of physics *will* ensure history remains consistent if a time traveler changes the past. I can't think of any other explanation that makes sense."

Yinuo looked out the bedroom window, deep in thought. Finally, she turned back to her father. "It *does* explain what we're observing.

But, Mum *died* in 2061. We both saw her get hit by that truck. How can that reality and her diary entries both exist?"

Kapono leaned back on the mattress and smiled soberly. "History won't be repaired all by itself. Some future event will do that." His smile widened. "And I know what that event is." Based on his understanding of Novikov's self-consistency principle, he realized it was possible that time would automatically repair itself. But he knew there was one way to *ensure* history was corrected. "But it will happen about 30 years from now. I'm quite sure I won't be around when it happens, to make sure it happens." He looked into his daughter's eyes. "I need your help, and An's, to ensure history is restored."

Yinuo's shock and anger were replaced by curiosity and determination. "What is this event? And what do An and I have to do?"

"You may not like this," Kapono cautioned. Then he explained his daughter's and grandson's roles in repairing history. As it turned out, Yinuo didn't like her father's plan at all.

"*No*, Dad!" she said vehemently as she shook her head. "I am *not* going to do that! And I don't think An will do it, either. You're asking us to make a terrible choice!"

"I realize that. But this is *not* what history was meant to be. You were supposed to have your mother for many years. An was supposed to know his grandmother. And," he added in a quieter voice, "there's more."

"What?"

"When I was in the future, I was told that there was very little crime, and virtually no violent crime. I was pretty amazed by that. So, I checked some statistics. I found out that in the 84 years between World War III and late 2141, there had been only 17 known deaths by violence."

Yinuo's look of shock returned. "In the *whole world?*"

Kapono nodded. "Yes, due to the Newton Effect having been reinforced and amplified by your mother's efforts on LOA." He paused; he was tiring, but he pressed on. "I checked those same statistics a few months ago. I found out that since November 2057, there's been 2,138 deaths by violence—over 2,100 more deaths, in only 49 years."

"But, Dad, 2,000-some deaths by violence for the whole world over nearly half a century is still very low!"

"Over 2,000 people died because of me!" Kapono cried. *I was an arrogant fool, to think I could replace Lai and her work on LOA.* He closed his eyes as he thought about his family, friends, and colleagues who had perished in World War III—and who'd haunted him in his nightmares for many years. In recent weeks, he'd had nightmares about the thousands of people who'd died by violence because Lai wasn't alive to prevent their deaths. He reopened his eyes and looked sorrowfully at his daughter.

"The blood of those people is on my hands. And who knows how many more will die because of me in the next 35 years, and beyond? More than that ... who knows what impact the deaths of all of those people will have on history?" He grasped Yinuo's right hand. "You and An must do this! History *must* be corrected!" He stopped to catch his breath. She looked at him for a few seconds, then she closed her eyes and nodded.

"All right. I understand what you're saying. If that's really what you want ... I'll do it. But, An's only 16. I don't know how we'd explain this to him right now—how he'd react."

"I agree. Now is not the right time to share this with An. It can wait until he's older—right before the event, even. But that means *you* will have to talk with him about it. Are you okay with that?"

"Yes. I'll tell him, when the time is right." She squeezed her father's hand. "I was wondering ... will An and I remember any of this timeline, once we correct history?"

Kapono furrowed his brow as he remembered something he'd said to Lai many years ago: *The loss of what is past.* "I don't think either of you will remember, honey. Spontaneous memory erasure is a ramification of Novikov's self-consistency principle."

"But, *you* remember details from before history was changed. And, another thing—how is it you're here *at all*, if history will be corrected?"

Kapono smiled slightly as he thought about the complexities of quantum mechanics and time travel. "That's because I reached both the future and the past through bends in spacetime. Thus the different realities were differentiated for me, I remember events from all of them, and I still exist in this timeline. There were no such bends for you or An, or anyone else. So you'll recall only the events that occurred before I changed them by traveling through time, because that's the only history that actually happened and for which everything works out consistently."

Yinuo nodded mournfully. "I wish there were some other way. I treasure all the time we've had together, Dad. I hate to think I won't remember any of it."

"And I treasure all of my years with you, from the day you were born until now. That's one of the reasons I wanted to return to the past. But although you won't have your memories of me, you'll have many more years, and memories, with your mother—and An with his grandmother. Plus, thousands of lives will be spared. I'd say that's more than a fair trade."

"Yes, it is," Yinuo agreed sadly. *Even so, it's going to be really hard to do what he asked me to do 30 years from now, even if it means setting history back on course.*

| 41 |

3 July 2106

Yinuo, Liam, An, and An's secondary-school sweetheart Linda Kim stood in the stern of the small cabin cruiser as it floated three nautical miles off Crescent Head beach. Liam, an experienced pilot, had rented the boat for the day. They could hear the mewing of the seagulls that circled over them in the blue sky dotted with puffy clouds, and the distant sound of waves crashing onto the beach. It was a chilly, windy winter day; there were only a few surfers in wetsuits riding the tall waves.

Kapono had asked his daughter to scatter his ashes at the beach where he and Liam had enjoyed many days surfing together. Yinuo and Liam had led a memorial service for Kapono at Elouera Beach the previous day. Over 250 friends and colleagues had attended, including former United Earth President Amanda Wong. She'd been escorted by 26-year-old Witi Ngata, who'd been elected to New Zealand's House of Representatives in 2104.

Yinuo looked down at the paper urn she held that contained her father's ashes. It was decorated with hand-painted yellow hibiscus flowers. She looked up at An and nodded, then she held the urn over the side of the boat and slowly released its contents into the sea as An read an old poem from an unknown author:

> *We heard your voice in the wind today and we turned to see your face;*

The warmth of the wind caressed us as we stood silently in place.
We felt your touch in the Sun today as its warmth filled the sky;
We closed our eyes for your embrace and our spirits soared high.
As long as the Sun shines… the wind blows… the rain falls…
You will live on in our hearts forever, for that is all our hearts know.

As An finished the poem, Liam rang the boat's bell eight times. Then each person picked up a handful of hibiscus blossoms from a bowl and sprinkled them in the water.

An noticed a tear running down his mother's cheek, and he put his arm around her. "Are you okay, Mum?"

She patted his hand that was on her shoulder and forced a faint smile. "She'll be right." But in truth, she didn't feel right at all, because she knew her father would *not* live on in their memories—or their hearts—forever.

| **42** |

18 October 2135

Charlotte Evans looked up from her desk as a slender, elderly woman, dressed in a black pantsuit and blue blouse, walked into the 22nd floor reception area in United Earth's headquarters in Auckland.

"G'day, Dr. Shen-Martin!" Charlotte said cheerfully to the familiar visitor. "How are you this fine afternoon?"

"I'm well, thank you, Charlotte," Yinuo replied in an unsettled voice that did not match her words. "How are you and your wife and children doing?"

"Everyone's great, thanks for asking. How are your son and daughter-in-law?"

"They're doing well, thank you."

"I'm glad to hear that. Shall I let the president know you've arrived?"

"Yes, please."

Charlotte tapped the pad on the desk in front of her. "Madam President, your 2:30 is here."

"Thank you, Charlotte. Please send her in," a woman's voice answered.

"Please go right in, Doctor," the president's executive assistant said as she motioned to the inner office door with a nod of her head.

"Thank you, Charlotte." Yinuo opened the door to the inner office and saw United Earth President Sumati Patel walking toward her in a dark blue saree with gold trim.

"Hello, Doctor! It's good to see you again. Thank you for coming," Sumati said cordially as she shook hands with Yinuo and motioned to a small, round glass table.

"It's good to see you, too, Madam President," Yinuo replied as she and Sumati sat down across from each other at the table.

"How is your son?" Sumati asked.

"He's well, thank you. He's busy working on the designs for the replacement bridges for Perth. He'll be going there soon to supervise their construction."

"That's good news—Perth really needs those bridges. And your daughter-in-law—how is she? She's in the Peace Corps, is that right?"

"Yes. She's on holiday now but will be starting an assignment in West Texas soon."

Texas ... that will be challenging—and not a little hazardous, Sumati thought. "I wish her safe travels. Please convey to her my gratitude for her service."

"I will, Madam President—thank you."

Sumati leaned back in her swivel chair. "So ... it's happened."

"Yes. The Wagamese Wormhole appeared in the constellation Triangulum Australe at 2:52 this morning. I was three minutes off on my prediction."

Sumati smiled. "Only you would mention such a small difference, Doctor." Then her expression became serious. "I read your report on the Prometheus Project. I understand the first attempt to travel to the future will be made just over five years from now, is that right?"

Yinuo nodded. "Yes—1,940 days from now, to be exact. But, as you saw in the report, that attempt will not succeed," she said, thinking of what her father had told her about her mother's near-disaster with *Chronos 2*. "However, nearly six years from now—on 26 September 2141—a second attempt will be made."

"And we're not sure if that attempt will be successful, correct?"

"That's right, Madam President," Yinuo lied. *I hate to mislead the president, but I have no choice—I certainly can't tell her everything I know.* "Apparently, the ship was damaged by a micrometeorite and may or may not have entered the wormhole. If it did, we don't know the condition of the spacecraft, or if the pilot survived."

"If it did not enter the wormhole, observers on Earth of the past would have been able to track it, would they not?"

"Shortly after the ship was damaged, the wormhole was destroyed by a tremendous explosion," Yinuo said dispassionately, trying to keep her emotions in check. "If the ship didn't enter the wormhole, it would have been destroyed by the blast."

Sumati looked at Yinuo with a puzzled expression. "Do we know what caused the explosion?"

"There's only one way it could have happened. We did it."

Sumati's look of puzzlement changed to shock. "What do you mean, *we* did it?"

"I believe that a powerful explosive device, most likely a nuclear warhead, was sent into the wormhole—our end of the wormhole—to purposely destroy it."

"But the Council hasn't even discussed doing that!" Sumati countered.

"Not yet. But obviously, it will. And it's clear their decision will be to destroy it."

Sumati considered what Yinuo had just told her. "Why would we do such a thing?"

"To prevent anyone from using the wormhole to travel through time. Specifically, to prevent the pilot of the second Prometheus mission, Dr. Kapono Ailana, from returning to the past. That was his mission: to learn what happened to Earth in the future and bring knowledge of the future back to the mid-21st century in hopes of resolving some of the immense problems Earth faced then."

Yinuo paused and cleared her throat before she continued. "And, Madam President, as chief physicist, I must tell you I think it would be a mistake to allow that to happen. A mistake that could threaten the future of the entire planet. You may recall the discussions I've had with the Council's science committee on that subject."

Sumati nodded slowly, "I do. So, you are in favour of this decision the Council made—*will* make—to destroy the wormhole?"

Yinuo hesitated. "Yes, Madam President," she said quietly.

Sumati thought for a few seconds. "But, what about Dr. Ailana?"

"There's a near-zero chance of his surviving the micrometeorite impact," Yinuo replied, still speaking quietly and without emotion. "And if he did survive the impact, he may not have made it through the event horizon before the wormhole was destroyed."

"I see," Sumati nodded slowly.

"However," Yinuo continued as she struggled to think of what she'd say if she hadn't agreed to follow her father's wishes, "it's only right we give Dr. Ailana every chance to make it safely through the wormhole, and reach Earth if he can. After that, we should destroy the wormhole."

"But, if we wait for Dr. Ailana's mission six years from now, isn't there a chance someone from the present will attempt to travel back in time, for what they believe is a very good reason?"

"Yes, it's possible—but unlikely. The wormhole is almost three billion kilometres—two billion miles—from Earth. With spacecraft available today, it would take nearly two years to reach it. And the ships that could make that type of voyage are, as you know, in very short supply."

"Yes, I know," Sumati replied. "Thus, I don't know how we could hope to mount a rescue mission for Dr. Ailana."

Yinuo nodded sadly. "I agree. We won't be able to send a ship to help him. But if his ship's Quantum Drive survived the micrometeorite strike, it's possible he could make it to Earth." She knew that was *not* possible, because of what her father had told her—but the president didn't know that.

Sumati thought in silence for a few seconds. "I don't know, Doctor. Given the very low odds of his reaching Earth—of being alive at all—I think it would be prudent to destroy the wormhole as soon as we can, to prevent anyone from attempting to reach the past and endangering the present—and our future. We could launch a probe carrying one of our asteroid-buster warheads now, and within two years the wormhole will no longer be a threat."

"But, Madam President, that would in itself change the past," Yinuo countered. Sumati looked quizzically at her. "History records the wormhole was destroyed on 20 October 2054—that's 26 September 2141 in our time. We must hold to that timeline to avoid changing the future in some unanticipated, and possibly tragic, way. Most importantly, we must allow the first Prometheus mission to happen, and to fail. Do you understand why?"

Sumati didn't understand. But then she recalled what Yinuo's report had said about that mission and its aftermath. "Oh! Yes, of course—I do understand. So, we need to wait about three years before launching the probe, to allow that mission to happen, yes?"

"That's right, Madam President—at least three years. But I believe we need to wait *four* years before launching the probe, to allow Dr. Ailana's mission to happen."

"I don't follow you, Doctor. I understand the importance of allowing the first mission to fail. But why can't we simply destroy the wormhole right after that flight—before Dr. Ailana's mission?"

Time travel is an incredibly sticky conundrum, Yinuo thought—as she knew better than any person on Earth. "It's complicated, Madam President. But the net of it is, *we don't know* what will happen if Dr. Ailana does *not* make that attempt. History could unfold in a much different way—with serious consequences for the entire world." *For one thing, it's possible the Love One Another movement would never have happened ... and maybe I never would have been born.*

Sumati nodded. "I think I understand what you're saying."

"Also, the timing of the wormhole's destruction is important."

"How so?"

"We know the Prometheus team was going to launch a rescue mission for Dr. Ailana. We must destroy the wormhole about two hours *after* Dr. Ailana's accident, but no later than that. That will avoid jeopardizing the rescue ship ..." Yinuo forced her voice to stay controlled, "... and give Dr. Ailana time to get a safe distance from the wormhole—if he can."

"That seems reasonable." Sumati looked down at the tabletop as she thought for a few seconds, then she looked up at Yinuo. "All right. I will ask the Council to wait four years before launching the probe with the warhead. And we'll carefully time the detonation, as you've suggested. We will give Dr. Ailana every chance to come home—albeit a much different home than he's used to."

"I think that's a good plan, Madam President," Yinuo said with sadness in her voice that was reflected in her eyes.

Sumati looked at her with concern. "Is everything all right, Doctor?"

Yinuo gazed out the window wall of the president's office toward the familiar bronze statue on the plaza below. "I was just thinking about my dad."

| 43 |

14 August 2137

Yinuo sat quietly on the couch in the living area of her small flat in Miranda. She took a deep breath to steady herself, then said into her phone, "Call An, voice only." Her son was still in Perth, working on replacements for two bridges that had collapsed during World War III. After a few seconds, An answered the phone call.

"G'day, Mum! How are you?"

"I'm well, thank you, An. How are you?"

"I'm good. I miss Linda, of course. I can't wait for her to return from Texas."

"Yes, it'll be great to see her again. How's your work on the bridges coming along?"

"Really well. We're at just over 80 percent complete on both of them. They should be open by early next year."

"That's good news." She paused, dreading the task facing her. Then she plunged ahead. "Are you alone right now?"

"Yes, I'm in my on-site office. Let me close the door—just a minute." After a pause, Yinuo heard the sound of a door closing, then An returned to the call. "What's up, Mum?"

"Linda is going to call you in two days about something she found in Texas."

"How do you know that, Mum?" Yinuo heard the puzzlement in An's voice.

I can't tell him what his pop told me—not just yet, anyway. "I just know. When you talk with her, you need to ask her to do something specific about her discovery."

"What do I need to tell her to do?"

"Are you sitting down?"

There was a short pause. "I am now. Why?"

"I'm going to tell you something you may not believe." *Or may not want to believe, at least.*

Yinuo told her son how his grandfather, Dr. Kapono Ailana, had traveled to the future through a wormhole to 2141, then found a way to return to 2054 and lived under an alias until he died in 2106. She also told An about the accident that had altered the course of history and had taken the life of his grandmother decades too soon, and had also resulted in the violent deaths of thousands of people. It took quite a while for An to come to terms with and accept what his mother had told him. After he'd done that, Yinuo told him what he needed to say to Linda when she called him.

"An, it's *imperative* that Linda does what you'll ask her to do. That's the only way to ensure history will be restored to as it should be." *The only certain way, at least.*

"But," An protested, "my pop—your dad!"

"I know," Yinuo said sorrowfully. "He understood that. It was his dying wish that we do this, to make things right." The thought crossed her mind that *to make things right* is literally what ho'oponopono means. She remembered what her father had taught her about that ancient Hawaiian practice of reconciliation and forgiveness when she was a teenager and having a difficult time dealing with the loss of her mother years earlier.

"What do you mean, 'we'? Do you have to do something, too—other than this call?"

"Yes. I've already done it." *Two years ago.*

"I see." There was silence on the phone for several seconds. Then An said, "I'll do it. I hope Linda trusts me about this. She's going to think it's whacko. I know I do."

"Thank you, An. Could you please call me after you talk with Linda?"

"Of course …. Mum, the lead project manager is knocking on my door. He looks anxious. I'd better run. I'll talk with you in a couple of days, Mum. I love you."

"I love you too, An. Goodbye," Yinuo replied as the call ended.

She set her phone down on the couch cushion, leaned back, and closed her eyes. She thought of a night 80 years ago, when she was snuggled in her bed with Qing Bao beside her, listening to her father read her favorite bedtime story. It seemed to her as if it were only yesterday. She focused on every detail of the memory. She realized that memory, and all other memories of her father, would soon be gone forever.

| 44 |

15 August 2137

The afternoon Sun blazed high above the West Texas prairie as the white solar-powered panel van moved slowly westward down Interstate 20 toward Colorado City, dodging the many ruts and potholes in the forlorn highway that hadn't been maintained for almost 80 years.

Myrt Reinhart gazed out the front passenger window at the native sagebrush, grasses and cacti dotting the desolate brown landscape. She was thinking about the people in the two towns she and her teammate Linda Shen-Martin had just visited: 11 families in Roscoe and six in Loraine. Although it had been three years since the last checkup visits in West Texas, everyone had told the two women they were doing "just fine" and didn't need any help. *Typical proud, self-reliant Texans,* Myrt thought. But she and Linda had been able to get the townspeople to agree to medical checks, and Myrt had convinced the adults to allow her to bring the vaccinations of their children up to date. Some of the adults had agreed to the injections, too.

Linda, who was driving, was thinking about the families they'd met in Roscoe and Loraine also. *It must be a hard life. But they seemed happy, despite their hardships. And at least their families are together.* She glanced at her teammate. Myrt's given name was Marie, but when she was a child, her grandfather had started calling her Myrt, and it had stuck.

"Hey, how are your mum and dad doing?"

Myrt turned toward Linda. "The last time I talked with them, about a week ago, they said they were doing good. But I know they miss me. They didn't expect their only child to start gallivanting all over the world right after finishing nursing school." Myrt wished she could talk with her parents more often, but intercontinental phone service was sporadic at best.

"I wouldn't call what you're doing 'gallivanting,'" Linda replied with an encouraging smile. She was old enough to be Myrt's mother. And as she'd worked with Myrt in the field over the past several months, she'd sometimes thought of her as the daughter she'd never had.

Myrt grinned at Linda. "How's the Master Builder doing?"

Linda smiled at Myrt's use of her husband's nickname. "He's still in Perth, overseeing the construction of the two bridges he designed. He'll be there a few months yet."

"Those are the replacements for the Matagarup and Narrows bridges, right?"

"Yes. I was hoping to take a short holiday and see him before my next assignment, but I'm not sure I'll be able to do that."

"That's a shame," Myrt replied sadly. "Do you know where you're going after we finish the checkups in Texas?"

"I'm trying to decide between Alberta and Northern California—the Sacramento Valley. I'm leaning towards California. How about you?"

"I've put in for Spain. I've always wanted to go there. It'll be the first Peace Corps mission on the Continent."

"That's ripper! And quite a challenge. I'm so proud of you, Myrt."

"Thanks," Myrt blushed. "I need to brush up on my Spanish, though. I may not always have a charged phone and its translator app with me."

"Oh, no worries. You'll do great."

It will be a challenge, Myrt thought as she returned her gaze to the prairie passing by her side window. *But I guess that's what I signed up for.* Then she noticed something odd off in the distance on her right, just ahead of them. It looked like a long, low building, barely visible through the native vegetation. *If I'd blinked, I would've missed it.*

"What do you suppose that is?" Myrt asked as she pointed in the direction of the shape.

Linda squinted through the windshield. "I can hardly see it ... a warehouse, maybe?"

Myrt looked down at the pad on her lap. "But according to the map, there's nothing there."

"Crikey. Maybe we should check it out—see if anyone's home." Myrt nodded in agreement, and Linda turned the van onto a badly rutted road that appeared to lead to the mysterious structure.

After about a mile, the road ended at what looked like a guard station. But it was obvious to the two women it hadn't been used in a long time. Its paint was almost worn away from years of Sun and wind, its windows were broken, and the entrance gate arm was lying in pieces on the ground.

Linda stopped the van to check out the guard station, then carefully drove around the broken gate arm toward the big, boxy, gray metal building. She noticed there was no signage or lettering; there was only a number in one corner of the building, near the top: 7. She stopped the van close to what looked like the main entrance, and she and Myrt climbed out and walked up to the door.

"Locked," Myrt said as she tugged on the handle of the steel door. She peered through a small window in the door. "Looks like a reception area. But I don't think anyone's been in there for quite a while."

Linda looked over the outside of the building. "Let's try the other end."

"Okay," Myrt agreed, and they walked around the huge structure, avoiding overgrown shrubs and windblown tumbleweeds.

When they reached the far end of the building, they saw a large sliding double door. Myrt inspected the padlock securing the door and noticed it was badly rusted. She picked up a softball-sized rock from the ground and looked at Linda.

"Breaking and entering?" Linda asked.

Myrt looked around. "I don't see anyone to report it," she replied with a sly smile. She whacked the rock on the padlock three times, and it fell away to the dirt. She opened the latch and tried to push one of the doors open—it refused to budge. Linda joined her in pushing on the door, to no avail. Then they tried the other side of the door and were rewarded by a loud squeal as the door moved an inch.

"Maybe if we try the Mak'tar Chant of Strength?" Linda joked as she remembered an old movie her husband An had saved from his grandfather's antique holopad.

Myrt's face scrunched into a puzzled expression, "Huh?"

Linda laughed, "Never mind. Let's try it again."

They both put their shoulders into the door and pushed with all their might, and the door shuddered open a few more inches—just enough for them to squeeze through.

Inside the warehouse, they blinked as their eyes adjusted to the low light. After a few seconds, they could see well enough to make out a hulking shape taking up most of the warehouse space: an immense semi-trailer, with the tractor truck at the far end of the warehouse. The trailer and truck's gigantic tires were flat. Lying atop the trailer was what appeared to be a huge cylindrical tank, strapped down and covered in tattered black fabric.

"That trailer must be at least 25 metres long!" Linda exclaimed, looking at Myrt. "I wonder what's on it."

Myrt grinned as she pulled her Swiss Army Knife, a gift from her grandfather, out of a pants pocket. "Let's find out!" She found an access ladder on the right side of the trailer, climbed up, and started cutting the frayed ties on the black tarpaulin with the saw blade on her knife. The ties were in such poor condition that it didn't take long to cut one end of the black fabric away. She looked down at Linda, "Give me a hand, please?"

Linda climbed part way up the access ladder on the left side of the trailer and started pulling on the tarp. Soon the fabric covering the back of the cylindrical shape fell away. Myrt and Linda climbed down and looked up in disbelief at their discovery, then looked at each other.

"What the heck is a *rocket* doing in the middle of nowhere?" Myrt asked incredulously.

Linda shook her head. *I have no idea!* But then she remembered something An had told her several years ago, and her face lit up with excitement.

"I think I know what this is!"

* * *

An's phone buzzed as he worked at the engineering workstation in his small office in Perth. The caller ID was a satellite phone number he didn't recognize. *It could only be one person*, he reasoned. *Still, I best not assume.* He picked up the phone. "An Shen-Martin."

"Hi, sweetie!" Linda's voice came from the phone's speaker, accompanied by static.

"Hi!" He got up quickly from his chair. "Give me a second, okay?" He closed his office door. "How are you, luv? How's Texas?" he said as he sat back down in his chair. Although it was nine a.m. on 16 August in Perth, he realized it was eight at night on 15 August in Texas.

"Myrt and I are doing okay," Linda replied. "No big dramas, yet. The people have been hospitable towards us. The roads are terrible, though—even the interstates. Slows us down quite a bit."

"I'm not surprised. Those roads probably haven't been touched since the war."

"Right. But the reason I'm calling—other than to hear your adorable voice—is that Myrt and I discovered something incredible out here, in the middle of nowhere! You'll never be able to guess what we found!"

Or I might, An thought. "What did you find?"

"An old spaceship! From what your pop told you about the attempts to traverse the Wagamese Wormhole in the 2050s, I bet it's one of those ships—probably *Chronos 4.*" Once the Prometheus Project had been declassified in the late 21st century, Kapono had shared some details with An and Yinuo—not mentioning, of course, that he had been aboard *Chronos 3*. "It's got a lot of dust on it, but otherwise it looks to be in perfect condition. Isn't that ripper?"

"Yeah, it, uh, it is." He closed his eyes and took a deep breath before continuing. "Linda, I need to ask you and Myrt to do something for me. And it's going to sound a bit whacko."

"Okay," Linda's voice said uncertainly. "What do you want us to do?"

"Does anyone else know about the spaceship?"

"No, not yet. We were going to report it to the Peace Corps at our next check-in. It looks like no one's been anywhere near it for many years—decades, even."

An exhaled with relief. "Good. Here's what I need you to do: secure the building it's in as best you can, and don't tell anyone else about it—ever."

There was a pause before Linda's surprised voice replied, "No one?"

"That's right. It's vital that ship does *not* see the light of day. When you get back home, my mum and I will explain everything to you. I'm sorry to keep you in the dark on this. I hope you can trust me about it."

"Of course I trust you, An. But, you're right—it *is* a bit whacko."

"I know. Do you think Myrt will be okay with it?"

"I think so. I'm positive she trusts me. And she's the kind of person who keeps her word."

"That's good to know. Thank you for doing this, honey."

"No worries. But I can't wait to find out what this is all about." An heard a woman's voice saying something to Linda, then Linda returned to the phone. "An, Myrt and I have some planning to do for our checkup visits tomorrow, then it'll be time for bed—we need to hit the road at sparrow's fart tomorrow. Besides, these satellite calls aren't cheap. So, I'd better say cheers now. I love you, dear. Give my love to your mum, okay?"

"I will. I love you too, sweetheart. Cheers." The call ended.

An stared out the lone small window of his office for a few seconds, then said into his phone, "Call Mum, voice only." After a few moments, Yinuo's voice came through the speaker.

"An, g'day. Did Linda call you?"

"Yes. It's done," he said in a voice tinged with sorrow.

"That's ... that's good," she said quietly. "Thank you for doing that, An."

"You're welcome. I just—I wish there were some other way."

"I do, too, Son ... I do, too."

| 45 |

26 September 2141

Kapono groaned as he tried to sit up in the command couch. He felt dizzy, and he had a splitting headache. *Chronos 3*'s master alarm was still blaring. He reached out to cancel it and felt dull pain in his arm and his back; then he realized most of his body hurt. Yet, he felt tremendous gratitude and relief. *I'm alive! But, where am I? And WHEN?* The last thing he remembered was Aileen, the spacecraft's AI pilot, saying they'd crossed the event horizon of the black hole fronting the Wagamese Wormhole.

"Aileen, are you still with me?"

"Aye, Kapono," Aileen's cheery voice replied in an Irish brogue. "How's the form? I didn't hear you say anything for a few minutes."

"I've felt better, but I'm all right. I must have been unconscious. Can you check communications for me—is it operational?"

"Naw, both primary and backup communications are down."

"I'm not surprised," Kapono said as he thought of the micrometeorite that had crashed through the ship before it traversed the wormhole, knocking out several systems and also the ship's oxygen supply. He already knew both guidance computers had been taken out by the micrometeorite; thus he needed to fly the ship manually and use the Aileen app on his hPhone. "How about radascan—is it still working?"

"Aye, radascan is nominal."

"Good! Does it detect any moving objects?" *Like a ship, maybe?* He hoped that, just as in Lai's dream after her aborted mission in *Chronos*

2, Earth of the 22nd century would know exactly when he'd arrive in the future and send a rescue ship. He preferred to not dwell on the alternative—that Earth of the 22nd century wouldn't be in any position to mount a rescue mission.

"Radascan detects no moving objects within range."

What if you travel to the future and no one's home? He was about to ask Aileen for Quantum Drive status, but he realized it didn't matter. He knew his G-suit had about nine hours of oxygen, and he'd already used some of it. He figured the trip to Earth would take at least eight hours at maximum speed, plus well over an hour for re-entry and landing—which would be extremely difficult if not impossible using only manual controls and no communications with Earth. But he tried to stay positive. *Maybe they're just running a little late. There might be lots of space traffic to navigate through in the 22nd century. I just need to chill for a little while.*

"Aileen, could you sing something for me?"

"Delira and excira to do so, Kapono. What kind of song would you like?"

"Oh, pretty much anything will do—just not *Daisy Bell.*"

"Why not *Daisy Bell?*"

Kapono chuckled, "Never mind—that was just a little joke."

"I'm sorry, I didn't get—oh! I get it, now. That was gas!"

Kapono thought for a few seconds. "How about an Irish folk song?"

"Grand. Let me search my music catalogue …. I think I've found something appropriate; I hope you like it."

Aileen started singing the old Irish folk song. But Kapono asked the AI to stop singing after the first verse and chorus because the lyrics surfaced memories of his sorrowful farewell to Lai early that morning.

There was still no sign of a rescue craft, so he asked Aileen for one more song—then another, and another. After many songs, he checked the ship's chronometer—Aileen had been singing for nearly two hours.

Suddenly the master alarm sounded; Aileen stopped singing. Kapono canceled the alarm and checked the alarm status screen. It displayed: PROXIMITY ALERT.

"Aileen, does radascan show anything close to us?"

"Checking …. There's a moving object, distance 981 kilometres, heading x-y 86, z 3, speed 2.1 kilometres per second. It's on a collision course."

Whoa! Kapono figured the object was approaching from the starboard side at nearly a right angle to the ship. He nudged the joystick that controlled movement in the x-y plane forward slightly for five seconds, and the ship's thrusters pushed it ahead. "Aileen, is the object still on a collision course?"

"Checking …. Naw, Kapono. The object is no longer on a collision course. However, it *is* headed directly for the black hole."

I wonder if it's a meteorite that got sucked into the black hole's gravity well, Kapono thought. *Let's get a look at it* …. He turned the x-y joystick slowly to the right to rotate the ship 89 degrees to starboard, so the approaching object would be visible in the right front window.

He peered out the window, straining to see whatever was heading for the black hole. After a few minutes, he saw a light gray dot that quickly grew larger and larger. Soon, it was close enough that Kapono could make out details. *It's a ship!* he realized with excitement and joy. *But it looks too small to be a rescue ship,* he thought as his excitement faded. *It looks more like a probe.*

He watched with increasing bewilderment as the sleek gray spaceship passed within 100 meters of *Chronos 3* and continued toward the center of the black hole's event horizon.

That's very strange, Kapono thought with extreme disappointment. *Why send a probe instead of a—*

The five-megaton thermonuclear warhead in the probe detonated, creating a huge, round, white fireball that was brighter than the Sun. The black hole collapsed and disappeared, and with it the Wagamese Wormhole.

After a fraction of a second, the fireball reached *Chronos 3*. It was instantly incinerated.

| 46 |

27 September 2141

Yinuo and An sat quietly in the Pacific conference room of United Earth headquarters in Auckland. It had been a long day for them, starting with an early morning flight from Sydney to Auckland, followed by a wait of several hours in the conference room. Charlotte Evans had brought them an early dinner about an hour ago. Yinuo was resting with her eyes closed and her head nestled on top of her arms on the conference table. An was browsing randomly on his phone, trying to avoid negative thoughts about the reason they were there.

He looked through the conference room's interior glass wall and saw United Earth President Witi Ngata walking down the hallway toward the conference room. "Mum," he said softly as he touched his mother gently on her arm. Yinuo's head popped up from the table.

"What is it?" the 86-year-old physicist asked her son. An looked toward the door, and Yinuo swiveled her chair in that direction as Witi opened the glass door and entered the room. An and Yinuo started to stand up, but Witi raised his right hand halfway, and they sat back down.

"I'm very sorry about your long wait," Witi apologized as he sat down next to Yinuo. She and An looked at him with hopeful eyes. "I finally have news about *Chronos 3* and Dr. Ailana." Yinuo and An both sensed that, based on the president's somber tone, the news wasn't good. He folded his hands on top of the table.

"The wormhole was destroyed a little over 18 hours ago," Witi began in a subdued voice. "Since then, there's been no sign of *Chronos 3*. If Dr. Ailana had been able to get a safe distance from the blast, his ship would have entered Earth orbit by now—or at least be close enough to Earth that we could detect it by radascan or telescope."

An looked at his mother, and she returned his sorrowful gaze. They both grasped what Witi was trying to tell them before he said it.

"It appears Dr. Ailana did not survive." He reached out and put his hand on top of Yinuo's as he looked at her and An. "I'm so sorry for your loss."

Yinuo reached out and squeezed An's hand, then she cleared her throat. "Thank you, Witi. I know how hard it is to deliver this sort of news."

"Is there anything I can do for you?" Witi asked gently.

"I don't think so—not right now. But, thank you for asking." Yinuo looked at An. His devastated expression reminded her of the dreadful day 24 years ago when she told him his father Liam had died. She turned back to Witi. "I think we'll start back to Sydney now." She stood up, and An did likewise.

The president stood up and nodded. "I understand." He embraced Yinuo, then An. "Don't hesitate to let me know if you need anything—help with a memorial service, for instance."

"That's very kind of you, Witi—thank you," Yinuo replied gratefully.

"Would you like Charlotte to see you out?"

Yinuo shook her head. "We know the way." She'd visited the headquarters building hundreds of times during her 35 years as United Earth's chief physicist.

"Of course. Safe travels." He opened the door for them as they stepped into the hallway.

They said nothing as they took the elevator down to the expansive atrium for the main entrance and went out the glass doors leading to the plaza. The setting Sun cast the tower's windows and pale brown Hinuera stone façade in a soft rose hue.

As they neared the statue in the center of the plaza, Yinuo stopped, and An stopped beside her. Although she'd passed by that statue over a thousand times, she felt it calling out to her in that moment.

As she gazed up at the familiar bronze sculpture, memories flooded her mind … happy memories such as bedtime stories as a little girl, her idyllic life on Ma'uke Island, growing up in Miranda, the joyous day United Earth was founded, graduating from the university in Caringbah, earning her PhD, her wedding day, An's birth, and the day she became chief physicist. But also, the unpleasant memories: the desperate flight from Minnesota after World War III, the typhoon, Liam's lengthy illness and his death, and then, Yinuo thought sadly as she looked at the face on the statue, *I lost you.*

She read the inscription on the plaque on the statue's Hinuera stone base, although she'd read it many times before:

Lai Shen, PhD
25 April 2019 – 25 December 2111
United Earth Founder and Chief Physicist
Beloved Mum and Nanna
"Love never fails"

"Are you okay, Mum?" An asked.

Yinuo looked at her son with love. "She'll be right. Let's go home." They walked slowly toward the light rail station as the red disk of the setting Sun disappeared on the western horizon.

Epilogue

9 November 2144

Aroha Whakatane sat slumped at her desk in the Antimatter Power Generation Research lab at the University of New South Wales Caringbah campus. Widely considered the most talented experimental physicist in Australia and perhaps all of United Earth, United Earth's chief physicist wasn't used to achieving anything less than exceptional results. _That's not going to happen this time_, she thought dejectedly as she tapped the stylus of her pad on the desktop and rested her tattooed chin on her left fist.

But there is ONE result from this project, the black-haired Māori scientist realized. _I think we've pretty much proven that generating usable energy from antimatter is impossible with current science._ Over the past three years, Aroha had worked with two physics graduate students from the Australian National University to design, build, and test a matter/antimatter reactor. While they were able to sustain reactions for a few milliseconds, itself a tremendous achievement, the results were far short of what was necessary for practical power generation. And, those tests had nearly used up their precious, costly supply of antimatter.

But Aroha wasn't a quitter. She sat up and tapped rapidly on her pad with the stylus. She calculated she _might_ have enough antimatter for a few more tests if she greatly reduced the amount used per test. She started to get out of her chair to prepare the reactor for a test using the smaller payload when she heard a _bleep_ from the particle detector on the table behind her. The device detected and recorded subatomic particles emitted from the matter/antimatter reactions.

That was too, too weird, she thought as she looked at the detector's display panel. It showed that one type of particle had apparently just been created by the quiet reactor. Aroha raised her thick eyebrows when she read the details off the screen:

Type: UNKNOWN
Quantity: 1.0574613e10

Eeeeeh? Over 10 billion particles—but of WHAT? She realized the detector shouldn't have reported *any* particles, with no activity in the reactor.

She prepared the test and ran it. Immediately the particle detector bleeped again, and she stared at its display:

Type: Neutrino
Quantity: 2.881020205e12

That's more like it, she thought as she exhaled with relief. Neutrinos were a typical by-product of matter/antimatter reactions. *But ... what were those impossible other particles?*

Before she could investigate that question, Yinuo Shen-Martin entered the lab. She'd been a volunteer advisor to the antimatter project since retiring three years earlier. Before retiring, she'd hired Aroha to lead the project, then convinced her to become the new chief physicist for United Earth.

"*Kia ora*, Aroha! How are the tests coming along?" Yinuo asked cheerfully.

Aroha smiled uneasily as she looked at the elderly woman who was considered the world's foremost theoretical physicist. "*Kia ora*, Yinuo. They are ... *very* interesting."

The unusual uncertainty in Aroha's voice surprised Yinuo. "What do you mean?"

"Just now I ran a test with an antimatter payload that was only one percent of what we've used for previous tests. I was trying to make the remaining antimatter last as long as possible. But," she continued as she turned toward the particle detector and pointed at its display, "*before* I ran the test, the detector reported over 10 billion 'unknown' particles."

Yinuo raised her eyebrows. "*Unknown?* That *is* interesting! Also, quite impossible. Unless …." She gazed out the lab's windows for a few seconds, then turned back to Aroha. "What were the test results?"

"The results were similar to earlier tests," Aroha replied as she scrolled the detector display with her finger. "Heaps of neutrinos."

"I see. What if you—" Suddenly the particle detector bleeped again.

"That's what it did the last time!" Aroha exclaimed. She studied the detector display. "Take a look—again, over 10 billion of those unknown particles were emitted by the reactor … somehow."

"That *is* whacko," Yinuo agreed as she looked at the detector's display screen.

Aroha ran a second test with the smaller payload, and the detector reported the expected number of neutrinos.

"Any ideas?" Aroha asked Yinuo. "I'm proper stuck on it."

"Was there any difference in the tests besides the much smaller payloads?"

Aroha shook her head, "No. Everything else was the same."

Yinuo sat down in a swivel chair, and Aroha sat down beside her. "I can think of just one explanation. But … it might blow your socks off."

Aroha was wearing sandals on the bare feet of her bionic legs, but she ignored that detail. "Go ahead, blow away!"

Yinuo looked directly at Aroha and said confidently, "It has to be tachyons."

Aroha's deep brown eyes opened wide in astonishment and disbelief. "But tachyons are only *theoretical*—no one's ever observed them!"

"Until now?" Yinuo smiled, tongue in cheek. "I can help you and your lab mates investigate this further, if you wish, but I can't think of any other answer that fits the results. I've probably never told you this, but my PhD thesis was on tachyon theory."

"I did not know that! I haven't studied tachyons since grad school. Why do you think that's the answer?"

"Good question. First, tachyons can only travel *faster* than the speed of light, never slower. That explains why they showed up on the particle detector *before* you ran the tests. Also," she continued, "the less energy that's applied to creating tachyons, the faster they go. By using a much smaller antimatter payload, it seems you provided just the right conditions to create tachyons."

Aroha sat back in her chair, somewhat overwhelmed by her apparent discovery after many months of dry holes. "It's incredibly exciting from a theoretical physics standpoint, but what would be the *practical* use for tachyons?"

Yinuo pondered the question for several seconds. "Theoretically, they could be used to send messages of some kind, or perhaps even matter, to the past. The quantum mechanics to achieve that would be incredibly complex. And then, of course, there's the practical matter that the Council has expressly forbidden time travel in any form."

"Legit," Aroha replied. *Time for the unpleasant news,* she thought. "Yinuo, before this apparent discovery of tachyons, I was going to let Dean Sushkov and you know that I believe we've proven that power generation from matter/antimatter reactions is impractical. There's simply too little energy generated compared to the cost."

"I'm sorry to hear that," Yinuo said sadly. Then, her expression brightened. "But not every experiment has the desired results. At least we know to not pour any more time or money into that idea. And," she added as she smiled proudly at Aroha, "your discovery of tachyons is groundbreaking in itself!"

"Fair dinkum. I was thinking about writing a paper on it for the *Australian Journal of Scientific Research.* What do you think?"

"Definitely!" *Maybe someone will come up with practical uses for matter/antimatter reactions and tachyons, someday.*

January 23, 1960

The *Trieste* hovered silently a few feet above the muddy bottom of the Challenger Deep. Inside the submersible's cramped, cold, and damp pressure sphere, neither Jacques Piccard or U.S. Navy Lieutenant Don Walsh spoke; each kept his thoughts at that historic moment to himself. A dense white fog of diatomaceous ooze, loosened by the iron ballast they'd just released striking the ocean floor, billowed up around the pressure sphere.

Walsh picked up the underwater telephone; it hadn't worked since early in their descent to the deepest point of the Pacific Ocean. *It probably won't work now, but there's nothing to see out there, yet,* he thought.

"Pittsburgh, Pittsburgh, this is *Trieste,* we are on the bottom of the Challenger Deep at six-three hundred fathoms. Over." Pittsburgh was the radio call sign for the *Trieste's* support tug, the U.S.S. *Wandank.*

To Walsh and Piccard's astonishment, a reply blasted from the phone's speaker 30 seconds later: "*Trieste, Trieste,* this is Pittsburgh. I hear you faint and clear. Will you repeat your present depth? Over," Lieutenant Larry Shumaker said, excitement evident in his voice. He was shocked that the *Trieste* had apparently reached a depth of nearly 38,000 feet, far deeper than anticipated.

"Pittsburgh, Pittsburgh, this is *Trieste,* confirming depth at six-three hundred fathoms. Over," Walsh answered. After a 15-second delay due to the seven miles of seawater above the *Trieste,* Shumaker acknowledged.

Walsh turned around to look out the aft hatch window. The white mud cloud had started to clear. As he looked up at the flooded steel and Plexiglas tube that connected the pressure sphere to the *Trieste's* main hull, his heart skipped a beat.

"I know what happened—that noise, that jolt," he said quietly to Piccard. At about 30,000 feet, Walsh and Piccard had been startled by a loud *CRACK,* accompanied by rocking akin to an earthquake. "It was the big viewing port of the entry tube that cracked."

"Oh!" Piccard exclaimed. Both men knew what that crack meant. If the entry tube's window failed and they were unable to blow the water out of the tube after surfacing, they would be trapped in the pressure sphere, 10 feet below the ocean's surface, during the four-day transit to Guam.

"I think we should surface as soon as possible, so there's maximum daylight to check on the entry tube problem," Walsh recommended.

"Agreed," Piccard replied as he nodded once.

"But first …." Walsh held out his right hand to his fellow explorer, and they solemnly shook hands. Then they pulled two flags from a small watertight bag: a Swiss flag for Piccard, an American flag for Walsh. While holding their respective flags, they took a selfie with a fixed camera supplied by *Life* magazine. Unfortunately, there were no exterior cameras to record for history what they were seeing at the furthermost depths of the ocean—a view never seen before by human eyes.

As Piccard turned to pull the ballast release lever, he glanced out the forward viewport. "What … what is *that*?" he exclaimed in surprise.

Walsh peered out the porthole. "I don't see anything out there," he told his fellow hydronaut.

Piccard looked out the viewport again. He saw nothing but black water. He rubbed both eyes with his hands and looked again. Still nothing. He shook his head in bewilderment. "I could *swear* I saw something out there."

"Being confined in a cold, tiny metal sphere underwater for many hours can do that to you," Walsh said empathetically.

"Yes, I suppose," Piccard agreed.

Walsh picked up the telephone. "Pittsburgh, Pittsburgh, this is *Trieste*. We're preparing to ascend now. The entry tube window is cracked, and we don't want to risk a longer stay. ETA …." He looked at Piccard.

"About three and a half hours."

Walsh checked his watch; it read 13:26. "ETA is 1700. If you could heat up the shower water, we'd greatly appreciate it. Over." Piccard grinned at Walsh.

After the usual delay, Shumaker's voice said, "*Trieste, Trieste*, this is Pittsburgh. 1700 and hot water, acknowledged. Congratulations to both of you for making history! We can't wait to hear all about it when you're back on the surface. Over and out."

"Hot showers, here we come," Walsh said as Piccard pulled a lever to release two tons of ballast, and the *Trieste* started rising slowly toward the surface.

References

Prologue

1. (Darkness is absolute and eternal …) Wikipedia. "Challenger Deep." Accessed December 12, 2024, https://en.wikipedia.org/ wiki/ Challenger_Deep.

2. (Jacques Piccard checked the fathometer …) Wikipedia. *Trieste (bathyscaphe)*." Accessed December 12, 2024, https://en.wikipedia.org/wiki/Trieste_(bathyscaphe).

3. (The Swiss engineer …) Wikipedia. "Jacques Piccard." Accessed December 12, 2024, https://en.wikipedia.org/wiki/ Jacques_Piccard.

4. (… U.S. Navy Lieutenant Don Walsh …) Wikipedia. "Don Walsh." Accessed December 12, 2024, https://en.wikipedia.org/ wiki/Don_Walsh.

5. ("What happened?" …) Polmar, Norman C. and Lee J. Mathers. *Opening the Great Depths: The Bathyscaph Trieste and Pioneers of Undersea Exploration*. Annapolis: Naval Institute Press, 2021.

Chapter 1

6. (… bionic legs were invented …) Davis, Maya. "Bionic leg restores natural walking speeds and steps: 'I didn't feel like my leg had been amputated.'" CNN, July 1, 2024. https://www.cnn.com/2024/ 07/01/health/bionic-leg-ami-neuroprosthesis/index.html.

Chapter 2

7. (Neutrinos were a typical by-product …) Graber, Jim. "How much energy is carried away by neutrinos in matter-antimatter annihilation?" Physics StackExchange, January 20, 2013. https://physics.stackexchange.com/questions/51679/howmuch-en-

ergy-is-carried-away-by-neutrinos-in-matter-antimatter-annihilation.

8. (But tachyons are only *theoretical* …) Wikipedia. "Tachyon." Accessed December 12, 2024, https://en.wikipedia.org/wiki/ Tachyon.

9. (… using tachyons to send messages …) Norton, John D. "Spacetime, Tachyons, Twins and Clocks." *University of Pittsburgh*, September 22, 2024. https://sites.pitt.edu/~jdnorton/ teaching/HPS_0410/ chapters/spacetime_tachyon/.

Chapter 4

10. (You've been a busy beaver …) Brubaker, Ben. "With Fifth Busy Beaver, Researchers Approach Computation's Limits." *Quanta Magazine*, July 2, 2024. https://www.quantamagazine.org/amateur-mathematicians-find-fifth-busy-beaverturing-machine-20240702/.

Chapter 6

11. (… the Novikov self-consistency principle …) Novikov, I. D. "Time machine and self-consistent evolution in problems with self-interaction." *Physical Review D* 45, no. 6 (March 1992). https://journals.aps.org/prd/abstract/10.1103/PhysRevD.45.1989.

Chapter 7

12. (… Hawaiian core values …) Campbell, Dave. "Nā Waiwai Aloha – 28 Hawaiian Values." *Temptation Tours*, February 22, 2023. https://www.temptationtours.com/na-waiwaialoha-28-hawaiian-values/.

Chapter 10

13. (I perform the minimally invasive …) Stacey, Dawn, Ph.D. "What Is a No-Scalpel Vasectomy?" *Verywell Health*,

April 9, 2023. https://www.verywellhealth.com/no-scalpel-vasec-tomy-906903.

Chapter 13

14. (They're hypothetical subatomic particles ...) Wikipedia. "Tachyon."

15. (... the loss of what is ...) Shakespeare, William. "Coriolanus." Folger Shakespeare Library, edited by Barbara Mowat, Paul Werstine, Michael Poston, and Rebecca Niles, 86-89. Accessed December 12, 2024. https://www.folger.edu/explore/shakespeares-works/coriolanus/read/3/2/.

16. ('What's in a name?') Shakespeare, William. "Romeo and Juliet." In *Folger Shakespeare Library*, edited by Barbara Mowat, Paul Werstine, Michael Poston, and Rebecca Niles, 46. Accessed December 13, 2024. https://www.folger.edu/explore/ shakespeares-works/ romeo-and-juliet/read/2/2/.

Chapter 14

17. (*Or, if there were ...*) Shakespeare, William. "A Midsummer Night's Dream." In *Folger Shakespeare Library*, edited by Barbara Mowat, Paul Werstine, Michael Poston, and Rebecca Niles, 143-151. Accessed December 12, 2024. https://www.folger.edu/explore/shakespeares-works/a-midsummer-nightsdream/read/1/1/.

Chapter 15

18. (... 'fought the good fight' ...) 2 Timothy 4:7 (New International Version).

Chapter 17

19. (*Daniel and Dr. King …*) Lee, Alicia. "Martin Luther King Jr. explains the meaning of love in rare handwritten note." CNN, February 9, 2020. https://www.cnn.com/2020/02/09/us/martin-luther-king-jr-handwritten-note-for-sale-trnd/index.html.

Chapter 18

20. (Nitrous oxide is quite popular …) Spencer, Christina, D.O. "5 FAQ about laughing gas for pain relief during labor, delivery." *Mayo Clinic Health System*, March 17, 2022. https://www.mayoclinichealthsystem.org/hometown-health/speaking-ofhealth/5-faq-about-laughing-gas-for-pain-relief.

Chapter 20

21. (Only God has the power …) Howell, Kenneth. "How Can a Priest Forgive Sin?" *Catholic Answers*, January 1, 2003. https://www.catholic.com/magazine/print-edition/how-cana-priest-forgive-sin.

22. (We believe that the peace …) Trese, Father Leo. "The Sacrament of Reconciliation: Rising Again to New Life." *Beginning Catholic.* Accessed December 12, 2024. https://www.beginning-catholic.com/sacrament-of-reconciliation.

23. ('No one has greater love …') John 15:13 (New Revised Standard Version, Catholic Edition).

Chapter 21

24. (Please be seated …) "Traditional Wedding Ceremony Script." *Universal Life Church.* Accessed December 12, 2024. https://www.ulc.org/wedding-ceremony-scripts/traditionalceremony-script.

25. (I, Katherine ...) Nowack, Hannah. "Traditional Wedding Vows From Religions and Cultures Across the Globe." *The Knot*, September 18, 2023. https://www.theknot.com/content/ traditional-wedding-vows-from-various-religions.

Chapter 24

26. ('Goodnight air' ...) Brown, Margaret Wise. *Goodnight Moon.* New York: HarperFestival, 1947.

Chapter 25

27. (... the biggest impact would be ...) Mills, Richard. "What would a nuclear winter look like?" *Ahead of the Herd*, January 26, 2024. https://aheadoftheherd.com/what-would-a-nuclearwinter-look-like-richard-mills/.

28. (We have no word ...) Eggers, John. "How do you say goodbye in Ojibwe?" *The Bemidji Pioneer*, April 26, 2014. https://www.bemidjipioneer.com/opinion/john-eggers-howdo-you-say-goodbye-in-ojibwe.

Chapter 26

29. ('For I was hungry ...') Matthew 25:35 (New King James Version).

30. ('Judge not ...') Matthew 7:1 (New King James Version).

Chapter 28

31. ('And anyone not found written ...') Revelation 20:15 (New King James Version).

Chapter 30

32. (Family and friends …) Montemayor, Christina. "8 Sample Wedding Ceremony Scripts to Guide Your Own Celebration." *Brides*, April 8, 2024. https://www.brides.com/wedding-ceremony-script-5074157.

Chapter 31

33. (… Randall-Sundrum II model wormholes …) Maldacena, Juan and Alexey Milekhin. "Humanly traversable wormholes." *Physical Review D* 103, no. 6 (March 2021). https://journals.aps.org/ prd/abstract/10.1103/PhysRevD.103.066007.

Chapter 33

34. (*My young man is taking …*) Ellison, Harlan, writer. *Star Trek.* Season 1, episode 28, "The City on the Edge of Forever." Directed by Joseph Pevney. Aired April 6, 1967, on NBC. *Paramount Global*, 1967, streaming.

Chapter 34

35. ('Love never fails.') 1 Corinthians 13:8 (New International Version).

Chapter 36

36. (The five permanent members …) "UN Security Council Working Methods." *Security Council Report*, February 13, 2024. https://www.securitycouncilreport.org/un-security-councilworking-methods/the-veto.php.

37. (The Security Council played …) "Security Council." *United Nations.* Accessed December 12, 2024. https://main.un.org/security-council/en.

Chapter 37

38. (WE THE PEOPLE …) "United Nations Charter (full text)." *United Nations.* Accessed December 12, 2024. https://www.un.org/en/about-us/un-charter/full-text.

Chapter 40

39. (Spontaneous memory erasure …) Appel, Jackie. "A Scientist Claims He's Solved a Major Time-Travel Paradox." *Popular Mechanics,* January 14, 2025.

Chapter 41

40. (*We heard your voice …*) van Rijs, Helen. "Poems & Readings for Scattering or Burial of Ashes." *Helen van Rijs Celebrant.* Accessed December 12, 2024. https://helenvanrijs.co.uk/poems%26-readings-ashes.

Chapter 44

41. (… Mak'tar Chant of Strength) Howard, David and Robert Gordon, screenwriters. *Galaxy Quest.* Directed by Dean Parisot, performance by Alan Rickman. *DreamWorks Pictures,* 1999.

Epilogue

42. (Neutrinos were a typical by-product …) Graber.
43. (But tachyons are only *theoretical …*) Wikipedia. "Tachyon."
44. (A dense white fog …) Polmar, Norman C. and Lee J. Mathers.

Timeline of Events

1960

January 23 - Trieste explores the Challenger Deep

1969

June 28 - Daniel Bennett is born in Boston, Massachusetts

1991

April 7 - José de la Cruz is born in Monterrey, Mexico

2006

May 5 - Ben Abwao is born in Nakuru, Kenya

2008

February 18 - The de la Cruz family emigrates to the United States
March 30 - Katherine Rose Etter is born in Ankeny, Iowa

2018

March 12 - The Abwao family emigrates to the United States
August 25 - Kapono Ailana is born in Maui, Hawai'i

2019

April 25 - Lai Shen is born in San Jose, California

2023

August 8 - Kapono's mother dies in the Maui fire

2024

December 6 - Federal Correctional Institution in Dublin, California is closed

2028

March 8 - Hannah Ochrankyne is born in Gainesville, Florida
November 7 - Aida Pendamai and Daniel Bennett are elected president and vice president, respectively, of the United States

2030

January 7 - Ben joins the Secret Service

2031

March 6 - Anong Wagamese is born in Red Lake, Minnesota

2032

November 2 - Aida and Daniel are re-elected

2034

October 2 - Ben joins Daniel's Secret Service detail

2036

January 7 - Aida resigns as president; Daniel takes the oath of office
January 31 - Aida dies
February 13 - American Security Act (ASA) becomes law
September 2 - Kapono begins studies at the University of California, Berkeley

2037

February 23 - FBI investigation of Lai's parents begins
May 9 - Lai is raped after her senior prom
September 8 - Lai begins studies at Stanford University
September 21 - Rebuilt FCI Dublin prison opens

2038

March 12 - Lai's father is dismissed from his professorship at Cal Berkeley

2039

February 13 - ASA protest at Stanford

August 1 - Lai begins serving her sentence at FCI Dublin

September 29 - Lai is released from prison

October 8 - Lai attempts suicide

October 31 - Lai is accepted into the physics program at the University of Minnesota

December 6 - Jared Levine is sentenced to 18 years in prison for the Stanford University firebombing

2040

January 17 - Lai begins studies at the University of Minnesota

May 12 - Kapono graduates from Cal Berkeley

June 4 - Kapono starts PhD program at MIT

2041

August 30 - Kapono earns his PhD in quantum physics at MIT

2042

May 9 - Lai graduates from the University of Minnesota

June 21 - Lai starts PhD program at Cambridge University

2043

August 28 - Lai earns her PhD in quantum physics at Cambridge

October 5 - Lai starts working at the Harvard Center for Astrophysics

2045

January 13 - Lai's parents are killed in an accident

2048

November 3 - Héctor Ramirez is elected president of the United States

November 12 - Anong Wagamese discovers the wormhole to be named after him

2049

March 22 - RAND Corporation's Top Secret study *The Future of Humanity* is released

May 3 - The U.S. government starts a Top Secret research project on the Wagamese Wormhole

November 1 - Lai starts working on fusion research at Lawrence Livermore National Laboratory

2050

June 12 - Hannah earns her undergraduate degree at Stanford

2051

July 19 - Katherine is confirmed as director of the Prometheus Project

2052

June 16 - Hannah earns her master's degree in Public Policy at Stanford

July 15-24 - Hannah swims in the Olympics

August 1 - Hannah joins the Secret Service

August 5 - Kapono joins the Prometheus Project as chief scientist

November 4 - Lai joins the Prometheus team, replacing Kapono as chief scientist

November 5 - Héctor Ramirez is re-elected

2053

December 10 - *Chronos 1* test flight is unsuccessful

2054

March 6 - Lai's flight on *Chronos 2*

May 21 - Lai has a dream and tells Kapono about it

October 5 - Lai and Kapono prep for his flight and go bowling

October 17 - Lai and Kapono talk over pizza in Lai's quarters

October 19 - Kapono's flight on *Chronos 3*

October 29 - Lai meets Daniel at his home in Boston

November 3 - Kaleo Peleke is re-elected governor of Hawai'i

November 10 - Lai and Daniel meet with Governor Peleke in Honolulu

November 11 - Lai meets Keone Ailana in Maui

November 12 - Lai returns to Boston from Hawai'i

November 23 - Lai's and Daniel's second meeting in Honolulu, with Governor Peleke and other officials

December 2 - Daniel, Lai, and Ben visit the University of Kansas in Lawrence

December 4 - Lai meets with Tony and Jared in California

December 7 - Lai and Daniel attend Governor Peleke's inauguration in Honolulu

2055

January 18 - Daniel and Lai speak at the University of Minnesota on MLK Day

January 20 - Daniel is killed while saving Lai's life in Honolulu

January 25 - Daniel's funeral in Washington

July 15 - Yinuo Shen is born in San Francisco

November 17 - Love One Another rally in Atlanta

2056

April 25 - Lai meets Pope Francis II in Boston

2057

May 19 - Katherine marries Patience in Kansas City; Lai and other Prometheus team members attend

November 6 - Hawai'i passes a referendum

November 13 - World War III

November 14 - Anong and Lai talk with the Red Lake Nation Tribal Council

November 15 - Lai et al. seek refuge in Alberta, Canada

2058

August 7 - Lai et al. board the *Centaurus*

August 19 - The *Centaurus* sails into a Category 3 typhoon

2059

October 27 - Lai et al. arrive in Sydney, Australia

2061

December 24 - Lai et al. go to see a movie in Miranda, Australia

2065

October 24 - United Earth is founded in Auckland, New Zealand

2088

October 11 – United Earth's Peace Corp is founded

November 10 - Yinuo marries Liam Martin in Caringbah, Australia

2090

April 9 - An Shen-Martin is born in Miranda

October 24 - A statue is unveiled outside United Earth headquarters

2106

January 8 - Aroha Whakatane is born in Queenstown, New Zealand

2111

December 23 - Lai records a video

December 25 - Lai dies

December 31 - An proposes to Linda Kim

2112

October 19 - An marries Linda in Miranda

2117

September 8 - Liam Martin dies

2135

October 18 - Wagamese Wormhole appears in the future

2137

August 15 - Myrt Reinhart and Linda make a discovery in West Texas

2141

September 4 – Yinuo hires Aroha to lead the antimatter project
September 26 - Kapono arrives in the future in Chronos 3
September 27 - Witi Ngata briefs Yinuo et al. in Auckland
November 1 – Aroha succeeds Yinuo as United Earth chief physicist

2144

November 9 - Aroha discovers tachyons
November 13 - Aroha wraps up the antimatter project

2145

January 23 – Aroha is married in Queenstown, New Zealand

2146

April 13 - Yinuo dies

Acknowledgments

There was never supposed to be a sequel for my debut novel, *The Lightning in the Collied Night.* I approached that book as a one-and-done story. As such, I was okay with the roadblocks I'd set up in it for a sequel, such as the destruction of the Wagamese Wormhole, the banning of time travel, and primarily, the deaths of many of the characters.

But then I realized there was much more of the characters' stories to tell. And I have to admit, I'd fallen in love with them (*most* of them, anyway—Irene Wilkes, not so much). Thus, I wanted to find out more about them. For example, what happened in the three years between the rally in Honolulu and World War III? How did Lai (and others) make it from northern Minnesota to Australia after that war? What happened to Kapono after he arrived in the future? What happened to Anong, Minwaadizi, and everyone else on the Red Lake Nation reservation? Were Lai and Pope Francis II really friends, and if so, how did that happen?

I decided that if I were going to write a sequel, it would have to include (almost) all of the characters from *Lightning*—all the main characters, for sure. But I wondered how I could do that, since at the end of the book, Kapono was 87 years separated from Lai, Katherine et al. I was certain I didn't want to write two parallel stories from different time periods.

Fortunately, *Lightning* is a science-fiction novel. And if we know anything about sci-fi, it's that *anything* can, and often does, happen. Our only limit is our imaginations ... and that pesky science stuff—the first part of *science fiction.* With that guiding principle in mind, I started outlining the story and characters for a sequel. After a few weeks, I thought I had a workable story.

Then, disaster struck: I realized I'd twisted the story into a temporal paradox with no apparent means of escape. (That can happen with stories that involve time travel.) I was despondent—*There goes the sequel*, I thought. But then I had an *Ah-ha!* moment and figured out a route around the paradox. Energized, I started writing chapters … only to run into *another* paradox that was worse than the first.

After stewing on that setback for a few days, I realized something I'd mentioned briefly in *Lightning* offered a way out of my paradox box. Was it perfectly clean? Well, no. Was it at least as clean as many other time-travel novels, movies, and TV shows I'd read or seen? I thought it was. So, I kept writing. Ultimately, readers will be the judge as to how well I handled these paradoxes.

I'm indebted to Norman C. Polmar and Lee J. Mathers for their excellent account of the bathyscaphe *Trieste* (see *References*), which was invaluable for this book's *Prologue* and *Epilogue*. As I did in *Lightning*, I used excerpts from some literary works (see *References*) in my sequel, and I paid homage to some of my favorite sci-fi books, movies and TV shows. And as in *Lightning*, there's one sci-fi TV show episode that plays a starring role—but this time with 180-degree twist.

The settings for this sequel are similar in time and location to those in *Lightning*—although, as you may have already found out, much of this book takes place in "the land down under" and involves several Australian and Kiwi characters. Although I visited Australia a few times about 20 years ago, I needed help to make those chapters of my book as realistic as possible. I supplanted my limited knowledge with research, and I was fortunate to get advice from a former colleague who lives in Australia, Vinod Ralh, on Australian slang and locales.

In addition to Vinod's help with Australian content, I'm very grateful to Martyne Backman and Jeff Evans for their valuable input on the entire draft; Reverend Matthew Malek for his expert assistance on Chapter 20 (Lai's meeting with Pope Francis II); and of course my editor, Barbara Kohl. And just as my wonderful, patient wife Joanna supported me while I wrote my debut novel, she put up with my long days huddled over my laptop as I wrote this sequel.

It's been said by authors such as Charlie Jane Anders that writing fiction can help us get through tough times. I certainly found that to be true with this sequel as a worked on it from mid-2024 to mid-2025. I'm thankful that I could retreat to the world I'd created for a few hours each day.

I'm working on a follow-on novel to this one, with publication planned for Summer 2026. It will be based on the universe of my first two novels and will be the conclusion to the trilogy I began with *Lightning*, but it will be a stand-alone story. It will pick up immediately after the first scene of the Epilogue in this book.

Thus, I must say farewell to several characters, including Lai, Kapono, Katherine, Daniel, Hannah, Ben, Anong, Minwaadizi, José, Kaleo, and Keone, from my imaginary world of the near future, and beyond. I'm going to miss them. I hope you've enjoyed getting to know them as much as I've enjoyed sharing them with you.

Aloha, a hui hou.

Dave Backman
Apple Valley, Minnesota U.S.A.
April 2026

About the Author

David Backman was born and raised in Minneapolis and has lived most of his life in the Twin Cities. However, he is also officially (by order of the governor of Texas) a naturalized Texas citizen, y'all. *The Loss of What Is Past* is the sequel to his debut novel, *The Lightning in the Collied Night*, which is now in its 2nd Edition.

Dave retired in 2023 from a 44-year career in information technology that focused on enterprise software architecture, design, and development. He wrote a lot during his career, including co-authoring a couple of books, but he didn't write fiction … at least, he didn't *intentionally* write fiction. In addition to writing, Dave enjoys volunteering and spending time with his wife Joanna and their three children. His main hobby is searching for a parallel universe in which the Minnesota Vikings have won a Super Bowl, or even played in a Super Bowl in the past half-century.

Dave is a life-long sci-fi fan. He earned a bachelor's degree in Mathematics (most of which he forgot a long time ago) and an MBA in Information Management. He holds certifications in several IT-related subjects including all the major cloud providers, which helps him keep his head in the clouds while writing.

https://thecolliednight.com/